DEVASTATION ERUPTS

BOOK 3 OF THE NATURE'S FURY SERIES

There's no running from fate when
it's determined to destroy all in its path

A.E. FAULKNER

INDIE OWL
PRESS

4700 Millenia Blvd.
Ste #175-90776
Orlando, FL 32839

info@indieowlpress.com
www.indieowlpress.com

DEVASTATION ERUPTS

Cover design by Michelle Preast
Indie Book Cover Designs / Michelle-Preast.com

Interior layout by Vanessa Anderson
at NightOwlFreelance.com

Manufactured in the United States of America

Paperback ISBN-13: 978-1-949193-03-9

For Jasmine

Wherever you go, chaos ensues. In the instant we met, you chose us. We love you beyond measure and hope to have many more years together. ♥

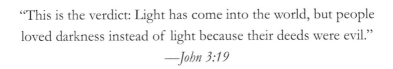

"This is the verdict: Light has come into the world, but people loved darkness instead of light because their deeds were evil."

—John 3:19

Contents

Chapter 1...Page 1
Chapter 2...Page 5
Chapter 3...Page 10
Chapter 4...Page 14
Chapter 5...Page 18
Chapter 6...Page 22
Chapter 7...Page 26
Chapter 8...Page 29
Chapter 9...Page 33
Chapter 10...Page 37

Chapter 11...Page 41
Chapter 12...Page 45
Chapter 13...Page 50
Chapter 14...Page 54
Chapter 15...Page 58
Chapter 16...Page 63
Chapter 17...Page 66
Chapter 18...Page 71
Chapter 19...Page 75
Chapter 20...Page 80

Chapter 21...Page 85
Chapter 22...Page 89
Chapter 23...Page 93
Chapter 24...Page 97
Chapter 25...Page 101
Chapter 26...Page 104
Chapter 27...Page 108
Chapter 28...Page 112
Chapter 29...Page 115
Chapter 30...Page 118

Contents

Chapter 31...Page 122
Chapter 32...Page 127
Chapter 33...Page 135
Chapter 34...Page 140
Chapter 35...Page 148
Chapter 36...Page 154
Chapter 37...Page 159
Chapter 38...Page 165
Chapter 39...Page 170
Chapter 40...Page 174

Chapter 41...Page 180
Chapter 42...Page 185
Chapter 43...Page 190
Chapter 44...Page 195
Chapter 45...Page 199
Chapter 46...Page 202
Chapter 47...Page 205
Chapter 48...Page 208
Chapter 49...Page 212
Chapter 50...Page 216

Chapter 51...Page 220
Chapter 52...Page 226
Chapter 53...Page 231
Chapter 54...Page 235
Chapter 55...Page 240
Chapter 56...Page 245
Chapter 57...Page 250
Chapter 58...Page 254
Chapter 59...Page 259
Chapter 60...Page 265

Contents

Chapter 61...Page 269
Chapter 62...Page 273
Chapter 63...Page 277
Chapter 64...Page 281
Chapter 65...Page 285
Chapter 66...Page 288
Chapter 67...Page 292
Chapter 68...Page 295
Chapter 69...Page 302
Chapter 70...Page 306

Chapter 71...Page 309
Chapter 72...Page 315
Chapter 73...Page 320
Chapter 74...Page 324
Chapter 75...Page 329
Chapter 76...Page 332
Chapter 77...Page 338

Author's Note...Page 341
Acknowledgements...Pages 342 – 344
About the Author...Page 345
Further Reading...Pages 347 – 349

DEVASTATION ERUPTS

Chapter 1

Time and surroundings fade to the far reaches as Riley and I clutch each other, sobbing. Untangling trembling arms and swiping away trails of happy tears, we slowly separate. My limbs tingle with pinpricks after fiercely clinging to my sister, as if she were the last life jacket on the Titanic.

Sergeant Bowen impatiently thrusts a box of tissues at us.

With awkward, nervous giggles, we both sop up spilled tears and runny noses. Riley cringes when she dabs a tissue over the scar that now brands her right cheek.

Pointing at it, I have to ask. "What happened?" Before she can answer, Bowen steps toward us. "So I just need to confirm, you two know each other?" With shaky emotions balancing on a tightrope of instability, we both burst into laughter. Narrowing his eyes, he states, "I know it sounds ridiculous, but I need verbal confirmation from both of you."

1

Raising my right hand to my temple, I salute him and give a stern, "Yes, sir!" Riley chuckles and answers with a simple, "Yes, this is my sister." We're both still running on the natural high, combined with the intense relief, of accomplishing what seemed impossible.

Clapping his hands together, he looks back and forth between us as he speaks. "First thing's first. You will have time to catch up with each other. But I have other matters to attend to, so I'm going to get you squared away for the time being and then we'll meet again tomorrow to determine our next course of action."

He takes a seat at the small desk I hadn't even noticed in a corner of the room. Riley follows my lead when I grab a chair and drag it to the other side of the desk. *I know how this works.* He fires up the computer and starts chicken-pecking the keys to pull up our files or something.

Although it's putting a damper on our reunion, I know he's got a lot going on. And he's right, now Riley and I have all the time in the world to be together.

We sit quietly, my foot tapping the floor nervously and Riley sitting on her hands. *Since when does she do that?* Finally, when Bowen finishes typing on the keyboard, he focuses on us.

"I'm going to ask you a few questions, Riley. And I would like the answers to only come from you," he shoots a pointed look my way. I shake my head slightly because I don't know what he's expecting. *Of course, I'm not going to jump in and answer for her.*

"Okay," she says softly.

2

"Who were you with when you arrived at the base?" *Oooh, right for the throat. Great question!*

She looks to me, but I stay silent. She releases a deep sigh and answers him.

"I came with two brothers: Dan and Jim Masters. Dan was injured and they brought him inside by stretcher." She glances at me, probably expecting my eyebrows to be in their current position: halfway up my forehead, framing wide eyes. *What happened to Dan?* I know I can't ask about it right now, but I make a mental note to get all the details as soon as we're done here.

Bowen nods and types her answer on the computer. Keeping his eyes on the screen, he asks, "And what is their relation to you?" She reaches for my hand and gives it a squeeze.

"None. They're just two guys that we knew from our family's summer vacations. They aren't related to us in any way." Her tone is strong and confident. *I like it!*

Narrowing his eyes, Bowen asks, "What is your last name, Riley?" Rolling her eyes, she crosses her arms.

"It's Whelan. Jim told the guy who entered our info here it was Masters and that we were married. I didn't correct him because he threatened me—and said he'd hurt Quinn—if I told the truth."

It takes about two seconds for her words to register in my brain. "I knew it!" I snarl through gritted teeth. Her sorrowful eyes force the wave of emotions within me to crest. Energy flows to my feet and they propel me out of my chair. I glance at the door, preparing to lunge. When I'm within a foot of the handle, a wall of muscle slides before it, blocking my access.

"Ms. Whelan, we do not tolerate violence on this base,"

Sergeant Bowen reprimands. "If you want this meeting to continue, you will return to your seat." Releasing a frustrated breath, I hold his gaze and sharply nod.

Keeping his eyes on me, Bowen waits until I sit down before he returns to his chair. *For a middle-aged guy, he's faster than I would have thought.*

"So you were brought here against your will?" He flawlessly slides right back into interview mode.

"Yes!" Riley answers assertively, punctuating it with a nod. She diligently answers each question he throws her way. He continues typing for a few minutes after she finishes speaking. *He's slow on a keyboard, but I guess I should just be glad he isn't pen-and-papering it again like when he interviewed me.* When his interrogation ends, there's only one thing left to do.

"Alright then," Bowen says, eyeing us both. "It's time that I get Mr. Masters' side of the story."

Chapter 2

Grabbing the walkie-talkie clipped to his waist, Bowen instructs a soldier to retrieve Jim and escort him to a nearby room. After giving the command, he assures us that Jim will not be joining us. Riley and I will wait here while the sergeant talks to him and sorts out the next steps.

Sitting in nervous silence, questions bounce around in my mind. I can't wait to talk to Riley alone. *What happened to her cheek? Did Jim do that? If I get my hands on him...*

Focused on the hands she's twisting in her lap, Riley gives me a side-eye glance. Maybe she's worried about seeing Jim again now that she's been able to tell the truth. I reach over and brush her arm, a silent signal that I'm here for and with her. Although it certainly doesn't hurt knowing that we're surrounded by soldiers with weapons. I trust in their ability to keep us safe.

We both jump when the walkie-talkie beeps and the soldier's voice fills the small room. "Sir," he hesitates. "James Masters is gone."

Bowen's face reddens as he attempts to remain composed. "Keep an eye out for him. I'll send a silent alert to personnel throughout the base. I don't want word of this getting out to civilians. He's not a confirmed threat and there's no reason to cause chaos."

"Yes, sir!"

"And Private."

"Yes, sir?"

"Alert the hospital. James' brother, Daniel Masters, is a patient there. I want you to verify that he is in his room and ask the staff there to alert me if James decides to pay his brother a visit. After you've searched the immediate area, take a walk over to the hospital. Keep your eyes open for him along the way and conduct your own search of the facility."

"Yes, sir!" With that, the conversation is over. The sergeant's hazel eyes betray his fatigue.

"Why did you say he isn't a threat? He kidnapped someone and lied about her identity. I'd call that a threat." I know this guy's trying to help us, but I can't hold back.

Heaving out a sigh, the sergeant turns to Riley. "Did James Masters cause you any harm or threaten you while you were with him?"

Wrapping her arms around her torso, she answers quietly. "Not really directly...he just, sort of...implied that he would hurt Quinn if he saw her again." Her brown eyes meet mine, although hers are clouded with guilt. *None of what happened was her fault. Jim should feel guilty, but I'm sure he doesn't.*

Rubbing his forehead, Bowen asks, "Based on the time you spent with him, do you feel that he poses a danger to anyone other than you or your sister?"

"No, I really don't think he would bother with anyone else unless they got in his way," she answers.

"Then we will proceed with standard protocol. Ladies, I will assign a soldier to secure a room for you and ensure that you are guarded until Mr. Masters is found." Peeking at his watch, Bowen pinches the bridge of his nose.

"We're not done here, but I have to be somewhere." *That's right, before we came to this building, someone called him on the radio and said there was a meeting about Yellowstone or Yosemite. Something out west.*

Without pause for a reply, he raises the walkie-talkie to his mouth again and asks the voice on the other end to come and collect us. A few minutes later, another camouflaged solider arrives and Bowen explains that we need a room and that it must be secured with a guard overnight.

Before his sudden exit, he turns to us. "We'll speak again in the morning. Until then, do not go anywhere on the base without an escort. There will be one stationed outside of your room. It's just a precaution until we can account for Mr. Masters' whereabouts."

He doesn't wait for a response. He nods at the soldier and ducks out the door.

Private Harris, the lucky soldier selected to babysit us, escorts us back to the intake trailer where Bowen initially sat our group down to talk. I almost forgot that I left Riley's bag, along with mine, there. I can't wait for her to see it. After everything she's been through, whatever it was, a small piece of the past should put a smile on her face, however brief.

As we trek along the pathways and road, my eyes volley from side to side. I don't like not knowing where Jim is. But overall, I feel pretty safe. I'm assuming all of these soldiers have guns or some sort of weapon that could protect us if Jim tried anything.

Playfully bumping into Riley's shoulder, I marvel at the reality that she's really here with me. Warmth swells in my chest. *I found her, I really found her.*

As we shuffle toward our destination, I whisper, "Where do you think Jim went? Do you think he's gone?" I feel like we can't speak freely in front of Harris. I don't really know if we're allowed to talk to him, but I doubt he knows many details about our situation.

"I'm not sure he'd leave with Dan still here," she says, her worried eyes watching for my reaction.

I return her look with one that says, "Spill it."

Glancing at our escort, she quietly elaborates. "Dan was in pretty bad shape when we got here. I think he fell asleep, he was keeping watch for us outside, and all of a sudden, he was screaming, and he had hundreds of fire ants crawling all over him. They were biting him or stinging him, or whatever they do."

She looks to the ground. "It was awful. I didn't know what to do to help him. Jim tried brushing them off, but it was too late. His skin was covered in nasty red welts and he was just…in so much pain."

Before I can respond, we arrive at the intake center. Private Harris directs us to seats while he takes one behind a desk and starts typing away. His fingers fly over the keys while I retrieve our bags. He stops typing for a moment, watching my movement.

"I left these here when I first came in." When I hold them up, Riley exhales a loud gasp and rushes toward me. "My bag! Quinn, you kept my bag!" She snatches it from my hands and hugs it to her chest. That must be all the proof Harris needs. He returns his attention to the computer.

"Thank you so much. I thought I'd never see it again." She smiles from ear-to-ear.

"I knew I'd find you; I just didn't know how long it would take." No need to tell her how much the Earth wanted to swallow that bag in the parking lot of Ton O' Fun.

"Is this a tear?" she asks, running her finger along the slightly split bottom seam. *Okay, maybe I will enlighten her on the Herculean effort it took to bring that stupid purple backpack all this way.*

Chapter 3

Within a few minutes, Harris finds space for us in one of the housing units. He explains that it's on the opposite side of the base, about as far away from Riley's previous room as possible. When the soldier asks if she has any personal items to retrieve from the room she shared with Jim, Riley adamantly shakes her head. Out of the corner of my eye, I see her casually cradle the backpack a little closer.

Staying close to our guard, we cross the base, passing other civilians and soldiers going about their business. We blend in with the others, no one really paying us any attention. I notice Harris' eyes sweep back and forth, in a state of perpetual alertness. It's comforting to think he is scanning for potential threats. Or one threat in particular.

When we reach the building, Harris leads us to the appropriate hallway. Stopping before our designated door, he unlocks the non-descript room and tells us to take our time getting settled. After presenting Riley with the room key, he assures us he will wait outside the door. We should alert him when we're ready to grab some dinner at the mess hall.

Enclosed in the safety of what feels like a drab dormitory, we drop our bags on one bed and plop down together on the other one. Staring up at the smooth white ceiling, we share details of our separate journeys. Focusing on the most important points, I tell her how we found Chris at Aunt Grace's trailer and how he tagged along with us.

She exhales a surprised sigh and narrows her eyes. "I'm surprised you were on board with that," she says. Rolling my eyes in response, I elaborate. "Okay, Aidan kind of made a big deal about not leaving the kid behind. I didn't necessarily agree it was the best idea, but…"

She finishes for me, "But those baby blues talked you into it!" She giggles and waves her hand in a circle. "Okay, continue."

We both fix our attention on the ceiling as I explain the lower points of the trip. I breeze over our little excursion to Ton O' Fun, where we got a brief break from the danger. Well, until a sinkhole ate our car.

I explain that Wes never made it to the base. Although my eyes threaten to spill tears, I manage to keep a steady voice. She audibly gasps when I describe our run-in with a gun-wielding homeowner who discovered us searching his house for supplies. Her hand flies to her mouth when I relay that Jasmine was shot in the shoulder when she jumped in front of Chris to protect him.

Riley listens in silence. Her sadness mirrors mine, but she

doesn't know these people like I do. Or did. *I hope to see them again.*

When I pause, tired of hearing my own voice, Riley offers her story.

Dan and Jim figured out we stole their bikes. Apparently, they knew about Aidan and Jeff coming around the trailer park, looking for supplies. The guys were keeping a close eye on Aidan and Jeff and even followed them "home" one night.

So, when we went missing, along with the bikes, Dan and Jim didn't really have any other leads. When they showed up at the campground Aidan and his friends were using as a temporary home, it was a jackpot: the bikes, Riley and I; it was all there.

Riley and I happened to be sleeping outside by the fire, which made us easy pickings. The guys grabbed Riley and, like she mentioned earlier, Jim threatened to hurt me if she didn't go with them. *My heart drops as she describes the fear she felt. And the helplessness.*

At first, she thought they were just going back to Dan and Jim's trailer to talk. Once there, the guys shared their real plan with her—to take her with them to Langley Air Force Base in Virginia until everything was cleared up in Delaware.

I interrupt to ask why they wouldn't just go to Dover Air Force Base. Riley explains that Dan and Jim wanted to put some distance between themselves and the trailer park. Dan admitted to her that Jim was responsible for what happened to one of the neighbors there, Mrs. Adams.

I knew it!

It was actually Aidan and Jeff that found Mrs. Adams' body. Desperate for supplies, they were scavenging around the trailer park, only entering homes they thought were empty. When they told us about the gruesome discovery they had made just a few doors down from our trailer, Riley and I had to see for ourselves. They were right. I found Mrs. Adams' lifeless body in her bed, red blots that oozed from stab wounds marring her white sheets. I make a mental note to ask how much Riley knows. *It couldn't have been an accident.*

I shiver, recalling what feels like a lifetime ago when I heard the scream in the middle of the night. I later discovered it was Mrs. Adams, the last hint of life leaving her body.

I slip back into silence as I contemplate this information. Of course, we suspected Dan and Jim were the ones to hurt Mrs. Adams, but for them to admit it…I just can't fathom how Riley endured her time with them, knowing what they were capable of. The more she explains, the more questions I have.

Did she even try to get away from them? Unless they kept her tied up, couldn't she just sneak away when they were sleeping? What the heck happened to her cheek?

Before either of us can utter another word, a sharp knock on the door startles us into upright positions. Reacting faster than me, Riley jumps up and yanks the door open. Private Harris swipes a curious gaze across the room. He's probably unimpressed by our lack of progress unpacking.

"Sorry to interrupt you, ladies, but I thought you should know. The mess hall closes in an hour." He pauses for a moment. When we don't answer, he elaborates. "And it's meatloaf night. Trust me. Not something you want to miss." He flashes an embarrassed smile when his stomach releases a low rumble.

"Of course," Riley says. "We'll be ready in five minutes!"

He dips his head and ducks back out into the hallway.

13

Chapter 4

After pulling a brush through my straggly hair and washing my hands, I'm ready for a hot meal. The last time I had a decent dinner was at Benny's, unless you count the pizza at Ton O' Fun. Although Riley and I had joined Dan and Jim for dinner one night at the trailer park, I believe they served us cat meat. I didn't touch it, so I'll never know for sure. *I wonder if Riley was able to extract any details about that from Dan? Maybe that's something to ask another time, like when we aren't getting ready to eat.*

I swear Harris' feet are in motion before the door swings completely open. We scramble to keep up as he leads us to the mess hall. Once again, my eyes shift to each face that crosses our path. Although I scan for beady eyes, a tiny mustache and slick black hair, there's no sign of Jim. *I don't like that he's out here somewhere, maybe even watching us or waiting for us in the shadows. I'd rather confront him and get it over with, especially when there's an armed soldier with us.*

The mess hall reminds me of our school's lunchroom. Although only about a quarter of the seats are taken, hearty laughter crescendos from a corner table. *At least it feels more welcoming than a high school cafeteria.* Harris beelines to the kitchen area entrance, waving his hand in a gentlemanly gesture, indicating *ladies first.*

I smirk at Riley. The poor guy is probably starving, but I dutifully follow his request, grabbing a tray and moving down the line. There are only a few others grabbing their dinner, so the line moves quickly.

Riley and I both gladly accept plates of meatloaf, mashed potatoes, and green beans. The mound of food looks enormous, but I can't resist grabbing a plated slice of chocolate cake with what appears to be peanut butter icing. *I didn't know they'd have dessert!* One iced tea later and I'm ready to dig in.

Harris sits at a table with us, but he looks longingly at the other soldiers. I'd suggest that he sit with them and just keep an eye on us from there, but I have a feeling he'd consider that shirking his duties.

The three of us eat in awkward silence. Riley and I still have a lot to catch up on, but we can't speak freely in front of a stranger. I find myself shoveling each bite into my mouth just to rush through the meal.

We all finish eating around the same time and quietly clean our table, disposing of trash, and balancing our used plates and silverware in their designated gray tubs.

As we weave around the mostly-empty tables, a heavily-accented voice calls out to my sister.

"Miss Riley, is that you?" We turn in unison. Riley's features immediately soften in recognition.

"Dr. Noori…hi," she verbally stumbles. A shy smile springs across her lips.

"Please, call me Safiya. You look like you are settling in well," the stranger says. She leans in closer and says in a hushed voice, "You look much happier than you did when we met."

"To be honest, I *am* much better now," Riley says, grinning. "Dr. No-, Safiya, I'd like you to meet my sister, Quinn."

Safiya eyes me cautiously. She looks like any other soldier here and they honestly all blend together. But I guess that's the point of wearing camo. *How does Riley know her? She didn't arrive here that much sooner than I did.*

Cocking her head sideways as if evaluating me, Safiya extends a hand. "It is very nice to meet you, Quinn. I am Dr. Noori and I had the great pleasure of meeting your sister at the hospital a few days ago." Then, as her deep brown eyes slide back to Riley, "I didn't realize you had any family on base."

With a nervous giggle, Riley answers, "Um, I didn't. Until today."

"Well, I am very happy for you both," she says. "Now, I must grab some food before the kitchen closes. I hope to see you around."

We both say goodbye and hoof it back to our room, led by our faithful escort. When we're about halfway across the base, Harris' radio buzzes to life. In one smooth movement, he raises it to his mouth and depresses a button.

"Go for Private Harris."

"Harris, this is Sergeant Bowen. Are you in a secure location?"

"Mid-base, sir. Approaching the housing unit."

"Okay. As soon as you are all behind closed doors, call me back. I have a status update to share."

Chapter 5

Harris affirmatively responds and calmly returns the walkie-talkie to his belt. Although he's unaffected by the brief message, Riley and I share a wide-eyed look. Our strides grow with each step until we're practically racing back to the room.

Once we cross the threshold and Harris secures the door, Riley and I plop down on one bed. We watch intently as he settles at the small desk and chair in the corner.

"I'm guessing you two are ready for me to make the call?" he asks, half smirking when we both nod vigorously.

Clutching the walkie-talkie, he calls Sergeant Bowen and confirms that we are back in the room. Bowen doesn't waste a moment.

"James Masters exited the base at fifteen hundred hours, during the time I was meeting with Quinn and Riley Whelan. Daniel Masters is an inpatient at the hospital and James has not made any attempt to contact him at this point."

Anger seethes through my veins.

"They just let him leave? No one even questioned him?" I demand.

Harris shoots me a surprised look and slowly shakes his head, as if to warn me.

"Ms. Whelan, I suggest you hamper your tone," Bowen responds. "Due to what is called civil rights, we do not force guests to stay on this base. Civilians are free to leave when they choose, unless they are deemed to be a danger or harm in some capacity. As you can understand, at the time Mr. Masters left, no one at the entry gates would have had reason to question his motives."

"So he's definitely gone? They're sure he didn't sneak back inside when no one was looking?" I ask, earning another disapproving look from Harris.

"I can assure you that this base is secure. No one comes or goes without us knowing." Breaking the brief silence as we contemplate what this means, Bowen adds, "Speaking of which, I will visit your room at zero nine hundred hours tomorrow to discuss your plans. Private Harris, your services are no longer needed as the subject in question is no longer on base." Before we can ask any other questions, he ends the call.

Harris springs to his feet and strides toward the door faster than a high jumper vaults over a pole.

"Is there anything else either of you need before I go?" he asks, clearly hoping we don't. Riley and I glance at each other. Her slight nod tells me she's got this.

"Just one question, sir. What time exactly is zero nine hundred hours, in normal clock time?"

Once we understand that the sergeant will show up at nine the next morning, we settle in for the night. The second the door closes behind Harris, we twist the lock so that we're safely sealed inside.

Even though we're far from home, we're very lucky to be here. Harris was able to arrange for us to get a fresh set of clothes and pajamas, the mess hall provides our meals, and Riley tells me about the places she's passed in the few days she's been here.

This place is like a small town. It has its own bowling alley and movie theater, and even a fast food restaurant or two. Riley spent most of her time in the room she had shared with Jim, at the hospital visiting Dan, or browsing the shelves at the library.

The best part is that this whole place resides within the safety of the perimeter fence. *It's nice to feel safe, especially with Jim gone, although I don't believe he'd just abandon his brother. I don't think he's the "lone wolf" type. He enjoys bossing around others too much.*

By the time I finish brushing my teeth, which feels absolutely amazing right about now, my body and mind ache for rest. Riley and I say an early goodnight, dim the lights, and lie in our respective beds. Within minutes, Riley's steady breathing reaches my ears from across the small room. *Who knew how much I could miss that sound?*

I practically ooze into the soft mattress, allowing myself to truly and completely relax for the first time in what feels like forever. We're safe. At this moment in time, we don't have to worry about sinkholes, finding food, or people trying to hurt us.

Still, as wonderful as clean clothes, hot food and a space of our own are, we can't stay. This isn't home and it never will be. I actually don't want to know too much about all the base has to offer. I don't even want to daydream about what we're missing if the trip home ends up being difficult.

I don't even know what we'll do once we get home. It's too much to figure out now. No matter what, we've got to get there. Our aunt must assume the worst; I imagine she's sick with worry. We haven't even been able to tell her we're okay yet.

And it wouldn't be so bad if we could catch up with Aidan and Jeff. They're both from Pennsylvania too. We can head north with them. Safety in numbers and all.

But after one solid night of sleep. Riley and I both need it. First thing in the morning, we'll figure out our plan so that we can tell Sergeant Bowen. Then we can try to find our friends and make the long trip home.

Chapter 6

A sharp knocking yanks me from a peaceful sleep. My eyes fly open and lead my sluggish body into a 180-degree turn. Non-descript gray walls meet a smooth white ceiling. The only décor is a stray crack or mark, but the bland surroundings trigger my memory. *The base. We actually made it to Langley.*

My heightened senses pick up a soft snoring, emanating from my practically unconscious sister. The sight of Riley sprawled out on a bed just a few feet away from me instantly warms my soul.

Just as I stretch my limbs into a deep yawn, the rapping on the door returns, nearly startling me out of my skin. Throwing the blankets aside, I stumble to the door and lean forward, angling my head to take full advantage of the peephole. *Crap. It's Sergeant Bowen, which must mean it's nine o'clock and we completely overslept.*

Without even waking Riley, I tug the door open. Narrowed hazel eyes land on me like an arrow hitting a target. Lowering my head in embarrassment, I step back and out of his way. As he crosses the threshold, he launches into a lecture.

"Miss Whelan, we had a meeting scheduled for zero nine hundred hours this morning. I have a very busy schedule, and I specifically carved time out of my day to discuss your predicament."

He waves a frustrated hand through the air. Just as he's about to speak again, his eyes land on Riley's sleeping form. *This isn't going to improve his mood.*

Bowen squints his eyes closed and rubs his forehead as if we've just given him a colossal migraine. Riley's snoring crescendos, perfectly punctuating his annoyance.

Eyes still pressed closed as if willing himself to stay calm, he quietly says, "I believe I need another cup of coffee. I'll be back in fifteen minutes and we'll discuss your plans at that time. I suggest you wake the other Miss Whelan for our meeting."

With that, he turns on his heel and strides through the door.

Rushing to Riley's side, I grasp her shoulders and shake. Her head lolls for a moment before her alarmed brown eyes snap open. "Riley, wake up. Now."

She chokes out a timid, "Wha-what's happening?"

Her blood pressure has probably shot through the roof, but at least she's awake.

"I'm sorry, I didn't want to scare you, but we overslept. It's after nine." Her eyes widen. "Sergeant Bowen was already here. We have fifteen minutes to get ready before he comes back."

There's no time, or need, for more words. We both jump

23

into hurried versions of a morning routine, brushing our teeth and hair and pulling on fresh clothes. By the time we finish our frenzied rush, the sharp knock returns.

This time we answer it together. The short absence has greatly improved the Sergeant's mood. When his eyes land on us, he gives an approving nod and says, "Nice to see you ladies. Awake and ready for the day." We step aside so he can join us in the room.

Once the door is closed, we sit together on a bed while Bowen plants himself in the desk's swivel chair. Resting his coffee on the desk's clean surface, he folds his hands and asks, "So, what are your plans?" His eyes shift back and forth between us. I imagine we both wear the same uncertain expression.

Bowen takes a long sip from his coffee as Riley and I face each other. *We probably should have figured this out last night before going to sleep.*

"Well, our home is in Pennsylvania and we do have relatives there, so that's where we're headed." Riley stuns me by not only answering for us, but also holding Bowen's gaze and nodding with confidence as she says the last few words.

"We just have one quick stop to make first," I add, turning toward my sister. "Remember Aidan and Jeff?" Of course, she does. Still, I wait for her affirming nod. "They were making sure Jasmine made it home, her parents live here in Virginia, but then they're going back to PA too. I thought we could meet up with them and travel together."

"Now, before you get too far with these plans, I have to ask," Bowen interrupts, rubbing his jaw. "Riley, how old are you? I need to verify that because our records do not confirm what

Quinn said upon her arrival on base. Are you, in fact, eighteen, or are you a minor?"

Chapter 7

Oh crap! She's seventeen, but if he knows we're both minors, what does that mean? Would he make my mom's sister, our Aunt Robin, come here to get us? Would they make us stay here until then? Training my eyes straight ahead, I don't dare look at Riley. I don't want him to think we're lying, but I REALLY want her to lie right now.

"I just turned eighteen while we were apart," she says. Although I don't dare look, I'm sure her big brown eyes look as innocent as a doe's. "So Quinn was right, then. The last time I was with her, I was seventeen. But now I'm technically an adult, so I can make decisions for both of us."

Her ease in doing so and willingness to lie evokes a two-fold emotional response. I hate that my sister had to go through so much when we were separated, but she's become a stronger person for it. The old Riley never would have lied so smoothly.

"I forgot," I add. Meeting Bowen's eyes, I sprinkle a bit of truth into the conversation. "It's a little hard to keep track of days when you're living like a nomad."

"Alright, given the situation, I can release you from the base as long as you're together. Now, have you given any thought as to your means of travel?" I swear relief washes over his hazel eyes. *Is he that glad to be rid of us?*

This time we both stutter. "Um, no, not really," Riley says. Shrugging my shoulders, I remember that we both arrived here under at least one similar circumstance. "Yeah, my friends were driving the car I came here in. And I'm willing to bet a bag of sour gummies that Jim didn't let you drive here." Riley laughs, shaking her head.

Steepling his hands and resting his elbows on his knees, Bowen rolls the desk chair a foot closer to us. "So, I'm guessing you'd appreciate a set of wheels to get yourselves, and your other friends, home?" *Here it is. When I first got to the base, I asked why he was helping me. He said he might need my help "on the outside" sometime soon.*

Riley nods vigorously. My cautious gaze slides over the sergeant, attempting to determine his motives. *What could he possibly want from us? We each own exactly one backpack and its meager contents.*

"While you are welcome to stay on this base while damage from the recent earthquake is being contained, I fully support your attempt to return home. And, I am able to provide you with a vehicle, supplies, and equipment that will enable you to reach your home in Pennsylvania."

He stops talking, his words and subsequent silence hanging

in the charged air. All of this help isn't coming for free; I'm not naïve enough to believe that. Riley turns toward me, her blazing smile confirming that she thinks we've just struck gold. *Nothing has come easy for us since our parents had died in the car accident. Why would it now?*

"Sergeant, this all sounds wonderful, and of course we want—and need—your help to get home. But why would you do all of this for us? I mean, you can't possibly do this for everyone who shows up here—why us?"

He stands, turning his back to us. "You're right, Quinn," he says. "I don't make this offer to everyone who walks through those gates."

My heart races, silently praying that we can deliver whatever it is that he wants from us. Stealing a glance at Riley, she hunches her shoulders, as if to say, "I don't know."

Bowen suddenly turns again, facing us. He rubs his chin as if in deep thought. After a few minutes of silence, which Riley and I don't dare break, Bowen fluidly rolls the desk chair out again and lowers himself into it.

Eyeing us both intently, he informs us that this conversation is confidential and asks if we can agree not to discuss it outside of these four walls. We both swear ourselves to secrecy.

Releasing a deep exhale, words tumble out of his mouth, more than I've ever heard him speak in one sitting.

Chapter 8

The serious soldier morphs into a vulnerable man concealed beneath the uniform. He explains that the base is about to go on lockdown. Several military personnel will be sent to Wyoming to deal with an issue there.

We launch question after question at him, unable to contain our curiosity. He's reluctant to disclose much, but after consistent pressure, he admits that the Yellowstone Caldera is showing signs of an impending eruption. The military will converge on the surrounding areas and begin evacuation efforts, which will leave this base understaffed.

Bowen twists the wedding band on his left hand as he explains that he lost contact with his wife a week and a half ago. They were mid-conversation when the phone disconnected. Since then, he's dealt with one obstruction after another in trying to reach her. All with no success.

"At this point," he begins with a defeated tone, "leaving would be considered abandoning my post." Rubbing his temples, he adds, "I can't do that."

Riley gently asks, "Where is home for you?"

"Towson, Maryland," he answers, "Not too far from the Pennsylvania border." His hazel eyes meet mine and I sense what's coming next.

"You think your wife is still there?" I ask. When he nods, I continue what feels like the beginning of an interrogation. "And you want us to find her?" *Even if we find her, he doesn't expect we'll come all the way back down to Virginia with her, does he?*

"I realize this is a strange request, but I believe our paths crossed at the right time. You need to get home and I need to reach my wife. We can help each other, and we'll all get what we want."

"What exactly do you need us to do?" I ask, even though it really doesn't matter. Glancing at Riley, I know we're both thinking the same thing—*whatever it takes to get a ride home, we'll do. It's not like we have any other options or offers.*

"I'll give you our home address. I just need you to go there, find her, and give her a message from me. And a phone...a satellite phone, so she can reach me."

"What if she isn't there?" Riley asks, eyes narrowed. "What would we do then?"

"If you can't find her, you call me on the phone I'm giving you," he explains. "If she isn't there, she didn't go far. You may have to ask around with the neighbors. But we'll discuss that if it becomes necessary."

"And what about our friends?" I ask. Both Riley and the

sergeant narrow their eyes in question.

"You know, the people I came here with?" I glance toward Riley, reminding her, "Aidan, Jeff, Jasmine, and Chris." She turns her head sideways, like a confused dog.

"Aren't they already on their way home, though?" Riley asks.

"Well, if we *hurry*," I avert my eyes to the sergeant, imploring him to understand, "we can probably catch up with them. They were going to Jasmine's house, and Aidan gave me her last name. He thought maybe someone here at the base could look up her address."

I wield my most desperate puppy dog eyes at Sergeant Bowen. He rubs his forehead, closing his eyes for just a moment. Releasing his frustration in a deep exhale, he settles an intense gaze on me.

"One day. You take one day to try and find your friends, but that's it." He shoots a pointer finger into the air to emphasize the order. "Then, whether you find them or not, you get on the road and head north."

With no other options and a growing desire to return home, my response comes easily.

"Deal! How soon can we go?" I ask, my adrenaline spiking with each word.

Riley's head volleys back and forth as she silently follows the conversation.

A slight smile curves on Bowen's lips and his shoulders drop into a relaxed posture. Visibly pleased that negotiations are over, Sergeant Bowen rises to his feet and slides the chair back under the desk with a sharp squeal. "I've got duties to attend to right now," he says confidently, starting toward the door. "Why don't you both gather whatever items you need from the room and meet me at Intake Office 3 at thirteen hundred hours." Raising an eyebrow, he throws me a glance, "You remember where that is, right?"

"Yes!" *Of course I do. It's where I said goodbye to Aidan. And the others.*

"Very well. I'll gather some supplies and we'll have you on your way. Any questions?"

Riley startles us both by responding. "Yes, sir, uh…what time is thirteen hundred hours exactly?" When he shakes his head in frustration, we both collapse in giggles.

Chapter 9

The door sweeps closed behind the sergeant, settling with a firm click as it latches closed. We contain ourselves for exactly four seconds before erupting with giddiness. Taking turns, we randomly call out thoughts. "We're going home!" "It's over, it's finally over!" "We're gonna see Aunt Robin and Snickers!"

The mention of our family dog instantly melts the smiles from our faces. Reality sweeps through the air, choking the last lingering drops of joy.

As far as we know, Snickers is fine and still at our Aunt Robin's house. But he isn't the only family member we're separated from. Riley's eyes glimmer with grief. The weight of our parents' deaths crushes my soul. It's never really gone; it just floats to the forefront of my subconscious sometimes, creeping from the mournful shadows drifting through my mind at any given time.

Our house is an empty structure that will never again hold holiday gatherings or birthday celebrations. At least not with our parents. It's a hollow shell of what was once a happy home.

Forcing my mind back to the present, I grasp Riley's hands. "Hey, let's get ourselves ready. We should stop by the mess hall before we leave."

"Yeah," she says, nodding. "Let's get outta here."

After a quick trip to the showers, we scour the room for any lingering belongings. We never unpacked our backpacks and nothing in the room belongs to us. We spend a few minutes tidying the room before we head out the door for, what I hope, is the last time.

Now that we have a plan, even though I don't know all the details yet, I can truly appreciate all this base has to offer. Several buildings, like the mess hall and the dormitory Riley and I stayed in, bear red brick exteriors. And the temporary structures—mostly trailers that function as offices—have simple, gray siding.

But other areas, like the child development center and the family housing blocks, are picture-perfect. You'd never know they were inside a large military base surrounded by ominous barbwire fences. Two-story houses, in varying shades of yellow, white, and red line manicured streets. Meticulously-spaced trees dot lush green lawns.

Camouflaged soldiers pass by, some in small groups casually sharing a laugh while others move at a faster pace with a clear destination in mind.

"Quinn?" I meet Riley's eyes until movement draws mine down to her waist. She's wringing her hands.

"What? What's wrong?" I ask. Her eyes shift past me. I follow her gaze to a rectangular, modern-looking brick building. A large awning directs visitors to the main entrance and tall block letters matching the brick label it: USAF HOSPITAL LANGLEY.

"Well, we're leaving," she brushes a lock of long brown hair behind her ear, "do you think we should visit Dan to say goodbye or anything?"

"No! He's part of the reason you're even here and you want to make nice and go say goodbye?" *Is she serious?*

Resting a hand on my arm, she levels me with a stern glare. "Look, you don't know everything that happened out there. Dan was going to help me get away. That is, until he got hurt."

Maybe she can forgive him that easily, but I can't. And who's to say he was even telling her the truth when he said he'd help her? I quickly decide that my argument won't help the situation, so I take another approach.

"Okay, I believe you." Those four words instantly soften her glare, but her eyebrows reach for the sky in anticipation of my next words. "But I still think it's a bad idea to visit Dan. For one, he'll be upset when he finds out that Jim is gone. And maybe he'll blame us. And besides that, what if he asks us about our plans, like how we'll get back home? We can't really say that we made a deal with Bowen. We're not supposed to tell anyone."

She crosses her arms and scrunches her face, grudgingly absorbing the truth.

"You're right," she says finally. "We can't." Without another word, we continue toward the mess hall. Just as we round the building's corner and face the main entrance, Riley yanks me back hard, nearly dislocating my shoulder.

35

"Ouch, what are—" I start.

"Shhhhhhh!!" she hisses in my ear. "Dan. I just saw Dan!"

Chapter 10

We scramble all the way to the next corner, crouching behind it. Keeping watch, we whisper.

"What was he doing?" I demand.

"He was walking out with someone. A soldier. He was wearing regular clothes. They must have released him from the hospital." She squints in concentration.

"Well, at least he was leaving. Let's just watch until he's gone and then we can go in and eat."

I haven't seen Dan since the night we stole his and Jim's bikes. I recognize his gait immediately. A lack of confidence slows each step he takes. Although, he was just in the hospital, so maybe he's still in pain too. His pasty pallor hints that the effort of walking is draining any reserve energy he may have had. I wonder if he should really be at the mess hall instead of reclined in a hospital bed hovering over a tray of food.

His clothing is completely out of character—sleek black pants and a short-sleeved button-down shirt. Must have been issued to him before he was discharged from the hospital.

The soldier accompanying Dan escorts him away from the mess hall, probably to an office or dorm room. Dan's shoulders slump and, for a moment, I almost feel sorry for him. Just as he's well enough to leave the hospital, he discovers the only family he's got left is gone.

If he wasn't partially responsible for taking Riley away from me, I just might feel enough sympathy to help him right now.

When they're safely out of sight, we rush inside the mess hall. Gulping down a quick lunch, we dash back outside and slink through the streets to the intake office. We earn ourselves a few suspicious looks along the way, but no one stops us.

Rushing around pays off. We arrive fifteen minutes early for our meeting with the sergeant. His stunned expression bears a hint of impressed amusement.

"Nice to see you two so punctual," he says, a genuine smile lighting his face.

"Well, we figured we owed you from this morning," I say, continuing the goodwill.

"That you did, young lady. That you did," he nods, an appreciative smile reaching his cheeks. I've never seen him this relaxed. He must be excited to finally have a plan to reach his wife.

He directs us to a familiar cluttered desk in the corner. As he steps around and sinks into the worn chair, he motions for us to sit in the folding chairs directly across from him. A twinge of nostalgia warms me. The last time I was sitting here, it was with the gang: Aidan, Jeff, Jasmine, and Chris. If they only knew how close I am to seeing them again. Well, honestly Jasmine would probably roll her eyes, but the guys would be happy about it.

Leaning back in his chair, Sergeant Bowen rubs his eyes. Tenting his hands, he leans forward, resting his elbows on the desk, and levels us with a serious expression.

"Remember, the information I share with you stays here," he motions a pointer finger back and forth between him and us. We both nod quickly. We want this to work out as much as he does.

Satisfied, he swivels the desk chair to the drawer opposite where we sit. He pulls out a soft black pouch about the size of my makeup bag. Slowly unzipping it, he reveals what looks like a half walkie-talkie, half cell phone. A stubby antenna sits atop its thick black body.

"This is a satellite phone," he explains. "It doesn't rely on cell networks, so it will still work even if networks are down." Thrusting it toward us, he explains how to dial out and how to accept calls. Then he makes us both repeat the instructions back to him. Once he's satisfied that we understand how it works, he moves on to our next lesson.

Swiveling toward the black computer monitor, he taps the keyboard a few times, prompting the printer to awaken and spit out two pages. Rolling his chair toward the other end of the desk, he retrieves the papers and thrusts them toward us.

"This is your friend Jasmine's address," he says. "Remember, you take one day to get there, let them know you're okay, and then head north." We nod in unison.

"I realize that your friends may no longer be there. And I also realize that teenagers sometimes let their hormones influence their decisions." His eyebrows arch in anticipation of a response. I swallow the two words priming to escape my lips: *Okay, boomer!*

Instead, my eyes explore every inch of the floor as my cheeks radiate crimson. Thankfully, he slices through the awkward silence a moment later.

"Now, this other paper," he releases a deep breath. "This is a list of numbers associated with each of your friends. Think of them as identifying numbers."

I slide this printout closer and examine it. Just as Bowen said, each of our names is listed in alphabetical order. He even included Riley. My name is listed too, but it's the only one without a number next to it. All of the others have a six-digit sequence of jumbled numbers and letters.

Pushing back in my chair, I scrunch my face in confusion. "How are identification numbers supposed to help us? And why does everyone have one but me?"

He huffs out a deep breath and pinches the bridge of his nose. "What I am telling you is confidential information. As soon as you find my wife, you forget this ever happened. And you don't tell anyone else what I'm about to tell you." His serious eyes slide back and forth between us.

The air around us swells with tension. Riley and I both answer stiffly, "Yes. We promise."

Chapter 11

Sergeant Bowen slides a drawer open, reaches inside, and places a black device on the desk's smooth surface. The rectangular block looks like an old Walkman, but without the little window where the cassette sits.

Pointing at the mysterious object, the sergeant simply states, "This is a tracking device. Everyone who was immunized…" he rubs his chin as his eyes focus on a memory. For just a moment, he's no longer with us in the present. With a quick shake of his head, his attention snaps back to the conversation. "Everyone immunized was actually injected with a nano-tech tracker in a carrier serum. This machine locates the GPS tracker in the serum, treating it like a locator, and displays the GPS associated with the identification numbers. If you type in specific identification numbers, it will lead you to those individuals."

We stare in stunned silence, prompting him to elaborate.

"The muscles absorb the injection," he blows out a deep breath, as if it's cleansing his soul to share the information. "It's not exactly perfected yet. It wasn't supposed to be deployed, but the earthquake made for an opportune time to pilot test it on the East Coast. Now that the West Coast is in jeopardy, I'm guessing the project will…escalate."

"But why?" Riley asks, her voice quivering. Without even turning toward her, I can sense tears forming. She radiates sadness and confusion. "Why would the military want to track people? Without even telling them or giving them a choice." The last part evaporates into a whisper.

He sighs. "Things are about to get worse." Each word is calculated but his hazel eyes lack the conviction his steady voice attempts. "People are going to be moving around the country, some far away from their homes, and the government will need to locate population pockets."

What does this all mean? Things need to get better. Not worse. He rubs his forehead as if an agonizing migraine has clenched his brain like a vise.

"Resources are going to become limited and this will allow us to manage and distribute them equally." His shadowed eyes betray the truth. He doesn't believe that line any more than we do.

"So…wait," I narrow my eyes. "Why didn't you vaccinate me then?" The typically confident soldier crumbles for just a blink. His shoulders hunch and straighten as his composure returns.

"From the moment you walked through these doors, you stated your intent to return home," he stares into my eyes raptly. "I needed someone who could move about freely on the outside." He places both hands on the desk, palms down. "I am about to give two civilians a vehicle, equipment, and weapons. If this is going to work, I had to make sure that no one could track you down."

"But Riley," I mutter. "She was injected. She can be tracked."

"That is what we call a snafu," he states casually. "She was vaccinated according to protocol and there is no way, to my knowledge, to reverse the tracking effect. So, we will just have to take our chances because I will not ask you to separate."

Riley exhales a deep rush of relief. "Thank you."

The sergeant doesn't respond and uses the break in questions to steer the conversation away from the vaccinations.

"Now, let's fire this thing up, and I'll show you how it works." We spend the next ten minutes learning the basics on how to input tracker ID numbers as well as how to view trackers that are within range. The satellite phone acts like a GPS, so we can plug in the sergeant's home address to find his wife. The tracking device also acts like a GPS, but its purpose is to lead us to those who have been injected.

After he finishes explaining the device and how it differs from the satellite phone, he makes us demonstrate our newly-acquired knowledge.

Satisfied that we've passed the "test," Bowen swivels away from the desk and rises. He retreats to a small closet. Although his back is to us, I can hear the metallic clinking of a key as it disengages a lock. His wrist flicks a squeaky handle open and he retrieves a small black duffle bag.

Quickly securing the cabinet, he strides back to the desk

and plops into his chair. He carefully unzips the bag. "I'm going to give you some weapons to protect yourselves," he explains calmly. "Arming civilians is not something I would do under normal circumstances, but these times are anything but normal."

Riley's eyes widen as mine creep along the zippered opening, anxiously anticipating what lies within. Reaching into the shadowed interior, he grasps a gun. Its sleek black body is unforgiving. Although it's about the size of my hand, it exudes a power that strikes fear to my core.

"This is a Sig Sauer P226 semi-automatic pistol. It's got ten rounds per magazine and I'm giving you three mags. So you've got ten shots before you have to reload. You probably won't even use that many, let alone have a need to reload at all." His eyes trace the metal from barrel to handle as he speaks. "It's ideal for self-defense." With those words, his eyes find ours. "And that is why I am giving you these weapons. These are for self-defense only. Don't show this to anyone unless you have no other choice."

He places the pistol back in the bag and retrieves a silver-handled knife. Its serrated blade blares a stringent warning. He nods toward Riley. "You have any experience with something like this?" I almost choke on the incredulous laugh churning in my throat. *Why would he ask her that?*

Chapter 12

Shooting me a side eye glance, Riley answers, "No, of course not." Bowen watches her for another moment but neither breaks the silent standoff.

"Aren't you going to show us how to use the gun?" I implore, smothering the rippling tension. "I mean, the knife is pretty basic, but we've never used a gun before." He quickly returns the knife to its hiding spot.

"Just one more thing and then we'll go to the car. I'll show you how to use the weapons there. It's a little more secluded and the last thing we need is someone walking in here, seeing me teaching you two how to shoot."

As if his arm suddenly pools with lead, he sluggishly slides it across the desk toward the monitor. Wistfully, he wraps a steady hand around a wooden picture frame and presents it to us.

"This is my wife, Rossana." A blonde woman smiles broadly, the spark in her green eyes radiating happiness. One arm is snugly wrapped around a chubby black dog with a white muzzle.

"All you need to do is explain that I asked you to find her and give her the sat phone. I need to work through a few more details about getting the car back, but I'll do that while you're on the road."

"Is that your dog?" Riley asks with a wistful grin, tracing a slim finger along the dog's outline.

She's probably thinking of our dog, Snickers.

"Yes, that's Millie. You find Millie, you'll find my wife."

"How will we find her?" Riley asks. "Does she have a tracker?"

"She does not," Bowen replies. His eyes land just above our heads as he returns to a memory we can't see. "She refused to leave the dog behind. Certain pets are not permitted on base. So she stayed home, with Millie, when I was sent here." After a breath, he continues.

"I wrote our address down on a slip of paper. It's inside the picture frame. After you find your friends—in one day—" he raises a finger in emphasis, "get back on the road, locate that paper, and enter the address into the satellite phone. It'll guide you there like a GPS."

"We can handle that," I confirm.

"One day," he repeats.

Geez, I get it. We both nod in agreement.

He gives us a brisk nod before turning toward the black keyboard. He chicken-pecks a few keys and the printer rumbles to life once more. He thrusts the mostly-white sheet toward us across the desk. This one has two names on it, along with their tracking numbers.

James Masters: 53A72C

Daniel Masters: 95X37H

"You can probably guess what these are. Hopefully, they won't show up on your scanner, but just in case, you should be on alert for those numbers."

"But wait, isn't Dan still here?" Riley whimpers, her face scrunching in confusion.

"He is, but he was a bit distraught when he was informed that James is gone. He has a guard, so he is accounted for, but we haven't been able to question him thoroughly on what happened while you were in their company. He claims he doesn't remember much before the fire ant incident."

Riley and I share worried glances. Bowen leans toward us, one hand splayed on the desk.

"I am going to show you how to use the weapons. Remember, they are only to be used for self-defense, but they will keep you safe." When neither of us replies, he tries again.

"You'll be in a car and you're going to find your friends, so that's more sets of eyes to help keep watch."

He's right. Jim wouldn't try anything if he was outnumbered four-to-one. He's dumb but he's not *that* dumb. Right now, we just have to make it to Jasmine's house. Safety in numbers.

Riley shrugs her hesitation off first. "Okay, so what's next?"

Bowen gathers a few stray papers scattered across the desk and shuffles them into a messy pile. He powers down the computer and rises from his swivel chair, gliding it back to its parking spot under the keyboard in one swift movement.

Eyeing us expectantly, he exclaims, "Well, that about does it here. Gather your supplies, ladies, and let's check out your wheels."

I'm not sure how long we've been in his office, but dusk seems to be riding our heels. "How is it already getting dark outside?" I wonder aloud. The sun still clings to the horizon, but it's as if we've turned the clocks ahead a few hours and lost daylight.

The others must be consumed with their own thoughts because no one responds to my question.

As we follow the sergeant through the dimly lit pathway behind the intake trailer, Riley questions him, "So what exactly do we tell your wife if we find her?" He pauses mid-step, turning and raising an eyebrow.

"*When* you find her, you will call me on the sat phone so I can talk to her. At that point I'll instruct you on what to do next," he pauses, but before another syllable tumbles out, a series of high-pitched beeps shriek from his hip. With wide eyes and deft fingers, he unclips the walkie-talkie and presses it to his mouth.

"Go for Sergeant Bowen." The sequence of beeps must have some meaning because he's answered that walkie-talkie in my presence before but this is the first time I've seen concern wash over his features as a result of it.

"Bowen, this is Staff Sergeant Owens. Are you in a private location?" Bowen doesn't even glance at us. His whole body is attuned to the radio. The deep voice on the other end oozes with urgency.

"Yes, sir." He turns his back to us, as if that will shield the conversation. It doesn't.

"I need you to meet me in Phoenix Room 2A. Yellowstone's reached stage two, inflation. We're going into lockdown at eighteen hundred hours."

Chapter 13

Bowen's shoulders hunch and his head drops for just a moment. Defeat radiates from his weary frame. A shaky hand raises the walkie-talkie one more time.

"Yes, sir, on my way." He stills before his shoulders expand as he ingests a gulp of air. When he faces us again, his hazel eyes exude determination.

"Follow me." His boots crunch gravel as he leads us toward a paved parking lot behind the office trailers. It's so small that you'd miss it if you blinked at just the right moment. Two enormous white vans sit next to each other, taking up four parking spaces each. *He can't possibly think we can drive one of those beasts out of here unnoticed.*

His footsteps quicken as we near the vans. Riley shoots me a wide-eyed glance. I crinkle my nose in return and shake my head. *We are not driving one of those things.*

Hidden behind the girth of the massive vans is a modest silver sedan. *Now that's more our speed.* Bowen stops abruptly at the passenger side door and turns toward us.

"You're going to follow this street out of the lot." He motions toward a road nearly bathed in darkness. One lone streetlight serves as our guide.

"Make a right and drive straight until you come to a restricted entrance." When my eyes flash with worry, he elaborates. "Tell them I processed your release and that I instructed you to take this exit. Tell them there's an Alpha Charlie waiting for anyone who doesn't let you pass."

I coax an unsure "Ooookaaaay" out of my mouth. Here's hoping an Alpha Charlie is enough of a deterrent that this will work. My pulse spikes when the walkie-talkie emits three sharp beeps. Eyes trained on us, Bowen's hand glides to the radio and silences it.

Suddenly, my vision clouds as if muting the world around me. My heart strains to pump blood faster than is needed. Surrounding sounds fade as an inner panic monopolizes my senses. The sergeant's beleaguered tone pulls me from the momentary haze.

"I've got to go. Now." His chest swells and billows with rapid breaths. "Remember, the address is in the frame. Do NOT lose that frame! Tell Rossana that she can bring Millie. I'll figure something out." His words erupt in a jumble of syllables and gasps. He turns to leave us, halfway caught between the next emergency and his only hope at finding his wife.

"Just one more thing. The government knew about that earthquake in the Atlantic, but they didn't warn anyone. And now this Yellowstone eruption is being kept under wraps too." His words shoot directly to my heart like sharp daggers. It feels like a betrayal. People could have prepared if they'd known. My parents could have prepared. But there's no time to fully process the information right now.

He strides toward us and grabs my shoulders, physically conveying the importance of his message. "I have a ham radio at home. When I talk to my wife, I'll tell her to give it to you. Take it and figure out how to use it. At this rate, it may become the only way left to communicate. If emergency broadcast messages are transmitted, you're going to want to hear them."

Shaking his head, as if suddenly remembering the whole reason we came here, he slides a rough hand into his pocket and retrieves a pair of keys. They clink as they dangle from a silver ring attached to a round white medallion bearing the U.S. Air Force logo.

I nod dumbly as he thrusts the keys into my hand. He leans in close for one last bit of advice. Warm breath wafts to my cheek as cautious words drift to my ears. "Drive carefully through the base but don't waste time. You've got to be outside the fence before the official lockdown order is announced."

He whirls away, boots scuffling along the ground. Headed back toward the Intake Office, his stride is so fast that he nearly matches a runner's pace. Numbly fixed in place, we watch his figure disappear into the shadows. Once again Riley and I are truly alone.

"Quinn?" Riley's voice sounds hollow and far away, as if she's speaking from the distant end of a tunnel. Turning toward my sister, I imagine our eyes reflect the same uncertainty. We both know what we're supposed to do, but my feet refuse to move.

"He…he didn't…show us how to use the gun," she stammers.

Crap! Silently inventorying everything he gave us, I'm relieved that we have what we need. Unfortunately, we don't know how to use it all.

"Riley, there's nothing we can do about it now. Besides, we've got to get out of here. You heard what he said."

Shrugging her shoulders dejectedly, she nods.

"You're right. Maybe Aidan and Jeff can help us figure out how to use the gun." I'm not sure we're supposed to tell them we have it, but I don't want to discuss that right now. We've got to go.

"Alright, Quinn, I'll take the keys," she presents an open palm, holding it out expectantly. My eyebrows jump in surprise. The old Riley would never make that offer in a potentially precarious situation like this. Acknowledging she's the more experienced driver, I drop them in her outstretched hand.

While she adjusts the mirrors and driver's seat, I load our supplies into the trunk. No need to show off our goodies. The base is still relatively silent and calm. I wonder how much longer it will bask in this tranquil state.

Chapter 14

Riley eases out of the lot, her cautious eyes bouncing in every direction. We inch past civilians and soldiers who casually stroll to and from buildings in small groups. They're probably grabbing an evening meal at the mess hall or looking to blow off some steam at the bowling alley.

Here and there, eyes land on us and track our movement. "I think we're going too slow. You should speed up a bit." Keeping her eyes glued to the road, Riley nods and accelerates. Slightly. Impatience seeps out of my right foot as it taps the floor, bouncing in place. If I was driving, I'd zoom right outta here at a whopping thirty miles per hour.

I attempt to squelch my annoyance by focusing on the scenery we pass. This should be the last time I see any of this.

"Look at these people, Riley," I say, motioning out my window, even though I know her eyes are trained on our route.

"None of them know this lockdown is coming. I wonder how long they'll have to stay here."

"Yeah, I guess we're really lucky that Bowen guy asked for our help. Otherwise, we'd be just like all of them: trapped lab rats."

Nervousness stifles the conversation and charges the air as we roll toward the gate entrance. Intermittent red lights flash along a bar that runs over the guard shacks. Their sporadic blinking display, along with the guard's leisurely pace, confirm that it is still business as usual.

Riley's hands drop from the wheel and find each other, twisting with anxiety. Fiercely, I hiss between closed lips, "Stop it! You look like you're hiding something!"

With a deep breath, Riley smooths her long brown locks from her scalp to her shoulders. She powers the driver's side window down and greets the soldier with a smile. His chiseled face remains stoic.

"Ma'am, this entrance is for authorized personnel only. I'm going to need you to turn around and proceed to the main gate." He starts pointing in the direction he's attempting to send us but Riley cuts in.

"I know this is a restricted gate, but we got special permission from Sergeant Bowen to use it." The soldier sighs, narrowing his eyes. Before he can challenge the statement, I blurt, "Yeah, the sergeant says he's got an Alpha Charlie for anyone who gives us a hassle."

The words bounce from my lips with a sing-song tattletale quality. *No such luck sounding intimidating.* The air blisters with anticipation as we await his response. As he cocks his head to the side like a confused dog, another soldier calls out from the other guard booth.

A bead of sweat descends along my spine as my nerves tingle. *Please let us go. Please let us go.*

"Everything okay over there, Kessel?" His eyes slide from us to the other soldier. Waving a hand in the air in an affirmative gesture, he turns back toward us and slams a flat palm down on the car's roof. Riley and I practically launch out of our seats in surprise. Kessel's lips part in a sly smirk.

"Alright, if the sergeant said so, proceed." He backs away from the car with two sure-footed steps and motions for another guard to let us through. We both inhale a deep breath and Riley rolls the car forward cautiously as the creaky mechanical arm swings open.

Once the last Langley Air Force Base sign we pass fades in the rearview mirror, the tension begins to erode.

"We did it!" I squeal. "We're going home!" Riley pounds the roof and my feet stomp the floor. After a few celebratory "Woots," Riley turns toward me, suddenly silent.

"Quinn! Where are we headed *right now*? I need to know where to drive!" I erupt in laughter but quickly wipe the smile from my face when Riley's death glare targets me.

"Okay, okay," I raise my hands placatingly. "Sorry, we're going to Jasmine's house to find Aidan and Jeff."

"How about an address or something?" she utters impatiently.

"Right! Can you pull over? I need to get the tracker out of the trunk."

After a quick stop, I scramble to fire up the tracking device with one hand while digging through my backpack with the other. Aidan wrote Jasmine's last name down for me and the sergeant was able to provide her address.

Riley drives in simmering silence, clearly annoyed by my lack of preparedness. The tension dissipates when a robotic voice rings out, "Destination located. Proceed on the calculated route."

My stomach churns with nervous anticipation as I scan the screen. We're only twenty minutes away from Jasmine's house. And Aidan. I hope.

Chapter 15

We pass a few cars and trucks as we drive, but we're too focused on our plans to pay them much attention. Now that we have clear directions, Riley's mood turns inquisitive.

"So, Aidan, Jeff, and Jasmine are all college friends, right?"

"Yep," I affirm. "They were heading south on Route One when the earthquake happened. So they were stranded like us." She nods.

"Yeah, I remember now. So it will be Jasmine, Aidan, Jeff, and then Jasmine's parents?" she continues, biting her lower lip.

"No one ever mentioned if Jasmine has any siblings, but I think one version of Jasmine running around in the world is enough. Oh, and don't forget Chris. You didn't meet him, but he should be there too. He's ten and he's kind of a pain but he should be Jasmine's parents' problem now. They're adults. They'll know what to do with him."

She nods, keeping her eyes fixed on the road ahead. "Quinn, how are we going to explain the car and supplies to everyone? I mean, we're sworn to secrecy but of course they're gonna ask how we suddenly have the means to get home."

I hadn't thought that far ahead. Which actually isn't very far ahead now, considering we have less than half an hour to figure this out.

"Well," I start, thinking as the words tumble out. "Maybe we can just be vague and tell them as little as possible."

"I know!" Riley exclaims. "We'll park the car a street away and walk to Jasmine's house. Then if we can just get the guys and leave, we'll tell them about the car and lead them back to it. We don't have to tell Jasmine's whole family about any of it."

"Yeah, I like that," I nod. "I really just want to head north as soon as we can. And, we're going to have to explain to the guys why we're stopping in Maryland to give someone a satellite phone!"

"Yeah, Bowen knows we're trying to find our friends so that we can all head home together. He must know we can't keep absolutely everything he said a secret." I silently nod in agreement, crossing my arms. *I didn't really think about all this when I was being sworn to secrecy.*

Silence engulfs the car for just a moment before Riley whispers, "Where do you think Jim is?" Thoughts swirl through my mind, just beyond reach when I attempt to grasp conclusions. With everything happening and the rush of leaving the base, I almost forgot that Jim is out there somewhere. *I wonder if he knows I'm the one they brought Riley to see. If he does, he's probably pretty ticked off at me right not.*

"I really don't know," I admit. "I never thought he'd just up and run. I figured he'd stay at the base with Dan. Maybe he actually figured out that kidnapping is a crime—even when the world goes to crap."

I glance out the window, as if Jim might magically appear because we're talking about him. Instead the city has faded into outskirts. Convenience stores and fast food restaurants crop up intermittently, interspersed among apartment buildings and boxy brick houses. Riley's voice pulls me from the scenery.

"When I was with them," she says slowly. "Dan told me that Jim is in love with me." She shoots me a side eye to gauge my reaction. My stomach churns as I process her words. I fight the urge to grind my teeth and ball my hands into fists. She doesn't need my anger, but it's blazing just below the surface.

"Seriously?" I question. "That asshat doesn't love anyone but himself!" I brace myself for the guilt she typically wields when I'm rude, but she surprises me with a short burst of laughter.

"You're right, Quinn. I think you were right about a lot of things when it comes to Jim." She pulls her eyes from the road to meet mine momentarily. I'm stunned silent. Right about now, the Riley I know would be lecturing me about only seeing the worst in people. *This new Riley isn't so bad.* When I don't respond, she continues.

"I bet he'll stay near the base, near Dan." The slight flicker of her eye confirms that she believes that statement about as much as I do. I'd like to agree with her theory, but the chill slinking along the nape of my neck says otherwise.

Changing the subject, Riley quietly asks, "Does it bother you that the sergeant is rushing us so much? If the guys are still at

Jasmine's house, we have to convince them to leave really fast."

"Honestly," I shrug. "All I've wanted since this whole mess started was to go home. The sooner we can get there, the better. And without the sergeant's offer, we'd still be sitting on that base wishing for a way home."

Keeping her eyes fixed on the road, she slowly nods in agreement. We fall silent as the robotic GPS voice commands our next moves. Following the directions, we wind our way over back roads and down neighborhood streets. The closer we get to Jasmine's house, the stronger my nerves jitter. I doubt Jasmine will be happy to see us, but obviously Aidan wanted me to find him again. I wouldn't even know where they were if he didn't write down Jasmine's last name so that I could look up her address.

Although dusk has fallen, and the streets are quiet, a sense of near-normalcy hovers just beyond our windows. A woman walks a leashed dog on the sidewalk. Vein-like cracks wind through the concrete. I'm guessing those are courtesy of the earthquake, or maybe the aftershocks. The pair pauses so he can saturate a collapsed fire hydrant. She waves as if we're neighbors. I hesitantly return the gesture.

Only small hints of destruction linger. Either this area wasn't hit as hard as the northern states or they were able to repair some damage rather quickly.

Two-story homes with lush green lawns line the street. Occasional patches of upturned grass suggest that something crushed the previously-healthy landscape, but has since been cleared away.

Beds of blooming wildflowers intersperse between

streetlamps along the sidewalks. Most are lit, but some appear to have shattered. No glass shards rest at the base, confirming that whatever dropped there was tended to, even if the bulbs have yet to be replaced.

As we roll past the occupied homes, I catch glimpses of normalcy within their walls. A family gathers for an evening meal. White light emanates from a static-filled television. A cat lazily glances out a window.

Jealousy tinges my thoughts. Were these people even remotely impacted by the earthquake that devastated so many others along the East Coast? Like us.

Most houses appear to have electricity. The people in this neighborhood have mostly restored their homes to order. Although we don't pass many cars or people on the streets, it's clear that life is chugging along just fine here.

The female guidance system voice cuts through the silence. "Your destination is just ahead on the right." Riley throws me a knowing nod and proceeds past Jasmine's house. We park the car around the corner a block away and stash our supplies in the trunk.

I lead the way to 16 Larkspur Lane. Depressing the circular doorbell, I step back and inhale a deep breath. Out of the corner of my eye, I catch the movement of Riley's wringing hands.

Chapter 16

Movement blurs behind the rectangular stained-glass center of the navy-blue door. Shadows swallow the warm background light as a figure approaches. The handle twists a moment before the door swings inward.

Surprise washes over a familiar face as her eyes widen and her mouth drops. In this moment, all prior misgivings are forgotten. Jasmine was never my favorite person, but finding her brings me one step closer to finding Aidan and Jeff. And once they walk through this door, we can set off on our journey home together.

A smile tugs at her lips. "You found us."

I return her smile and nod my head. "We did. And we found each other."

"Who is it?" a deep male voice calls from inside the house. Ignoring it, Jasmine remains planted in place, focused on her unexpected guests. She shifts her attention from me.

"Riley?" A smile blazes across Jasmine's face. "It's really you?" Riley nods shyly.

As if suddenly remembering proper etiquette, she swings the door open wide and waves her hand as if presenting her home to us. "Come on in, the guys are still here. And you can meet my parents."

Her parents. A twinge of jealousy slices through my initial feeling of triumph at having found the others. Riley and I take two hesitant steps over the threshold when the owner of the deep voice that called to Jasmine earlier appears.

"Jasmine, are these the friends that went to Langley?" he asks, towering over us. I'd guess he's nearly 6' 6" tall. His intimidating frame is balanced by a welcoming broad smile.

"Yeah, Dad," Jasmine answers, turning toward him. "This is Quinn and Riley." Tilting her head back to us, she adds. "And this is my dad."

His dark complexion mirrors Jasmine's, yet he radiates a genuine friendliness that his daughter does not. At least not upon first impression. He runs a hand over his bald head before extending it toward us.

"It's nice to meet you girls. I'm Lucas. I heard how you stuck together to get down here safely. That was a smart move." He begins to mutter under his breath before Jasmine jabs an elbow into his ribs, abruptly stopping the flow of words. "And a certain young man's been talking about one of you almost nonst—"

"Dad!" Jasmine warns, shooting him a threatening glare. Releasing a chuckle, he runs a hand over his head again. *Maybe that was a nervous habit from when he had a full head of hair.*

"Right, anyway, come on in," he offers, beckoning us further

64

into the house. Like magnets, my eyes are drawn to Riley's in a side glance. We don't have time for this. I just want to get the guys and get on the road. As I'm about to explain that we can't stay, clomping footfalls echo through the hallway before us.

"Quinn!" Smiling eyes peek out from behind shaggy blond bangs. Chris hurtles toward me and throws his arms around my waist. I recover from the momentary surprise at his warm welcome—I barely know the kid. He appears to be the same unpredictable ten-year-old that barely bid me farewell a few days ago at the base.

Glancing around self-consciously, my tension melts when I see Jasmine and her dad smiling at Chris warmly. Riley just watches raptly. She never met Chris. Aidan and I had found him at the trailer park when we were looking for Riley.

"Hey, Chris," I begin, "this is my sister, Riley. You didn't get to meet her yet." Riley bends down to his level, but before she can say anything, he grabs my hand and pulls me down the hallway, calling back.

"I know that's your sister. Come see Aidan and Jeff!" In an effort to ensure that my shoulder remains in its socket, I loosen my instinctual resistance and let the kid drag me away.

Chapter 17

Although the surroundings are mostly a blur as Chris tugs me down a hallway and around a corner, I catch snippets of vibrant colors and modern décor. He stops abruptly when we reach a sunken living room.

Unfortunately, my legs receive the message a little too late, and my body crashes into his, sending us both stumbling down the hardwood steps. We both catch ourselves, thankfully, before either of us collide with the glass coffee table.

As I catch my breath and smooth the hair out of my eyes, a familiar voice confirms my suspicion that an audience had witnessed our grand entrance.

"There's the graceful girl I remember! Quinn, how the heck are ya?" Jeff jumps up from an indigo, wrap-around couch, springing to my side.

My cheeks scorch to a deep crimson. "Hey, Jeff, good to see y—" he pulls me into a bear hug, practically squeezing every last molecule of oxygen from my lungs. When he releases me, I take an unsteady step backward to maintain balance and take in his appearance. His short brown hair is starting to grow out, reaching a slightly unwieldy length. His hazel eyes radiate happiness as he shifts focus.

Jeff brushes past me to approach my sister. "Riley?" His eyes twinkle with amusement while a smirk dances across his lips. She nods shyly and he rests a hand on her shoulder. "It's great to see you again too." She flashes a toothy smile in response.

"Quinn...is that you?" My stomach flutters and my cheeks flush. It's only been a few days, but I'd know that voice anywhere. I slowly turn toward him.

Aidan and a middle-aged version of Jasmine teeter on the top step leading into the living room. Their arms are loaded with snacks: a bowl of popcorn, a plate of chocolate chip cookies, and a platter of cheese and crackers.

The woman hops down the two hardwood steps and plops the refreshments on the coffee table. Aidan follows and quickly empties his hands too. They face us, wearing matching expressions of curious disbelief.

"Well, hello," she says, reaching out for a welcoming hug. "I'm Jasmine's mom, Celina. I've heard a lot about you girls," glancing at my sister, she adds, "both of you." After a brief but warm embrace, she sidesteps to Riley and does the same.

Aidan takes her place before me. The smile spreading across his lips reaches his blue eyes, which blaze with wonder. My insides twist with nervous exhilaration. He leans in close and speaks softly, as if his words are meant only for me.

"You did it. You found your sister and you found us." He shakes his head in mock disbelief. Pride swells within me, painting a goofy smile that must dominate my face.

"Well, you know, I had a little bit of help along the way," I remind him in a near-whisper. In that moment, the room and everything in it fades away. The only sounds come from within: a deep thudding in my chest and the rapid exhalations escaping my mouth.

A strong arm wraps around my shoulder, yanking me from the dream-like trance.

"Hey, guys," Jeff announces. I notice his other arm is draped over Aidan's shoulder. "You know, there are like six other people here! Maybe you could take a detour to Couplesville later and join the rest of us now."

Once again, my cheeks flush crimson and the adrenaline rush commands me to seek an exit. The long orange-and-white paisley curtains dangle just over the hardwood floor. If there was some sort of distraction, maybe I could dash behind the bright swaths of fabric and hide for the rest of the night.

When Jeff retrieves his arms, Aidan and I both take an instinctual step backward.

Without hesitation, Jasmine's mom breaks through the awkwardness with animated gestures. "Everyone, sit. Sit down and relax." Her hands fly through the air faster than her words, motioning everyone toward the lush couches and recliners. We scramble to sit, as if the tune was just cut off in a game of musical chairs.

I land on the middle cushion of the sofa, planted between

Riley and Jeff. Jasmine's parents lead the conversation, asking us about our time on the base. Riley and I answer as vaguely as possible, but each answer leads to another question.

Chris scamps about the room, swooping toward the coffee table every few minutes to swipe a cookie. But otherwise, he doesn't pay much attention to the discussion. I can't mask the smile tugging at my lips as my eyes trail his gleeful movements. He looks genuinely happy, in complete contrast to the uncertain, lonely kid Aidan and I first met at the trailer park.

For a moment, I wish my biggest concern was how many cookies I could stuff into my mouth before my stomach threatened to revolt. I shake my head, willing myself to return to the adult conversation.

Jasmine's dad is explaining that he's a doctor, and he's not too pleased to hear about the required vaccination for anyone entering the base. The whole topic sends rushes of heat through my core, seemingly spiking the temperature in the room to an unbearable level. My palms slicken and my forehead beads with perspiration.

I hate knowing the truth and not being able to share it. These are obviously good people and withholding what I know feels like lying. Like a betrayal. But telling them would break my promise to the sergeant. And without his help, we wouldn't be here right now. And we wouldn't be one step closer to getting home.

I'm yanked from my internal struggle when the voices around me rise. Jasmine's dad questions her. I get the feeling this scene has played out several times over the past few days.

"Did they tell you what they were injecting you with?" he

asks impatiently. "Did they ask if you had any allergies? Because that's the first thing to consider."

"Dad, they didn't really ask. They just told us we were getting the vaccine," she explains.

"For what purpose?" he demands.

"I told you already. They said that they had to protect all the people on the base, so they didn't get sick from being exposed to all kind of germs from people showing up."

"But you specifically told them you weren't going to stay, so why would they still vaccinate you?" he questions. Jasmine's mom steps between them, placing a gentle hand on her husband's arm.

Guilt sinks in my gut like lead. My gaze drops to the floor in a lame attempt to avoid meeting anyone's eyes. I know we can't tell them what the sergeant told us. I barely know Jasmine's family, but they deserve to know what their daughter was injected with.

"Lucas, that's enough. She's already told you what she knows." He rubs his face with the palms of his hands. Visibly relaxing, he steadies the tone of his voice.

"You're right," he agrees. Turning to Jasmine he says, "I'm sorry, honey. It just bothers me so much that they did that, and we don't even know what it is or what the potential side effects are."

"There's nothing we can do about it now," Jasmine's mom says quietly. Placing his hands on his hips in an attempt to look stern, he shakes his head in defeat.

"I have half a mind to go down there myself and demand to know what they're injecting people with," he says.

Jasmine rolls her eyes. "Do that and they'll inject you too!" Her words shatter the tension and the room erupts in laughter.

Chapter 18

The laughter subsides, inviting a natural break in the conversation. Jasmine's mother rises and starts to gather what's left of the snacks. Her husband jumps to his feet and follows her lead, collecting plates and napkins. Together, they retreat to the kitchen.

Riley asks where the bathroom is, and Jeff offers to show her. Chris zooms back into the room and tugs Jasmine down a hallway. It's just me and Aidan. Alone. We shyly meet each other's eyes, which ignites fireworks in my chest.

Holding my gaze, he stands and moseys over to the couch, plopping down next to me. Like attracting magnets, we turn toward each other, angled so that our knees are just centimeters apart. I focus on holding still. A nervous energy attempts to escape, inciting my limbs to twitch. My nerves are tingling.

He rests an arm along the top of the couch cushion and runs a hand through his hair, sending dark tufts skyward.

"So, I think everything is starting to go back to normal," he begins to say, watching me intently. I force my face to remain expressionless. *That's not what Sergeant Bowen said*, I think to myself.

"Electricity is being restored in some places. And…phone lines too. I got to talk to my parents," he says, breaking into a wide grin.

Sharp tendrils of jealousy clamp around my heart. "That's great!" I cringe inwardly as my voice cracks with forced enthusiasm.

His smile falters and the deep blue pools of his eyes reflect shamed sorrow. Guilt washes through me. His luck has nothing to do with my loss. I'm glad that his family is okay, but the reality of it scrapes at my invisible wounds that will never fully heal.

"I'm sorry, Quinn." He thrusts a hand through his dark messy hair again. His pained expression makes me feel worse. I reach a shaky hand out and gently squeeze his shoulder.

"You have no reason to be sorry. Nothing that happened is your fault. And I *am* happy for you. I'm glad you reached your family and I hope you can get back to them soon."

Grateful eyes meet mine as a weak smile brandishes his lips.

"It took some convincing to keep my dad from driving down here to bring us home. I told him the family shouldn't be split up even more. He needs to be home with my mom and sisters. I was able to hold him off—for now, at least. So that means we've got ourselves another adventure."

Once everyone has wandered back to the living room, Jasmine's dad gets to the point.

"Well, kids, this old man is getting tired, so we best discuss your plans." He leans forward, elbows resting on his knees, and rubs his palms together. He shifts his focus from me to Riley to the guys, maintaining eye contact with each of us in turn. "Now you're welcome to stay here for as long as you'd like," he says, waving his hands around. "But I'm guessing that's not what you want to do."

Riley and I share a glance. She throws me a quick nod, silently encouraging me to respond. Inhaling a deep breath, I rest my hands in my lap. "Well, we were actually planning to get on the road tonight still." I turn to Riley for support, but her smile deflates as the air practically crackles with tension.

A chorus of protests erupts around us. "It's getting late and it's dark outside."

"No, you can't go now! Wait until the morning."

"Just stay the night. We'll get you set up in a spare bedroom."

Jasmine hops down from the poufy footrest she's curled up on and rushes to Jeff's side. I tune out the other voices for a moment and focus on them. Alarm shades her eyes when she reaches the recliner he's lounging in. "You can't leave already!" He nonchalantly shrugs his shoulders.

Although he remains unfazed by my announcement, Jasmine and her family are clearly distressed. *How did this become a big deal?* I shoot to my feet to ensure that I've got everyone's attention.

"Okay, okay," I hold my arms out. They all stop mid-sentence, awaiting my next words. "We can wait until the morning. We're just, you know, eager to get home."

DEVASTATION ERUPTS

A relieved hush permeates the room. It dissipates just as quickly as it descended when a small voice slices through the fleeting silence.

"You know, I've been thinking and…I want to go home, too. I'm coming with you."

Chapter 19

All eyes turn to Chris, who lingers just at the edge of the living room. He slowly edges toward a hallway that I assume leads to the bedrooms.

"What?" Lucas stands, running a thick hand over his forehead. "You want to go back home, son?" His kind eyes are calm, but sorrow lurks behind his dark irises. Chris nods meekly.

My head automatically twists toward Aidan and his bewildered eyes meet my glare. Chris practically begged us to take him away from home. We were afraid to leave him behind because he seemed determined to leave and we didn't want him to find and go with the wrong people, who would have no intention of helping him. And now that he's out of there, he wants to go back?

Jasmine's mom slowly rises and glides toward Chris, lightly touching Jasmine's shoulder as she passes her daughter. She kneels down to meet Chris' eyes.

"Honey, if that's what you want, you can go home. We don't really have any right to keep you here. And your parents must be worried sick." She turns toward Lucas and he gives her a sad nod. Heads slowly turn toward me and Riley.

"Girls, would you be willing to take Chris with you and make sure he gets back home?" she asks. Frustration threatens to spill out of my mouth but thankfully Riley answers.

"Of course, we'll keep him safe." She smiles as I silently seethe. Once again, this kid is going to delay my mission. This means we'll have to bring him back to the trailer park, or his home—wherever that is. If not for this, we would be heading straight to Sergeant Bowen's wife. That was supposed to be our last stop before Pennsylvania.

With the adults distracted, Chris tears off down the hallway. Words flutter around the room, but none come into focus. I'm two breaths away from crossing my arms and stomping my feet when I realize every other face in the room bears a genuine smile. Even my sister, who just met Chris and is just as anxious to get home as I am.

Guilt slithers through my mind, hampering selfish thoughts. Chris is just a kid and he probably didn't think much beyond the adventure of tagging along with us. I'm guilty of the same.

I agreed that he should come with us, but I didn't really think about what would happen to him or the others after we got to the base. I had one goal in mind: to find my sister. Now that I have, it probably wouldn't hurt to put some good karma out there and hope it comes back around.

The conversation dwindles and relief descends upon the room. Lucas releases a satisfied sigh and slaps his knees. "Well,

I'm glad that's settled. Now why don't we all get some rest." It's more a statement than a question. As we all rise to our feet, Jasmine's mom reaches out toward Riley and I.

"Come with me, I'll get you girls set up for the night." We nod gratefully. All this planning is exhausting. I never would have admitted it, but they're right. We need sleep. Morning will come soon enough and then we'll finally be on the road to home.

Jasmine's mom leads us down the hallway and sweeps open the door to a lavish aqua bedroom. The cool décor is inviting, as if invisible arms guide us inside. *I guess this isn't so bad.*

"Thank you," Riley says graciously. "This room, and your whole home, is beautiful." Jasmine's mom smiles, thanking her. Riley returns the smile, but it catches on her right cheek. The scar is healing nicely, but I wonder if that side of her face will ever return to its former smoothness.

"Girls," Celina's smile fades and her tone turns serious. "I know it probably seems odd that Chris wants to go with you tomorrow, but he's been talking about home lately. I don't believe he fully understood what he was asking when he begged to tag along with you. I won't belabor it, but...just be patient with him, okay? I think he's confused and just needs to be back where he belongs."

Riley and I nod. I don't understand the kid, but maybe I should at least try not to begrudge him for being an inconvenience. Confident that we're accepting the responsibility of taking the kid with us, Celina points across the hallway.

"You girls are welcome to shower if you'd like, either tonight or in the morning. It's up to you, but the bathroom's right there.

Just help yourself to towels in the linen closet."

"Thank you," we both say. It's probably not a bad idea to wash up so we're all ready to go in the morning. After a final round of bidding everyone goodnight, Riley and I take turns showering. By the time we've both climbed into the double bed, my eyes begin to drift closed. My sister's urgently whispered words yank me from the fringes of sleep.

"Quinn, this is probably our last chance to talk. Alone. Until we get home, I mean." Her words ride on a wave of worry, spilling faster with each syllable. "How are we gonna keep everything Bowen told us a secret?"

"I don't know," I sigh. "I don't think we can. We need the GPS, so we can't keep that a secret. Maybe we tell the guys about Bowen's wife after we drop Chris off. Then they'll only know for a little while and by the time they get home, they'll be so happy to see their family that they'll forget all about our little side mission."

"Yeah," Riley starts, building onto my idea. "And we probably won't even need the weapons. We can just leave them in the trunk. The guys will never know we have them."

"Good idea! That's probably the best we can do at this point. It seems like anytime we have a plan figured out, everything goes haywire."

Agreeing that there's no point in detailing what will probably go wrong anyway, we settle into the fluffy pillows and tug the teal bedspread up to our shoulders. Moments later, I drift to another plane, comforted by the rhythmic, relaxed breathing that floats to my ears.

When sunlight invades the room, I rouse Riley from sleep. We rush to dress and ready for our road trip. Retracing our steps, we make our way to the dining room. I guess we're not the only ones ready to start this day. Jasmine and her parents prepare a mini feast of eggs, bacon, pancakes, and coffee, while Aidan, Jeff, and Chris gather their belongings, depositing them in a pile by the door.

The hot breakfast is delicious, and the conversation is clipped. Anticipation hangs in the air around us. Lucas and Celina impose some typical parenting advice: drive safely, go straight to the trailer park to get Chris home, don't talk to anyone on the way. They even instruct Chris on how to explain what happened and where he spent his time away from home—in hopes that no one gets angry with us for taking the kid in the first place.

When the last slice of bacon and the last gulp of coffee are swallowed, everyone helps clean up the table. Lucas turns serious when he realizes no one has asked about a mode of transportation. I was kinda hoping no one would think of that until we were at least a few miles down the road.

Riley breeches the hushed air with lies that roll off her tongue like smooth caramel, "Oh, our dad was in the service. When we explained to personnel on the base what we were trying to do, they loaned us a car and gave us strict instructions for how to return it to a military facility once we get home. I think they felt kind of obligated to help us. You know, for everything our dad did."

When did my sister get so good at lying?

Chapter 20

Aidan squints his eyes in obvious disbelief but keeps quiet.

Thankfully.

When our arms and packs are loaded with belongings, the hugging commences. Jasmine's parents pull each of us into an embrace as though we've known them all our lives. The familiar parental expression sends a surge of sadness through me. It's not the same as hugs from my parents, but it's close enough to be a painful reminder of all I've lost. I swallow the grief and try to focus on my ultimate goal of returning home. The last thing I want to do right now is start crying.

Almost like an assembly line, we exchange parting well wishes and appreciation for our hosts' generosity. Before long, tears spill and the hugs turn fierce, especially when it's time for Jasmine to part with Jeff and Aidan.

"You couldn't get something a little sportier?" His eyebrows jump in question. "Maybe a convertible or at least something with a sunroof—maybe something a little brighter than concrete?"

I turn to Riley. "We should've just left them here and went straight home!"

The clear, promising sky lumbers in stark contrast to Bowen's parting words. I want to believe that our small part of the world is recovering from nature's recent wrath, but his clear warning niggles at my brain.

The government knew about that earthquake in the Atlantic, but they didn't warn anyone. And now this Yellowstone eruption is being kept under wraps too.

Riley beelines to the driver's side and unlocks the car. She pops the trunk open. As it slowly stutters upward, I grasp it and toss my backpack inside then move aside so the others can do the same.

Aidan and Jeff pitch their bags into the trunk without hesitation. Chris meanders over next, his eyes wandering from one side of the carpeted space to the other. *Now what's the problem?*

"What's that stuff?" he asks, pointing toward the supplies Sergeant Bowen gave us. Shooting him the sternest look I can muster, I point toward the backseat. "Nothing for you to worry about. Now get in the car so we can get outta here." He crosses his arms and paces to the backseat. A snarky utterance drifts to my ears, "I knew her sister was the nice one."

For someone who wanted to come with us again, the kid sure doesn't act appreciative. *We're going out of our way to drop him off and he's giving me attitude?* I shake my head as if it will ward off my heightened annoyance.

Checking the trunk one last time, my eyes sweep over the supplies. I realize that we need the GPS. Everything else can stay for now. Yanking the case out, I sling it over my shoulder and slam the trunk closed. *Finally. Let's go!*

Striding to the passenger seat, I stop mid-step when I notice the squabble outside of Riley's open window. Aidan and Jeff are debating over which one of them should drive. My sister smiles at them both. "Uh, guys, *I'm* driving, so no need to argue." She dangles the keys in the air, the jingling sound mocking their pointless discussion. Jeff turns on the charm, sauntering into a lean, casually resting his elbow on the door.

"You sure you don't want to just sit back and relax and let me worry about getting us there?" he asks, waggling his eyebrows. As if that will change anything.

"And I'm navigating, so I get the front," I announce.

The guys fix their attention on us, clearly dissatisfied. Realizing they're not getting anywhere in the quest to command the wheels, they shift gears. "So you're seriously not gonna tell us how you got a car?" Jeff asks, crossing his arms. Aidan's eyebrows jump in anticipation. Riley and I share a knowing smile and shake our heads. *Nope, not yet. We can't.*

"Girls in the front and boys in the back!" Chris proclaims, his mood suddenly matching the sun's rising rays. Looking defeated, Jeff and Aidan follow the kid as he scampers into the back seat.

Finally. We're ready to go.

Chapter 21

As the boys choose their seats, I nonchalantly unzip the satellite phone's bag and slide the device onto my lap. Just as I depress the button to turn it on, Riley throws her door open.

"I almost forgot something! Be right back." She pops the trunk open one more time and dashes outside.

The phone emits a faint beep. "Hey! What was that?" Of course Chris would hear it. Before I can conjure an explanation, he leans forward, eyes darting around the front seat. "Hey! What is that thing?" He launches a pointer finger toward the phone. Aidan and Jeff lean forward, two sets of questioning eyes bouncing between the device and me. *How am I gonna explain that we have a satellite phone?*

Riley bursts back into the car, unfolding a paper map as she settles into the driver's seat. She capitalizes on the hush that has overtaken the vehicle. *At least it distracts from their questions about the phone.*

"So, I…had an idea." Her eyes shift to each of us. My shoulders sag in anticipation of words I won't want to hear. *We don't need any new ideas. We've got a plan. All we need to do is stick to it.*

She inhales a deep breath before unleashing a stream of thoughts.

"So, when I was…*with*…Dan and Jim," she pauses to slip some stray hairs behind her ear. "We stopped at this place. This guy's place. And he had dogs. Like, a lot of dogs."

"That's great and all, Riley, but maybe we should—" My attempt to jump start this trip is thwarted.

"So these dogs are part of a fighting ring." Her tone rises with a slight tremor. "They're chained outside all the time, and they're forced to fight each other." Squeezing her eyes shut tight, her voice drops to a whisper. "They're starving and probably dehydrated, you guys. They aren't really living. They're tortured prisoners."

From one breath to the next, her sorrow sparks into fury. "We've got to help them." She turns in her seat, toward each of us individually as if willing us to understand and agree.

"Riley, you know we promised…I mean, we've got to head north. We don't really have extra time." Already I've got to filter my thoughts to avoid telling the guys about Bowen's instructions.

Running a hand through his hair, Aidan slouches back into his seat. "Well, things are finally starting to get back to normal." He motions toward Jeff. "And we both talked to our parents so they know we're on our way. It probably wouldn't take that long to make a quick side trip. I don't know, I kinda think we could do it."

"Yeah," Chris jumps in. "I agree. Aidan's right."

Who gave the kid a vote?

"Shouldn't we just report it?" Jeff interjects. "I mean, besides being cruel, it's illegal gambling. Police investigate that stuff." He raises his arms in question. "Why would we go all *vigilante* when we could just call the cops?"

"Do you really think they have the time to deal with this?" Riley's tone hinges on frustration. "And how long will those dogs have to suffer until someone can get around to it? And what if another earthquake or something happens and everyone's dealing with that?"

I flash Riley a look of warning. We cannot talk about Yellowstone. Besides, I really want to believe that Bowen was wrong. That it's just a big misunderstanding.

"Either *we're* going or *I'm* going," Riley huffs, crossing her arms. Dread pits in my stomach. *Are we ever going to get home?* The guys turn away in uncomfortable silence.

This is not my sister. I mean, I love dogs too, but what can we really do? We're a ragtag bunch of kids. We're not law enforcement officers. I lean closer, asking what is only meant for her ears.

"What happened to you out there? This doesn't sound like something you'd want to even try."

Averting her eyes outside the window for a moment, she takes a breath before responding.

"Quinn, every choice we make out there right now," she pauses to point out the window, "is going to either help or hurt others. I will fight to keep us safe, but if I have the ability to help someone in the process, then that's what I'll do. I've been paralyzed by everything that's happened over the past few weeks and I'm done. I have to help those dogs."

Tearfully, the Riley I know returns briefly, "They can't save themselves like we can."

Aidan returns to the conversation. "How many dogs are we talking about? And where are they?"

"Not far from here. I think it's practically on our way back home," Riley answers with a weak smile. "And it's just a few dozen dogs. Oh, and some puppies."

"Puppies?" Jeff asks, eyes wide. He stretches an arm over the seat, giving my shoulder a gentle shove. "Come on, Quinn, no one can resist puppies."

Crossing my arms, I give Jeff the stink eye. Of course they're all right, we can't leave the dogs—and puppies—to suffer. I just wish it didn't have to be us. Why can't someone else help them? We have our own problems.

"Fine," I concede. "Let's do it."

Riley and I practically eject out of our seats when Jeff hollers from the backseat. "Buckle up, ladies! Adventure awaits!"

Chapter 22

"Okay, so we'll go there. Then what do we do? We can't exactly take dozens of dogs home with us," I point out. "And they might be vicious—rightfully so."

"We just set them free," Riley says. "Trust me, anything is better than the life they have right now." The look in my sister's eyes tells me that ignoring their plight will haunt her for the rest of her days. There's no other choice. Sighing, I point toward the map her slender fingers cradle.

"What's the address? I'll plug it into this thing so we can finally start moving. You all figure out how we're going to get the chains or collars off them without having a limb torn off."

Forty minutes. We have forty minutes to figure out a plan. With our first destination entered into the GPS, Riley finally shifts the car into drive.

Aidan and Jeff huddle in the backseat troubleshooting options. "What if we get an axe and chop the chains off?" Jeff asks, eyebrows raised.

"Giving you an axe will definitely not make this world a better place." Aidan shakes his head, signaling the need for a better idea.

"Maybe we could get some treats. One person can distract them and then someone else can take the collars off," Chris suggests.

"Hey, Riley, did you notice anything about the collars? Were they leather or chains?" Aidan asks, perking up.

"All I noticed were thick chains," she glances in the rearview mirror to meet his eyes. "but I didn't really pay much attention. There were a lot of outbuildings, though, like sheds and small garages. Maybe there are tools inside those that we could use?"

"Yeah," Jeff jumps in. "The dirt bag that chained them up must have a way to remove the collars. I mean, when they fight, they probably aren't wearing chains and collars."

Aidan leans forward, rubbing his palms together. "Okay, so we park a short distance away and sneak onto the property. Magic hands over here," he motions toward Jeff, who smiles proudly, "can pick some locks on the sheds and we'll cross our fingers and toes there's something in there we can use."

"What about treats? We need something to keep them busy," Chris reminds us. "And I'll bet they don't ever get treats."

"Some of these places we're passing look like they're open," Riley mutters. "Anyone have any money?" It dawns on me that I can't remember the last time we needed to buy something. When Riley and I first got to our Aunt Grace's trailer, we had a stash of food and supplies that our parents had packed for vacation.

Then, when everything turned upside down, I ended up relying on others for what I needed—Rose gave us breakfast, we "borrowed" some food from a bowling alley and a pizza place, and we found a house that was free of people but loaded with food.

"I do," Aidan announces. "Lucas slipped me some cash just in case we needed gas or something for the ride home." Jeff crosses his arms and tilts his head in mock annoyance.

"Why didn't he give it to me? I'm way more trustworthy than you."

"He probably did eeny-meeny-miny-moe and I was the big winner," Aidan says, shaking his head again.

"Alright," I interrupt their banter. "So why don't we stop at the first place we see and buy dog treats. We'll be there before we know it." *Let's just get this over with so we can get back to our real goal—making it home.* I'd question whether we should really be doing this, but I've never seen that kind of determination in my sister's eyes before. Ever.

"Okay, guys," Riley says nervously. Her eyes flash between the rearview mirror and me. "There's a mini-mart up ahead. I'll stop there. Who's running in?"

"Since I'm the one with the money, I'll go. Quinn, why don't you come with me?" Aidan's blue eyes drill into mine, clouding any coherent thoughts. I nod dumbly.

"I'll go!" Chris yells, practically throwing himself out the door when we pull into the lot. Aidan shakes his head, but the smirk spreading across his face proves he's nowhere near as annoyed with Chris as I am. The kid's been so moody since he tagged along with us. Again. One minute he's thoroughly inconvenienced by where we parked the car and the next moment, he's practically jumping out of it to go buy dog treats.

Taking our cue from the kid, Aidan and I stumble out of the car and catch up to him. Two other cars linger in the parking lot. It sheds a touch of normalcy to the situation. Still, a month ago, I didn't even know these people and now I'm walking into a store with them to buy treats for dogs my sister wants to rescue. All because of an earthquake. A major earthquake along the Eastern seaboard that yanked my family tree from its roots. And the government knew about it. My parents were pretty cautious people. If an earthquake warning had been issued, they would have delayed our trip, no matter how much Riley and I whined about it. Glancing toward the sky, I shield my eyes from the sun's harsh rays. It shines as if nothing bad is on the horizon. Could Bowen's source be wrong? Maybe everything is getting back to normal. Or maybe I'd just really like to believe that.

Chapter 23

The clerk calls out a half-hearted greeting as we enter the store. It's barely discernable over the jingling bell wrapped around the door's handle. Aidan responds with a slight hand raise, throwing an awkward wave toward the man behind the counter.

Chris dashes up and down each aisle, searching for what is bound to be a meager assortment.

"I found 'em, guys!" Chris' announcement draws bored glances from customers gathering their slushy and cigarette purchases.

His fingertips leave a trail along the dusty shelf, tracking between a stack of slightly dented cans of dog food and exactly four boxes of bone-shaped crunchy treats. They'll have to do. Chris reaches toward them, pausing to look over his shoulder for our unspoken approval. Aidan gives him a single nod.

After a quick monetary exchange, we're back in the car buckling up for what's left of the drive to our first stop.

"So, do we know anything about who lives at this place?" Jeff asks.

"Yeah," Aidan adds. "If nobody's home can we just walk right on the property, release the hounds, get back in the car, and head north?"

Riley's shoulders noticeably slump. Her eyes remain glued to the road. Queasiness seeps from my stomach to my toes. She knows who lives there and it isn't good. Not that I really expected the homeowner to be a kind, misunderstood person who just happens to make dogs fight to the death.

Shooting me a side eye, Riley nervously answers. "I don't know much. Jim took us there, trying to get some help. I just walked around outside. That's when I saw all the dogs. Jim went in the house to talk to his friend, Vic. He owns the house and runs the dogfighting. All I know is that Jim came running back to the vehicle with his tail between his legs and couldn't seem to drive away from there fast enough."

She nervously laughs at the memory, covering her mouth with one hand, as if the reaction is inappropriate. Emotions in the car run a bit warped, fueled by the impending danger. Before she can silence the giggles, Chris and I join her. The three of us share a common hatred of Jim, thus we also share an inherent pleasure from hearing about him narrowly escaping misfortune.

My laughter dissolves when I realize that we're heading to the same place. I can only hope our outcome is very different. This would be a great time for karma to step in and let us do a good deed unscathed.

Seventy-four Newport Lane. The robotic GPS voice slices into my thoughts, announcing that we're five minutes from our destination. Jeff reiterates our plan. My nerves tingle with apprehension.

"We should start looking for a place to park," he says, eyes scanning both sides of the road. The rolling hills of the countryside morph into upturned dirt, downed trees, and scattered construction equipment.

"What's all that?" Chris asks, pointing out the window.

"Someone's building a pipeline here," Jeff answers. "Should we try to hide the car behind some equipment?"

"The driveway's pretty long. I was thinking we could just park toward the end of it and walk from there," Riley says.

"Maybe some of us should stay in the car and wait." Aidan runs a hand through his hair nervously. "I mean, the more people running around out there, the more likely we are to draw attention."

Riley and I lock eyes. Mine widen in surprise when I detect a determination that matches my own. The guys think we should wait in the car while they do all the dirty work—*or pretend to and expect us to be naïve enough to believe the charade.*

"Nope!" I start. Riley completes my thought. "Not happening!"

"Oooookkkaaayyyy," Aidan says, hunching his shoulders and raising his palms in defeat. "It was just an idea."

"So I guess we'll just take Chris out there with us," Jeff muses. "Instead of keeping him in the car, where it's safer."

Riley's narrowed eyes meet his in the rearview mirror. "That's a good point. You stay with him in the car. Quinn, Aidan and I will be back as soon as we're done." I nearly burst with laughter when she flashes the guys a sweet smile.

"Fine," Jeff concedes. "We *all* go!"

Chapter 24

As we creep up the driveway, hugging the edge where stones meet worn grass, it's clear we're not alone. A deep thrumming rents the air. Although my ears can't distinguish a song, the pounding rhythm overwhelms my senses, forcing my heart to race even faster than it was when we stepped foot on the property.

We gather behind the closest shed between the driveway and a massive white house. A thundering bass radiates within its walls, spilling outside and polluting the otherwise peaceful air, like a murky haze.

I scan the endless backyard, swiping the beads of nervous sweat from my forehead before shielding my eyes from the sun. Trees and bushes dot the far perimeter, but just like my sister said, the land before us bears the sorriest-looking bunch of dogs I've ever seen. From what I can tell they're all pit bulls.

Each is chained to a pathetic structure that's probably meant to resemble a doghouse. Some are attached to barrels resting on their sides with square openings cut into the round lids. Others are tethered to wooden boxes with shabby roofs.

Whatever grass may have once grown within the chain's radius has worn down to random patches of dying yellowed grass, dusty dirt, and the beginnings of exposed tree roots.

Although any sounds we make are likely muffled by the blaring music, a few nearby dogs sniff the air cautiously, as if sensing our presence. Aidan presses a finger to his lips in a "Shhh" signal.

I carefully lower the treat boxes to the ground and kneel, wedging a finger between each seal and sliding it to separate the cardboard. We've got to be ready to deploy our secret weapon when necessary.

Jeff tilts his head, motioning toward the closest shed, before he and Aidan slink away. Their mission is to investigate it as quietly as possible while Riley, Chris, and I stay rooted in place, watching for threats—human or canine.

Hopefully, they'll find something useful without having to search more than a few structures. At least half a dozen shack-like sheds litter the property, as far as I can see. The guys peer through the dirty windows and, satisfied with their choice, drop to their knees and set to work on the lock.

Less than two minutes later, Jeff raises his hands in victory while Aidan slowly pushes the door open. I take a quick inventory of my elite team.

Chris' eyes bounce from one dog to the next while his fingers dance as if he's silently counting them. Riley studies a treat box as if instructions for this mission hide in the nutritional details.

Confident I'm not needed, I investigate the shed with Aidan and Jeff. Tiptoeing toward the open door, I peek around it. My heart warms at the sight.

They found the mama dog and puppies. Wasting no time, Jeff moves around them carefully, fingers reaching toward dusty wooden shelves as he inspects random objects to evaluate their usefulness as tools.

He spots a partially-crumped sheet of paper and immediately stiffens. Smoothing it out on the teetering shelf, his eyes dance across it quickly. Shifting focus to the next shelf, his fingers deftly fold the paper and slide it into his back pocket. When he turns to catch me watching, he waves a free hand toward me dismissively and nods as if saying, "Go about your business."

Aidan kneels close to the mama dog. His lips move but the words are muted by the cascade of vocals—from low whimpers to screaming lyrics. Still, his demeanor says more than words ever could, from the dopey slant of his smile to the gentle arc of his hand as he lavishes the dogs with affection. And those piercing blue eyes. They radiate kindness and…

"Quinn!" Riley whisper-shouts. "What are you doing? You're supposed to be helping me!"

"Sorry." I stumble toward my sister. "Okay, what should I do?" With an audible sigh, she points to piles she's assembled on the ground before us. Leave it to my sister to divide out the dog biscuits evenly for each dog.

"We'll each partner up with one of the guys. We'll distract the dogs with treats while the guys remove collars." She pauses, smirking. "And I'm guessing you'll want to pair up with—" she raises her eyebrows. It's a very Chris-like move.

"Hey, where'd Chris go? I thought he was right here with us?"

Her eyes widen in panic when we both realize the kid is gone.

Chapter 25

Twisting in every direction, we scour the surroundings, alternatively hissing questions and commands. "Chris!" "Where are you?" "Come back here!" My thoughts jump to the property owner. What if the kid wandered too close to the house and Jim's friend has a hold of him right now? Bile lingers at the back of my throat, threatening to erupt.

Panic flares and I practically launch into the clouds when a hand clamps around my elbow, yanking me from my post. A sigh of relief escapes when I realize the hand belongs to Riley, who peers around her side of the shed, blindly reaching for me.

I scramble to her side, my jaw dropping when I spy our missing comrade.

Knees planted in the dirt, Chris leans against a muscular pit bull, one arm wrapped around the dog's back. My heart freezes while my nerves scream to look away. *That kid has no idea what these dogs are capable of.*

Just as I'm about to call out to him, the dog's ears relax and the stub occupying his hind quarters where a tail should be wiggles, as if he's trying to wag it. Bliss radiates from him, not aggression. Riley shakes my elbow, as if we're not seeing the same thing.

"Look at that!" She flashes me a smile. "These dogs aren't going to attack us. They actually crave human touch. Kind human touch."

"Well, *that one* anyway." I don't want to assume that all the dogs are this friendly. We watch as Chris and the dog bask in each other's attention. I'm so engrossed that I don't notice, or expect, Aidan and Jeff sneaking up behind us.

Aidan taps my shoulder, sending my heart into a fresh wave of panic. I clamp a hand over my mouth but not before a startled shriek escapes. It's loud enough for Riley, Jeff, and Aidan to hear, but thankfully, blaring music masks the sound.

Riley points toward Chris and the dog. The guys peer around the shed, their features fluctuating from concern to surprise in seconds. Jeff motions us in for a group huddle.

"We've already been here too long," he eyes each of us, rubbing his chin. "Forget about trying to distract the dogs. If they're all as friendly as that one," he motions over his shoulder toward Chris' new best friend, "then it'll be much faster if we spread out and free them individually instead of working in teams."

"And what if some aren't friendly?" I ask. "What do we do?"

"Skip them," Jeff says. "We can take care of them last. Right now, let's just focus on getting as many free as we can."

"What about Chris?" Riley questions. "Should we have

him wait in the car?" Aidan and Jeff share a glance, passing an unspoken message between them. Aidan shakes his head.

"No. The little man can help too. Without him, we'd still be wasting our time breaking into sheds."

After several minutes of trying to tear Chris' attention away from the dog, Riley motions for him to join the group. We explain our plan: run around to each dog and, as long as it doesn't act like it wants to tear your arm off, remove its collar and then move on to the next one. Meet back here behind the shed when you don't see any more dogs chained.

Just when I think we're about to put all of our hands in a circle and raise them together in a team high five, Aidan and Jeff turn away and sprint across the lawn. Chris returns to his new friend, and Riley and I dash in opposite directions. We all avoid the area closest to the house.

The first dog I reach cowers slightly in fear. I stroke her head and talk softly, explaining what I'm doing as my fingers work the leather collar. It's faster and easier than I ever expected. It takes just a few minutes and each successful release fuels adrenaline for the next one.

Staying low to the ground, I scan the area, searching for any dogs that are still chained. Seeing none, I start racing toward the shed. When I'm halfway there, the music stops abruptly. It takes a moment to process as the pounding rhythm continues in my head. The only thing worse than the sudden silence is the voice that explodes through it.

"Who the hell are you and what do you think you're doing!?"

Chapter 26

Eyes wide with horror, I anxiously scan the yard. The only sound is the rush of blood in my ears and the throbbing of my frantic heart. Movement bursts from every direction. Thankfully the others are all running toward me. I'm just the first to make it back.

No one answers the guy yelling. Riley makes it back to me first. She thrusts the car keys at me, trying to speak between gasps for oxygen.

"You're…the…fastest. Get…to…the…car…and…start…it." I nod, snatching the keys and sprinting toward the driveway. When I'm just a few yards from the car, I steal a peek toward the house. Trees block much of the view, but sounds paint a chilling picture.

A door slams. Moments later, shouting erupts, and the echo of gunfire shatters the air. My fingers fumble with the keychain as I clumsily yank the door open. I slide into the driver's seat and jam a key into the ignition, the engine wailing in protest as I force the shift into drive and stomp on the gas pedal.

Clouds of dust swirl from the back tires, creating a wake of stones and dirt. Riley, Chris, Aidan, and Jeff race down the driveway. In fear of colliding with one of them, I pump the brake pedal, skidding to a stop. They throw doors open and pile into the car within seconds. Before the last door slams shut, I steer the car into a sloppy three-point turn, tearing up grass that lines the driveway in the process.

When the last part of the turn is complete and I shift the car into drive, my eyes catch movement in the rearview mirror. An irate man charges toward us, screaming obscenities and waving a sleek black gun in the air. Reaching his free hand into the back pocket of his jeans, he retrieves a cell phone.

Slamming the gas pedal to the floor, the tires spin in the gravel for a moment before catching. Afraid to watch, but unable to look away, I see the man snap a picture of our car with his phone. *The license plate. He knows our license plate now.*

The car shoots forward, the momentum jostling us around the small space. As we crest the end of the driveway, a cracking thunder rents the air and the car swerves right, hard. The steering wheel jumps in my hands as I struggle to right the car.

"Get down! He's shooting at us!" Jeff's warning is the last thing I hear before a flurry of bullets pelt the car. It swerves again, this time to the left.

"He shot the tires out!" Aidan shouts. My hands clutch the steering wheel with all the strength I can muster. I suddenly wish I had put up more of a fight when we talked about coming here.

"That must be Vic," Riley mumbles. Leaning forward in the seat, she grips my shoulder. "Even Jim was afraid of him."

"Well, don't worry, cuz I'm not stopping this thing!" Popping erupts as bullets chase our retreat: some miss their target, but several pierce the trunk and back end of the car. It rings in my ears like stones pelting steel. Or balloons popping. Well, deadly balloons that want to puncture my skin and tuck me in for a dirt nap.

As the car fishtails, I focus every ounce of adrenaline-laced energy on forcing the gas pedal to the floor. The tires sputter as metal meets pavement. Friction and resistance permit only meager acceleration but we're outpacing Vic. And that's all that matters right now.

Eventually, he's a distant speck in the rearview.

Jeff rubs his forehead and squints at Aidan. "You know how to replace tires? I mean, not that we have any equipment."

Aidan blows out a pent-up sigh. "No, and even if we did know *how* to do it, we don't have tires. Or enough money to buy some. Jasmine's dad gave me plenty of money to get home but not enough for car repairs."

Jeff slaps his palms on his thighs in finality. "Well, we've got no other choice. We're gonna have to ditch the car," Jeff says. "Once we get some distance between us and that house."

"What do you mean *ditch the car*? We need this to get home!" My voice pitches higher with each word. Aidan turns to me, gently brushing a palm over my white knuckles that clench the steering wheel with a death grip.

"That guy has a picture of our license plate. I don't know what kind of connections he's got—or how long it's gonna take him to get in his own vehicle and catch up with us, but I really don't wanna find out." His voice is calm, soothing.

Great. And who's gonna be the one to tell the sergeant that we're already failing our mission? Riley takes the moment of peace to chime in.

"Quinn, you know the next place we're heading, right?" I slowly nod. *We're taking Chris home.* "Well, we don't want to lead Vic or any of his friends there."

Chapter 27

My adrenaline surge deflates like a punctured balloon. A dull ache throbs beneath my temples as a renewed panic threatens to spike my heart rate. *This is what we get for trying to do something good?* We should be on the way home right now and instead we're arguing about whether to keep going or not. And it sounds like they're all on the same page. Except for me.

My eyes shift to the only quiet one—the kid. He's sandwiched between Jeff and Riley in the back seat. His eyes bounce from one side of the car to the other before he twists in his seat to peer out the back window. Thankfully, there's no sign of anyone following us.

"Quinn! Someone trusted you with this car. Now it's got bullet holes, blown off tires, and possibly destroyed rims. We've done enough damage to it already, don't you think?" Jeff's harsh tone wields guilt that creeps into my limbs, consuming every cell in my body. *He's right.* Bowen loaned us supplies and the car.

"Besides," Aidan adds. "It's not safe to be driving around in it anymore. If that Vic guy finds the car—with us in it—we're sitting ducks."

"So what do we do?" I ask, shaking my head in frustration. "We just leave the car somewhere?"

His posture relaxes as he realizes I've accepted my defeat. Wiggling his eyebrows and wearing that signature smirk, he says, "I've got a plan."

Reaching into his back pocket, Jeff tugs on a tattered square of paper, carefully unfolding and smoothing it out on the seat.

"What's that?" Aidan darts an arm into the back seat, unsuccessfully trying to snatch the paper from Jeff.

"So this," Jeff flaps the paper in the air, "is evidence. It's one of their stat sheets. It's a list of their top winning dogs and their bloodlines." He pauses for a moment, shaking his head in disgust. "I say we find the closest police station, deliver the flyer, and leave the car there."

"And what do we tell the police? We borrowed this car and got it shot up, but there's nothing questionable going on here," Riley's voice cracks as worry trickles through each word.

Aidan raises a hand in a calming gesture. "No. We can't tell them anything or they'll keep us there and ask us all kinds of questions. I say we park the car in the back, fold the flyer into a paper airplane, send it in the station and high-tail it out of there before anyone notices."

"Yeah! I can make an airplane out of it!" Chris exclaims. *At least this is a distraction for the kid.* A flash of relief calms my tense muscles.

"Anyone have a pen and that asshat's address? I need to add details to this paper so the cops can find him," Jeff concludes.

"The address is on that map up front," Riley points toward the passenger seat. Aidan finds it on the floor and thrusts it back toward Jeff.

"Now, as far as a pen, we'll need to pull over so I can grab my bag." Riley eyes me in the rearview mirror. Inwardly I cringe. My instincts scream to put more distance between us and Vic's smoking gun. Riley senses my hesitation. She leans forward, quietly sharing words only meant for my ears.

"I think we should show the guys all of our supplies. If we're ditching the car, the weapons and satellite phone may save all of our butts."

She's right. I nod, signaling my agreement, and she slides back in the seat.

Within a few minutes we approach a deserted roadside vegetable stand. I ease the gas pedal, which slightly calms the protesting tires. I shift the car into park when we're sufficiently hidden behind the rickety wooden shelter.

Riley jumps out of the car to retrieve her bag, along with the various supplies we were given before leaving the base. As she presents Jeff with a pen, one bag spills open, the picture of Bowen's smiling wife landing at Chris' feet.

"Who's that?" Aidan asks. "And why are you carrying around a framed picture?"

There, less than twenty-four hours after we promised secrecy to Sergeant Bowen, Riley and I spill the beans. For the most part. We conveniently forget to mention a few details—like the fact that the "vaccines" given on base are actually tracking devices.

At least it's a bit less of a betrayal.

As we explain, the guys' reactions range from disbelief to disappointment that we didn't tell them sooner. We field their questions as vaguely as we can. By the time the last word is spoken, we have yet another new plan.

Chapter 28

Before we do anything else, Aidan insists on calling his dad. He refuses to get back in the car until his family knows what's happening. I completely understand. If I still had parents, I'd want to warn them and let them know that I'm trying to get home as soon as possible.

Thankfully, Aidan's dad offers to alert Jeff's family, so that saves us some time. Although Jeff would rather call them himself, he sees the value in wrapping up this little errand of ours so that we can get back to our true mission of getting home.

Instead of searching for a local police station, we decide an animal shelter would be a better place to leave the evidence. No police officer is going to let us just turn in a flyer with an accusatory note on it and then send us on our merry way. They're going to question us—and showing up in a car riddled with bullet holes won't exactly bolster our innocence.

We figure that an animal shelter would be much easier to slip in and out of without being noticed. We'll just leave it in their hands to investigate or call the cops.

Besides, Riley and I are hoping to keep at least one promise we made to the sergeant—that we'd find his wife as soon as we could. Hanging around a police station to be interrogated doesn't really play into that plan.

With a strategy in place—again—we introduce the guys to our collection of gadgets. Chris' eyes widen with each revelation: the pistol, the knife, and the satellite phone. Jeff and Aidan mirror his enthusiasm.

Although they briefly saw the phone when we first left Jasmine's house, we know it's time to show them how much it can do.

The three of them are like kids tearing into presents on Christmas morning. They *ooh* and *ahh* over the weapons, but they practically salivate over the phone.

"Why don't we get moving?" Riley asks. "Once we ditch the car, you'll have plenty of time to play with the phone while we're hiking our way out of here."

Although Jeff thinks we'll be able to find another car to *borrow*, I have my doubts. This is already the third vehicle we've had that isn't ours. I'm starting to feel like a cat living its ninth life. Plus, right now people think everything is returning to normal. They're leaving their homes, going to stores and jobs. We don't have the cover of an emergency right now, where people mostly retreat to their homes. And, when the next emergency does arise, I'm hoping we're safely locked in our home by then.

"Let's go!" Jeff races to the car, satellite phone in hand. He jumps into the passenger seat, signaling his intent to navigate. "I found the closest animal shelter! It's just a few miles away."

Riley takes the driver's seat while I hop into the back with Chris and Aidan. The short drive is slow but uneventful. The tire rims seem to diminish further with each rotation, imposing their sluggish pace on the front tires, hampering our progress.

Rolling into the parking lot, Riley cautiously pulls around to the back of the building and shifts the car into park. Hopefully this isn't its final resting place.

We scrutinize our surroundings and, confirming no one else is around, set our plan into motion.

Riley, Jeff, Aidan, and I scramble to the trunk. We sling every bag and backpack over a shoulder or across a back before darting toward a thinly wooded area behind the building.

Chris flutters past us, waving the one item in his possession—the flyer. We're sending the kid inside.

Chapter 29

He slinks along the building, clearly delighted to be chosen for this assignment. Flashing us a toothy smile, he gives a thumbs-up and dashes toward the entrance, disappearing inside.

"Have you guys noticed how moody Chris has been?" I ask. "Like one minute he's giving us attitude and complaining and then the next he's all excited to be here."

"He was pretty happy at Jasmine's house, but he got quieter when we left," Jeff interjects. "I don't know what we expected, though. It's not like they can just keep him like he's a stray that showed up on their doorstep."

"He's ten. He doesn't know what he wants," Aidan adds, running a hand through his hair.

"I barely know him, but I'm guessing he's very confused right now," Riley says. "His situation was bad enough, at least in his mind, that he was willing to do anything to escape it. But once the novelty wore off, he probably missed some aspects of the only life he knew. So even if he was treated much better at Jasmine's house, there's still comfort in what's familiar."

My sister was meant to work with kids. She spent nearly every Friday or Saturday night babysitting at various neighbors' homes. The weird thing is, she absolutely loved it. And weirder yet, none of them ever asked me to babysit.

Once she reached high school, Riley decided she wanted to be a child psychologist. Maybe she can still do that if this world would just straighten out.

Jeff taps my shoulder. "Yeah, so lighten up, Quinn! Give the kid a break."

Before I can respond, bounding footsteps stall the conversation and electrify the air. Chris flashes before us, briefly slowing to prompt us into action.

"Run!"

With no hesitation, we race after the kid. I quickly overtake Chris and follow a wooden path leading away from the building. The woods are fairly thin, but the trees offer some cover. Throwing a quick glance over my shoulder, slight relief washes over me—everyone's following and, so far, there's no sign of anyone chasing us. The shelter staff probably have more important things to do than chase down and interrogate a kid who wandered into their lobby.

Our feet pound along the narrow dirt path while low brush and reaching branches lash our legs. When the path widens, leading toward the rear parking lot of another building, I slow my pace and turn around. The others taper to a full stop, alternating between swallowing lungfuls of oxygen and scanning the sparse foliage for movement.

Other than our collective gasping breaths, the area is relatively quiet. An occasional car motors along the adjacent road; otherwise, we're alone.

"I don't think we're being followed. What happened in there, Chris?" I ask as I regain even breathing.

"I snuck in and stuck the flyer on the counter, but when I tried to leave, some lady stopped me." He raises both hands in frustration. "She was asking me all these questions, like what I was doing there and where my parents were. I told her to just look at the paper and I tried to leave."

"You did good, buddy," Jeff encourages him but the kid shrugs.

"She started coming closer. I think she was gonna grab me and make me stay until I answered her questions. So, I just…I ran."

"I think any of us would have done the same thing," Riley reassures. "Don't be so hard on yourself, Chris. You completed your mission. You delivered the evidence, and now someone will make sure that dogs never have to fight there again."

The kid's cheeks blaze with a genuine smile. "I was right. You are the nicer sister."

Chapter 30

With no wheels, we rely on the only mode of transport left: our feet. We use the satellite phone to navigate north. Riley leads the way. Surreal memories swirl through my mind as we hike in silence. Less than a month ago, I was just a typical teen heading to the beach for a family vacation.

Since then, my parents perished in a horrific accident, I lost and found my sister, and we're walking home—it's just a couple hundred more miles. Miles that would be rolling along beneath the tires if we were still in the car. I bet if we hadn't stopped at Vic's house we'd be in Maryland by now. Annoyance flares, which I attempt to deflect by focusing on my physical grievances.

I'm already tired of walking, and the mid-afternoon sun bakes my skin. We haven't had any strange weather lately, but the heat just doesn't lay off. As I swipe the beading sweat from my forehead, a mechanical melody bursts from the phone, startling all of us.

"It's ringing! This thing is ringing!" Riley eyes the phone in her hand, as if it's coated in acid. *There's only one person that could be.*

Jeff pushes the receiver and motions for one of us to speak.

"Hello?" It takes every effort to form that one word. My cheeks slightly redden when my shaky voice quivers.

"This is Sergeant Bowen. With whom am I speaking?" His voice bears no hint of concern, only authority.

"It's us, sir." Riley tries. "Riley and Quinn Whelan."

"You are together?" he questions, although it sounds more like a statement. We confirm in unison. "And you are separated from the vehicle?" *Dammit. How can he know that?*

"Um," Riley's eyes shift to me nervously and her hands twitch. If she wasn't holding the phone right now, I'm sure she'd be wringing them. "Yes. We had a little issue with the car."

"What sort of issue?" Frustration brims in his tone. Our faces contort with matching grimaces, neither wanting to explain.

"The car got slightly damaged," I begin. "We sort of ran into someone who had a gun and wanted to shoot us."

Riley narrows her eyes and scrunches her face as if that's the dumbest thing I have ever said.

I raise my palms and scrunch my face. *I don't know what to say,* I mouth to her.

"You crashed into another vehicle?" Bowen booms.

Riley rushes to answer him. "No! No, we didn't crash into anything." She twists a long brown lock of hair pensively with her free hand. "We just had to get away from someone who was shooting at us. And we did, we got away, it's just that he kind of shot up the car in the process. Including the back tires."

"What?!" I visualize a throbbing vein protruding from

119

his tensed forehead right now. He can probably sense that he's on speaker phone right now too, but he doesn't seem to care. I'm guessing shock and frustration have overruled his characteristically controlled temperament.

"Yeah and we didn't want to ruin the car's rims," I add, "so we parked it at an animal shelter, and we were going to tell you as soon as we had a chance." My attempt to redeem our actions fails.

Fury radiates through the receiver. "And what are your plans now?" he asks through audibly gritted teeth.

"Well, we're going to hike north and hope we find a way to get another car." Riley's meek response further weakens our case.

"Hope to find another car?" Bowen mutters under his breath. Then much louder, he says, "You don't have time to find another car. Look, Yellowstone is on the verge of eruption. When that happens, all hell's gonna break loose out west and you know where the chaos will head? East. People will panic and they'll flee as far as they can. You have *got* to get to my wife. Now. Do you understand?"

Aidan and Jeff remain silent, but their eyes widen with this influx of new information. We were going to tell them about finding Bowen's wife after we dropped Chris off.

"Yes, we understand," Riley says miserably. Her defeated tone softens his anger slightly.

"Look, I'll try to find you another car, but I don't know if I can. Just keep heading north and I'll call you again when I have news."

Our confession boosts my confidence enough to ask what I've wondered since he called. "Sergeant, how did you know we weren't in the car?"

He releases a sigh.

I'm not sure if it's born of frustration or exhaustion.

"The car has a tracking device in it. When I saw Riley's tracker move farther and farther away from it, I figured something was wrong."

Chapter 31

Awkward silence descends. *We hadn't told the guys they weren't actually injected with a vaccine.*

Guilt slithers through me, hampering my ability to meet Aidan's or Jeff's eyes. *We should have told them. They should have heard about it from us.*

"Alright, head north. I'll be back in touch soon. Keep the phone close, and *don't* get shot!" Bowen's raised voice crackles through the satellite phone.

The instant the conversation ends, the guys descend upon us, questions blazing.

"What does he mean by *trackers*?" "Are they watching us!?" "Why did he say you have to get to his wife?" "What else aren't you telling us?"

Riley raises her palms as if shielding us from the barrage of questions. "Look, we were sworn to secrecy," she pauses, glancing my way, "but I don't see how we can keep secrets any longer. Quinn, you agree?"

"All in," I say, my soul weighed in shame. Like a dam bursting, we release all the details we've been holding back. About our side mission to find Bowen's wife and give her the satellite phone. How the "vaccines" at the base were actually injectable tracking devices that will be used to monitor the population.

"Lucas was right!" Jeff announces. He shares an incredulous look with Aidan. "We thought he was just being paranoid, but he was actually right!"

"Yeah," Aidan agrees. "He couldn't let that go—that we were all *"vaccinated"* on the base," he says, using air quotes. Shaking his head, he mutters, "What the hell is inside me?" Wielding a pointer finger around the group he adds, "What's inside all of us?" Jeff tilts his head and crosses his arms, awaiting an explanation.

Riley and I look at each other nervously. We should have anticipated the anger that would accompany this flood of new information. I hitch a shoulder up and answer honestly. "We really don't know. Bowen didn't tell us much about it. He just said it was a tracking device and the carrier fluid absorbs into your muscles."

I place a hand on Aidan's arm and meet his eyes, then shift my gaze to Jeff. "I swear, if I knew anything more about it, I'd tell you." Riley rushes to affirm.

"I know we haven't been open up until this point and I'm sorry," she begins. "But really, guys, the sergeant was telling us so much and trying to get us out of there so fast. We didn't really have a lot of time to ask questions. He didn't even get a chance to show us how to use everything he gave us. The base was going on lock down and we had to leave quickly or be stuck there until they decided to open it up again."

Chris scrunches his face up and crosses his arms. The kid's been silent, either listening to our words intently or zoning out completely. I'm not sure which.

"I wanna see my tracker!" he demands. Riley smiles weakly.

"You can't see it, buddy, it's inside you." The kid has no respect for reason.

"If they can see where I am, then I wanna know what they see!"

Riley shoots me a side eye and removes the tracking device from its bag. I throw her a small nod.

With shaky hands, Riley powers on the device and unfolds the printouts Bowen gave us.

"What are these?" Aidan asks, squinting at the papers over her shoulder.

"It's your ID numbers," I answer. "In case we had trouble finding you. The sergeant gave us a list of your numbers and Dan's and Jim's."

Jeff scratches his chin in thought. Five sets of eyes remain fixed on the device. It powers on quickly, a small green dot illuminating next to each tiny letter-number sequence. We must still be within range of the base because a quarter-sized cluster of dots hovers in the lower part of the screen.

I scan the screen for Jim's number. That's the only one I'm truly interested in anyway. It doesn't jump out at me, but it could be jumbled in with all the others near the base. Just as I'm about to suggest we type the number in, Riley tugs the device toward the space between us.

She points to a sprinkling of dots that overlap. "See those four dots. That's us," she says. For a moment, the distraction

124

seems to be diffusing the guys' anger.

"Why is it only four?" Chris asks. "There's five of us." The guys' scrunched faces and shifting eyes bounce from one person to another, but Riley's steady gaze lands on me. One-by-one they notice the shift in her attention from the phone.

"Um…the sergeant…he didn't…vaccinate me." The words tumble out awkwardly. "He didn't want me to be tracked because he decided early on that he was gonna ask for my help to reach his wife." Their staring eyes implore me to continue.

"He can't leave the base and he knew that I was just there to get my sister and then leave. And his home is in Maryland, so he thought I could get a message to his wife on my way home. Riley was already vaccinated at that point and he didn't know a way to reverse that, so he just kind of left it as it was."

I don't know what else to say. Silence drapes around our little group like a thick curtain. "Guys, I'm sorry we didn't say anything." *I need them to believe that we'd tell them if we knew anything else.* I shake my head miserably. "I really am." Aidan rakes a hand through his messy hair. His blue eyes pin me in place. He doesn't smile, but he doesn't narrow those eyes at me in frustration either.

"Hey!" Chris' green irises widen as he jabs a finger at the tracking device. "Why is that dot so bright?" We all step closer for a better look.

"He's right, that one dot is shining like a spotlight," Jeff says, shrugging as he taps the black device.

Riley glances at the printout, now slightly crumpled within her grasp. "Look! That's Jasmine's ID." Shaking her head, she adds, almost under her breath, "Why would hers be different?"

"Do the others all look the same on there?" Aidan asks, pointing at the screen.

"There are a few extra-bright ones but, overall, there aren't really that many dots," Jeff notes. "We've got clusters around the base, but I'm guessing not that many people are vaccinated yet. Well, their definition of *vaccinated* anyway."

"Since Riley shows up and her signature isn't super bright, we know it's not just about gender," Aidan notes.

"What about age?" Chris asks innocently. "Is Jasmine older than you guys or something?"

Before Jeff or Aidan can answer, Riley shakes her head and responds. "How could a tracker determine how old she is?" After several minutes of useless contemplation, we fall silent again, each of our minds scrambling to solve the puzzle.

"I know, I know!" Chris shouts. "It's the bullet. She's got a bullet in her!"

Chapter 32

After a brief pause, Jeff's words flow deliberately, as if he's thinking out loud. Rubbing his chin, he speaks softly, staring into the distance. He's not speaking directly to us, we're just witnessing him slide the pieces of a puzzle together in his mind. "If a bullet can trigger the tracker to shine brighter, there must be some chemical reaction between the tracer and the slug. So if a soldier were wounded, that signature would alert the team and it would make him easier to find if they needed to extract him?"

It's interesting, but it doesn't really help us. Impatience coils in my stomach.

"That sounds believable," Riley agrees. "But the sergeant said we should keep moving. Maybe we should just head north. I mean, we don't even have a plan other than hoofing it for the next hundred miles."

With no other option, we use the satellite phone to point us in the right direction and walk. We follow the same path we would have taken with the car. And although we barely progress, the neighborhoods and small businesses slowly fade as commercial buildings materialize. Cars and trucks pass by, mocking the loss of our vehicle.

The sun is our constant companion, brandishing its harsh rays across our exposed skin. As if the situation isn't bad enough, I'm guessing this day will end with at least one sunburn. Thankfully, we all got to shower at Jasmine's house or else we'd probably have clouds of body odor hovering around us.

A dull ache throbs in my head, like a drum keeping time with each step. My throat grows more parched by the second. *If we had just headed north when we left the base, we'd already be home by now.*

I tamp down the thought before it unravels into blame. We plod onward in silence. If the others' thoughts match mine, we're all silently contemplating where we'd rather be right now.

By mid-day, my legs burn with exertion. And I was conditioned to run miles for sport just a few weeks ago. I wonder how the others feel, but I don't ask—don't want to open up any floodgates for complaining. I have a feeling Chris would be the first in line for that.

When our pace slows to a sluggish meandering, we agree to stop for a rest. A small community park offers the perfect space—a covered pavilion with picnic tables. We spread our belongings atop the splintered wood and claim seats within the shade.

Although I'm shielded from the sun and my legs savor the reprieve, the gravity of our situation lingers. The pounding behind my temples builds, threatening to cripple my brain. I lie flat on the seat and swallow my self-pity.

"Hey, you guys hungry or thirsty?" Tears spring to my eyes with Jeff's words. I feel like I've trekked through a desert for days and he just found an oasis. We all nod mutely, except for Chris, who yelps an enthusiastic, "Yes!"

Unzipping his bag, Jeff explains that Jasmine's slipped him a secret stash of snacks and drinks. She insisted that he take them. I guess she understands just how quickly a simple trip can turn into a nightmarish plague of detours.

Like a trick-or-treater proudly displaying his bounty, Jeff dumps the loot, sending water bottles rolling across the table's surface. Snack-sized bags of cheese crackers, popcorn, and chips tumble out, landing close to their drop point.

The temporary windfall makes the guys giddy. Jeff starts cracking jokes. "Hey, what did the baby corn say to its mom?" With raised eyebrows he searches his audience for a taker. Chris practically jumps out of his skin. "What? What?"

"Where's my pop corn?"

Chris doubles over laughing, sending Jeff and Aidan into their own fit of chuckles. While I'm grateful for the slight recharge, the last thing we can afford to do right now is sit around laughing at corny jokes. *Literally.*

"Did you hear the urgency in Bowen's voice?" My tone is harsh, but I'm starting to ache all over, and it feels like we should just claim defeat. Walking isn't going to cut it. We need a faster way to get home. "What are we gonna do?" My voice cracks, teetering between hopelessness and hysteria.

Aidan slides a palm across his face, wiping the smirk off of it. "You're right. We need a plan."

"What about public transportation?" Riley asks. "Do we have enough money for bus tickets? I mean, I don't even know if there's a bus station around here, but if your phones are working, maybe you could look it up?"

Jeff whips his cell phone from his pocket, waving it around like a magic wand. "Let's have a look here." He swipes the screen once, scrunches his face in confusion and swipes it again. His shoulders slump in realization. He runs a hand through his hair and focuses on the ground.

"Um, I guess I left it on after I charged it and it's kinda dead." When I still had my phone, I was acutely aware of where it was and when it needed to be charged. At all times. I get the feeling Jeff's one of those people who never seems to know when his battery's about to die. Aidan pats him on the back.

"It's okay, man. I've got mine." He pulls his phone out and powers it on. How responsible of him—actually saving the power when he's not using it. He swipes a few screens before glancing up, a smile spreading across his face.

"There's a bus terminal less than two miles from here, north. So it's kind of on the way. Who's up for one more hike?"

It's not much of a pep talk, but it's enough. A cascade of affirmations meets his question.

"Let's do it!" "Come on, let's hurry." "I'm in."

With a renewed purpose, we swallow every last bite of food and gulp every last drop of water before gathering our bags.

We hustle toward our destination, guided by Aidan's phone.

"Anyone know how much a bus ticket costs?" Riley asks. She's met with four shaking heads.

"We should probably figure out how much money we have," Jeff suggests. Our pace naturally slows as everyone but Chris digs into either a wallet or a backpack. Riley fishes the lavender wallet out of her matching backpack, brandishing twenty-six dollars.

Jeff's cheeks flush crimson as he slides a measly seven dollars out of his wallet. I can't criticize, though. I was fully planning on sponging money from my parents on our vacation. My fingers clasp around a loose ten-dollar bill floating around in my backpack amongst the random items I've deemed as necessities.

Jasmine's dad, Lucas, had given Aidan forty dollars just in case we needed cash on our way home. After paying for the dog biscuits, he's got about twenty-six bucks left. Adding his own money to the stash, it brings our combined net worth up to a hundred and nine dollars. Somehow, I doubt we'll be able to buy five bus tickets with that amount.

Hope deflates just as quickly as it skyrocketed. We continue in silence, seeking brief respite from the sun under the sparse trees lining our path.

By the time we reach the bus terminal, it's no longer the beacon of hope we briefly believed it to be. We all huddle around the ticket booth and lob questions at the bored-looking woman behind the window. She alternates between yawning and eye rolling as we explain our need to reach Delaware.

The terminal is nearly empty. Few feet pass over the shiny, waxed floors. With a few quick pecks on her keyboard, she informs us that the closest drop-off point along the bus route is Dover. And the one-way ticket would be fifty-one dollars. Per person.

We release a collective sigh when the woman asks, "Would you like to purchase boarding passes?"

"We don't have enough money," Riley says miserably. The woman purses her lips and a brief moment of sympathy passes over her features. It quickly returns to her previous bored stance.

"Please step aside then. I've got to assist the paying customers."

We skulk to the side of the open space, careful to avoid blocking the ticket window from the hordes of nonexistent customers this woman must anticipate. Once again blame slithers through my mind. *If we didn't stop to free the dogs, we would still have a car and we'd be that much closer to home.*

Aidan runs a hand through his ruffled hair. "Now what?"

"We could try to *borrow* a car," Jeff says, waggling his eyebrows.

"I don't think that's a good idea," Riley whispers, her eyes sliding back and forth as if police might spring from the corners and arrest us for even thinking about stealing a car.

"Alright, let's go outside since we're clearly not making any progress in here," Aidan suggests. Shuffling to the parking lot, we plop down on parallel benches, brainstorming exactly zero options.

My eyes catch movement as a muscular guy with a shaved head turns the corner of the bus station. He throws us a bored look before proceeding to a parking space, starting his truck, and peeling out of the lot.

About a minute later, a tall, lanky guy with a baseball cap

pulled down all the way to his eyebrows follows the same path. *How many other people are back there? And what are they doing?*

This guy notices us too. He does a double take before slinking toward us, like a used car salesman about to close a deal. He narrows his eyes and levels us with a cautious gaze.

"Are you here to make a purchase?" he asks. *What?*

"I don't think we're in need of what you're selling," Jeff answers for us. *Oh my gosh. Is this guy a drug dealer?*

Glancing around the group, as if seeking approval, Jeff adds, "But maybe there is something you can help us with."

My stomach churns with apprehension as I listen to the negotiations.

"Look, we need to get to Delaware, but we don't have enough money for bus tickets," Jeff explains. "Any chance you offer a taxi service?"

Baseball cap guy admits that he's got a car and he wouldn't mind making some cash. When he asks how much we have, Aidan confidently states, "Forty. We have forty bucks."

I bite back the smirk that wants to broadcast the lie. The guy narrows his eyes in disbelief but doesn't challenge it. He can't be that much older than the guys. I'd guess he's in his mid to late twenties.

"Alright. I'll take it, but we leave right now. I've got other business to attend to this evening," he announces. Riley's wide eyes express her disbelief. I hitch a shoulder up.

The lump gathering in my throat begs me to protest but I know we have no other choice at this point. We can't sit at a bus station all night. Money isn't going to magically appear for tickets.

Jeff looks to each of us and, other than Chris, we all give tentative nods. The kid just shrugs his shoulders and throws his hands out at his sides in an over-exaggerated *I-don't-know* gesture.

With pinched features, Aidan blows out a defeated breath. "Yep, you got yourself a deal."

Chapter 33

The guy leads us through the parking lot to an old maroon boat of a car. He smiles, tossing a palm toward the clunker as if he's presenting a chariot. I glance at the scripted text on the tail end. A Plymouth Fury. *This thing looks ancient.*

"Here's our ride," he says. "Hop in, let's go."

With one last apprehensive glance our way, Aidan yanks the passenger door open. The door squeaks on its hinges, groaning with effort. He motions for Chris to crawl in the front seat before he follows.

Jeff, Riley, and I pile into the back seat. The stench of stagnant cigarette smoke and must hover within the interior. The ceiling material—it looks like felt—hangs like a loose layer of skin in random spots. The seats and floor harbor dark stains every few inches. My stomach recoils with disgust.

I glance toward Riley, who has always been a bit of a neat freak. Her delicate fingers twitch. When she catches my eye, she wrinkles her nose. I can tell she'd love to clamp her nose shut, warding off the odors buried deep within the fibers of our latest ride.

Jeff shakes his head slowly, a silent warning for us to keep quiet. He slides into the middle and motions with a pointer finger on each side for us to "Sit!"

We oblige, sulking just so that he understands our level of suffering right now. Technically this guy could drive us anywhere and we'd have no way to stop him. At least we outnumber him five to one. That brings me a tiny bit of comfort.

As soon as the last door slams shut, our driver wakes the engine and turns to Aidan.

"So, you the banker here?" Aidan slowly nods, waiting for the guy to elaborate.

"Then why don't we just settle up now? Get it over with." This guy gives me the skeevies. He's outnumbered, though, so at least we have that going for us. Aidan reluctantly hands over two twenty-dollar bills. The guy snatches them from Aidan's hand, thrusts them into his pocket, and throws the car into drive.

The guy says his name is Ace. I'm guessing that's not his real name, but I have no desire to learn anything about him so it suffices. Aidan introduces us and they make small talk in the front seat. I tune it out and focus on the passing scenery.

We roll past a bank, post office, laundromat, and apartment buildings. We're finally moving! As much as I would love a hot, decontaminating shower, and clean clothes right now, I'm grateful that we're finally making some progress in our trip.

Shuffling through the bags at my feet, my fingers seize the printouts Bowen gave us with the ID tracker numbers. Now's as good a time as any to see where Jim might be. Besides, we're heading north and I'd sure like to know if he is too.

Dipping my hand into the other bag, I close my fingers around the tracking device. Silently, Jeff's hand shoots over and wraps around mine. He leans closer and whispers, "No. Don't take that out now. I don't want this guy to know what kind of equipment we've got. If that thing starts beeping or something, he's gonna ask about it. As soon as we're out of this heap on wheels, we'll check. I promise."

The seriousness in his eyes stops me in my tracks. I'm not used to it. I nod slowly and he slides the device and papers out of my hand. He smiles, a reassuring signal that I've done the right thing, and quietly returns the items to their place.

I sink further into the cloth bench seat, my eyes focusing on points in the distance while greenery, metal, and glass flash by just beyond the window. My nose and throat grow numb to the smell. Within minutes the outside world fades and my body descends into a dreamless oblivion.

Shouting yanks me from the darkness. My eyes fly open, searching for anything that might prompt recognition of where I am. Jeff sits next to me and Aidan's directly in front of me. We're still driving and the guy—Ace—throws an accusatory finger toward Aidan. "I *know* you have more money than that!"

It's pretty obvious we aren't dealing with the most upstanding citizen, but still, the guy's tone is overly-hostile. I saw Aidan pay him, so there shouldn't be any issue.

"We had a deal. You agreed to forty bucks and that's what we gave you." Aidan's voice remains steady, but there's a fierce edge in it that I've never heard before. His shoulders stiffen, as if his whole body is alerted to the rising threat.

"That's just gonna cover the gas. You know, once I drive you there, I still have to turn around and drive back home!"

Jeff leans forward, resting an arm on each front seat, and chimes in. "Then I guess you should have thought of that before you made a deal with us."

"Hey! This is my car and what I say goes. So you better cough up some more money or I'm stopping this thing and you can all get the hell out and walk."

Riley presses both palms to her forehead as if her brain is suddenly clenched in a tightening vice. Although her voice carries just above a whisper, her plea is clear. "Just do it. We have to."

Aidan twists in his seat, narrowed eyes fixed on Riley. He shakes his head in disbelief before looking to Jeff. Once again, the guys communicate wordlessly. Jeff leans back in the seat for a moment, then lunges his long arms to the floor, rummaging through the bags at our feet.

"Look, I don't got all day," our chauffer informs us in a slightly less agitated tone. "I think you should listen to the chick and just give me the money. Without me, you ain't gettin' home and without more money, I ain't taking you."

"List—" I start, prepared to fully educate this Ace guy on the hazards of referring to my sister as a "chick," but before

I can finish even one word, Jeff waves a hand in my face and shoots me a look that screams, "Stop!" *What's he got up his sleeve?*

As if I can make the whole situation disappear, I drop my head forward and squeeze my eyes shut. *Why does life still feel like a nightmare? And when can I wake up from it?*

The crisp click of metal, chased by a buzzing sound, yanks me from my pity party. Snapping my head upright, my heart stutters when the black pistol comes into focus.

Chapter 34

Riley openly sobs, wringing her hands in her lap. Jeff levels our gun about four inches away from the back of Ace's skull. His voice deepens, radiating a gritty quality I've never heard before.

"You are going to uphold your end of the deal." Ace's irises slither to Jeff's reflection in the rearview mirror. "We don't have much money and we can't give you everything we have. After you drop us off, we still have a ways to go. Do you understand?"

Ace's forehead crinkles when his eyebrows jump. I guess he's not used to being reasoned with. He probably expected a counter-threat.

"Fine," he says grudgingly. Casting his narrowed eyes to the road ahead, he goes silent.

Tension occupies every molecule of air within the malodorous car. Jeff rests the gun on his leg, keeping it aimed toward the driver. Knowing that it's loaded makes my nerves jittery. Thankfully, Jeff's demeanor has turned serious since he retrieved the gun.

Silence seems to stretch into days, making the ride that much more uncomfortable. I'm not sure which of us is the most anxious to reach our destination. I think we're all vying for that title.

Chris turns toward Ace. I don't like that the kid has to sit next to that guy, but he definitely fits in the space between the driver and passenger seats better than Aidan would have.

"Could we listen to the radio?" Chris asks innocently. Ace raises his lips into a sneer that quickly turns sickly sweet.

"Sure, kid. Have at it." He flashes a smile at the rest of us. His superficial pleasantries raise the hairs on the back of my neck. There's no need to act, we all know he's a slimeball.

Chris cranks the volume up, neutralizing the lingering hostility. He scans for music. When the radio lands on a news report, Aidan halts the search.

> *While the East Coast wraps up final recovery efforts resulting from last month's great earthquake, roadways have been cleared and power has been restored to most areas impacted by the disaster.*
>
> *Although some damaged vehicles and belongings have not yet been claimed, they have been removed from the roadways. Contact your local police station for assistance in recovering items lost or left behind.*

DEVASTATION ERUPTS

The steady female voice falls silent for a moment. Chris raises a hand to hit the scan button again, but Aidan quickly lifts his palm, pausing the kid's action.

The voice returns, this time slower and lacking the confidence portrayed just a moment ago. It's as if the announcer disbelieves her own words:

> *This just in, we're receiving reports of unusual geothermic and seismic activity in Yellowstone National Park in Wyoming. A spokesperson from the Yellowstone Volcano Observatory has stated that there is no cause for alarm. The agency monitors seismic activity, changes in the land surface, and chemical signals from gases released in the area.*
>
> *Yellowstone is one of the world's largest active volcanic systems. While it has been thousands of years since the last major eruption, future eruptions are likely.*
> *A major or super eruption would likely have global consequences—shifting weather patterns, disrupting food production, and temporarily cooling large areas of the Earth.*
>
> *We'll report more as additional information is released. And now, back to the music.*

The announcer's abrupt transition leaves us in stunned silence. Bowen was right, but he said the government was keeping this from the public. Somehow it leaked. If news stations are getting conflicting reports, they probably don't know what to say. A strong warning could cause a mass exodus or panic. But no warning at all would leave so many vulnerable if the threat really was imminent.

My heart races as I contemplate the words we just heard. Jeff squeezes his eyes shut and rubs his forehead as if the information physically pains him. Riley's fearful eyes seek mine. She clutches her hands together, nervously shuffling one over the other.

"How would a volcano make the Earth cold?" Chris asks. I wasn't sure how much of that the kid understood. Aidan raises his eyebrows and shoots the backseat dwellers a side eye. He's definitely most qualified to answer.

"Well, when a volcano erupts, it releases ash into the air," he explains. "They're like little particles of dust and they can stay in the atmosphere for months. They block sunlight and that makes the Earth cooler than it would normally be."

Ace shoots a hand toward the dash and powers off the radio. "No way that's happening, so quit boring me with your speech. You keep that up and I might fall asleep at the wheel."

Maybe, just maybe, if this guy wasn't a total ass, we would warn him that this is a very real possibility. But the more time we spend with him, the more convinced I am that he wouldn't believe us anyway.

Although the ride is mostly silent, hostility charges the air. Ace fixes his eyes on the road, occasionally sliding a glare our way in the rearview mirror. When we cross the Delaware border, elation seeps through my cells. *I've waited a long time for this.* I glance toward Riley and her smiling eyes meet mine.

The passing scenery awakens memories. We're actually

143

getting close. We navigate around the sections of highway that still display evidence of the Route One gridlock caused by the earthquake. Besides unmoving vehicles, additional damage remains—billboards that have toppled over and bridges blocked off and closed. I'm sure recovery continues. I would find comfort in any progress if I hadn't been warned of what's coming.

At just a few miles from our destination, the satellite phone chirps to life. Riley rummages through a bag on the floor and depresses the receiver. She starts to answer with a hesitant hello, but she's cut off mid-syllable.

"This is Sergeant Bowen. Looks like you got a ride. I see you're in Delaware." His voice is frantic as he barely pauses between sentences.

Ace's eyes widen. Wanted or not, we've got his full attention.

"Yes, we got a ride," Riley answers cautiously.

"Good. Now listen carefully. Some media outlets are starting to sniff around Yellowstone. So far, they've found very little information, but I don't know how much longer that will be the case. If radio or TV stations start issuing warnings, people are going to panic. It'll be utter chaos everywhere. The clock is ticking, ladies. Get to my wife and then get home."

"We understand," Riley answers before she stutters out a question. "So, um, is this eruption, um, really going to happen, do you think?"

"Our best estimates put it at T minus seven hours."

Still clutching the gun steadfastly, Jeff murmurs. "Seven hours until all hell breaks loose."

"What?" Ace practically yelps. "What the hell's—"

Aidan reaches around Chris and jabs Ace's arm to silence his potential rant.

Bowen knows we're with the guys, but he doesn't know about the con artist chauffeuring us. I'd rather keep it that way. Besides, this guy doesn't exactly exude credibility, so even if he did start telling people, they'd probably just laugh it off.

"We'll deliver the phone to your wife, Sergeant," I state with a confidence that's just out of my grasp. I know what we need to do. Somehow, we've got to make it happen.

"The next time we talk, you'll hear her voice, too." A calming steadiness overtakes my voice. I inhale a deep breath, releasing a silent prayer that I'm not making empty promises.

Riley's head snaps in my direction. She tilts it slightly, as if questioning what I'm doing.

"I hope you're right," Sergeant Bowen says solemnly. "Be careful but be fast."

The moment the call disconnects, voices erupt within the small confines. Ace demands to know who called us and how he knows this is really happening. Chris rides his coattails, hurling questions in general about what's going to happen.

Aidan, Riley, and Jeff scrutinize my word choices, wondering how I could make such a promise when nothing has gone right since we started this trip.

The overlapping conversations threaten to swallow me whole. I pour my determination into one word.

"Hey!" I repeat it until a hush spreads from the back seat to the front.

"We are out of time! We *have* to make this happen. Yellowstone isn't going to wait for us to be ready. Just like that earthquake didn't wait. It came and it took away people we care about and we can't let that happen again."

"You're right, Quinn." Aidan's blue irises, deep pools of sorrow, bore into me. "I wish we could warn everyone. But all we can do right now is take care of ourselves."

"Hey, we're almost there," Riley announces. I can't believe we're almost back at Aunt Grace's. It feels like it's been forever since we were last here.

Ace attempts to extract information from us as Riley directs him to the trailer park where we first met Chris. Thankfully he drives steadily, too distracted to remember his goal of extorting more money from us.

Luckily the ride is short, and we manage to evade giving Ace any solid information by the time he rolls to a stop. As he depresses the brake pedal, Aidan and I fling our doors open. Fresh air washes over my senses, embracing me. It's glorious. Although it makes me wonder how much longer we'll have fresh air to breathe.

Riley and Chris slide out of their seats and rush toward us. Before the last door slams shut, the car slowly starts rolling away. Jeff peers through the closest window, his eyes lighting up as realization dawns: apparently, we missed grabbing all of our belongings. Reaching for the handle, he shouts. "Wait! One of our bags is still in there! Stop!"

Either not hearing or not caring, Ace peels away, a trail of stones and dust spraying from the tire traction. Jeff vaults away from the flying debris and attempts to give chase. He slows after just a few yards when it's obvious Ace isn't about to stop.

Gasping for breath, Jeff lopes back toward us. "One of...the bags…we left…in the car."

"Which one? What did we lose?" Riley's voice turns shrill as she frantically rifles through the bag slung over her shoulder.

After a quick inventory, we determine what we still have: the satellite phone, the tracking device, remnants of the snacks Jasmine's mom packed for us, and our personal belongings.

"The weapons bag. And I don't see the printouts of the ID numbers. We left those in that scuzzball's car," I announce. Riley's hand flies to her mouth.

Chapter 35

J eff reaches for his waistband. "Good thing I kept this baby close to me. Just in case that asshat tried anything else." He brandishes the pistol. Well, at least we have one weapon. Although my brain tingles with warning. *Was one knife the only thing left in that bag?*

Tugging his backpack over his shoulder, Chris speaks as if we've just returned from seeing a movie.

"Okay, guys. I'll just go home now." He turns, tossing a slight wave over his shoulder. The rest of us squint in confusion. After everything we've been through with this kid, he's just brushing us off?

Jeff laughs, rubbing his chin. "Not so fast, buddy! You're supposed to be my little brother, remember? Like we told the people at the base."

Chris stops and turns toward us, a smile playing across his face.

"Look, I didn't want to ask your address in front of that Ace guy," Aidan says. "But I figured you must live close enough to walk since you used to come to the trailer park all the time."

"Yeah, I live close by," Chris admits, shifting in place as if he's bored.

"Then let's do this," Jeff says enthusiastically. "We'll keep you company and walk you home."

"Okay, I guess. I thought you were in a hurry, though." All eyes land on me. Of course we're in a hurry, but I feel like we're still responsible for the kid. Like we need to make sure he gets home before all hell, or lava, breaks loose.

"Hey, we have time to make sure you get home okay." I nod to him, and the others.

"You guys mind if Quinn and I wait at our aunt's trailer?" Riley asks. I wonder what she wants there, but it won't delay us since we would just be tagging along with the guys anyway, so I'm fine with it.

Aidan bobs his head. "Sure, we can just come get you there when we get back."

Riley hunches down and extends her arms toward Chris. She bids him goodbye and whispers encouraging words when he grudgingly stumbles toward her, accepting the hug. The kid is clearly not interested in long, emotional goodbyes.

Reluctant to inflict unwanted affection on him, I rest a palm on his shoulder when he escapes Riley's embrace.

"Take care of yourself," I say. "Stay with adults, okay? Maybe Aidan and Jeff can explain to your...parents...that something is about to happen that will change everything."

Both respond with solemn nods. I have no idea what Chris'

home situation is, but hopefully, whoever he's returning to missed him and is capable of protecting him from what's coming.

"Okay, bye," he calls, pushing past Aidan and Jeff, who stumble after him. Aidan throws us a passing wave before hustling to keep up with Chris. As much as he worked on my nerves, I'm going to miss that kid. Although I believe going home is the right option for him, his departure is one more loss for our little group.

Riley and I head toward Aunt Grace's trailer. The last time I was there, we were looking for Riley but found Chris.

"Why do you want to go back to the trailer?" Visions of damage within its walls flash through my mind. Aidan and I went there after the tornado tore through the area, leaving collapsed steps, smashed shelves, and broken windows.

Her brown eyes intently seek mine. She thrusts two fingers in the air for emphasis. "Two things! Did you know Aunt Grace keeps a cookie jar under the sink?"

I squint my eyes in confusion. "No. Why?"

"I think it's got some cash in it," Riley says. "Before we'd leave to go home each year, I'd see Mom toss some money in it. I asked her about it once and she said it was just a little "thank you" collection for Aunt Grace, to help pay for water and utilities."

I nod, following her train of thought.

"I'm not stepping foot in another car with a guy like Ace. Paying someone else more would have been worth every penny," Riley says.

I nod in agreement. "So what's the other thing?"

"Remember the photo album in mom and dad's bedroom closet?" Memories flood my mind. Aunt Grace had bought an empty album probably a decade ago and stored it in the main bedroom's closet. She asked that each family who stayed there—all relatives—add a picture of themselves while vacationing, essentially creating a memory book of all the happy times that revolved around the trailer.

"I'd love to have that," I mumble, slightly dazed from the euphoria that thoughts of the album triggers. I wrap an arm around her as we close the distance between us and the structure that harbors so many family-vacation memories. For as long as I can remember, they had started here.

"Okay, I'll get the album and you get the cash," Riley says. "Take all of it. It's not like anyone else will need it. And we just might."

A touch of normalcy has returned to the community. Branches and greenery that previously littered the roads and path have been cleared away. *I guess some residents have returned.* The last I knew, most, if not all, took shelter at Dover Air Force Base when the tornado threat forced an evacuation.

Mounds of debris dot driveways, boasting progress. Still, wood peeks through windows, replacing glass that obviously didn't weather the storm.

Shadows fall over us and the surrounding homes, drawing our attention skyward. Roiling clouds in deepening shades of gray tumble over each other, as if vying for the title of most vengeful. A flash of lightning illuminates the darkening sky.

"Where'd that come from?" I ask, pointing up. Just a few hours ago the sun was practically roasting us and now it's nowhere to be seen.

"I hope the sergeant was right," Riley mutters. "What if his timing is off? What if it's erupting right now?"

"Let's just hurry! Come on!" I tug her hand and jump over the caved-in steps. The door to Aunt Grace's trailer hangs on its hinges. I swing it open gently, careful not to knock it off its last lifeline to the frame. A rickety creak beckons us inside.

Riley beelines to the bedroom our parents would sleep in. I dash to the kitchen and throw open the cabinet doors beneath the sink. Sure enough, a chipped blue cookie jar sits in the corner. Painted white seashells dance along its cylindrical front. I gently lift the lid and dunk my fist inside. Grasping the wad of paper bills, my eyes graze over the cash before I stuff it into my pocket. I replace the delicate lid and return the jar to its resting place.

Satisfied from successfully completing my small mission, I return to the living room.

Riley joins me, gently resting a hand on my arm. She sees what I see. Emptiness. There's nothing here for us anymore. Happy memories haunt every corner, phantoms of our former life.

"Be right back!" She dashes down the hallway and quickly returns with the photo album, its cover boasting a golden sun setting behind the backdrop of a sandy beach.

Smiling, she continues right past me. "I'm just gonna check the dresser drawers in our room, make sure we didn't forget anything that we might want." I follow as Riley strides to the dresser we used to share.

My eyes slide from a corner to the dresser to the beds, scanning the surfaces for anything we may have left behind. Blankets litter the floor, salt-stained bodyboards rest in the closet, and unzipped suitcases spew clothes, spilling from open flaps. Shards of glass lay scattered, clustered below one of the windows. A gangly branch protrudes through the open pane, a victim of the tornado.

As I watch her slide the bottom drawer open, the trailer door creaks. After a moment of hesitation, it slams shut.

"I guess the guys are back. I'll let them know we're just about done here." I turn toward the hallway.

"Back here. We're just about ready," I call out. When I'm met with silence, I sidestep down the short hallway toward the living room. My heart seizes as a sleek black handgun aimed at my head blurs into focus. Fury pits in my stomach when my eyes land on Jim's smug smirk.

Chapter 36

Riley scuffles into the living room. "What is—" Her words drop mid-sentence when she notices our visitor. Her stance wavers, as if the floor below her had suddenly shifted. Tears spring to her eyes, perhaps evidencing a mixture of fear and defeat.

"Well, there's my girl," Jim says, full-blown smile blazing. Eyes shifting from me to the gun and back to Jim, Riley shakily asks, "What are you doing here, Jim?"

That must have been the right response because his demeanor turns animated. Bobbing his head and planting the free fist on his hip, he answers as though Riley's a game show contestant who just won the Showcase Showdown prize. "Well, I'm glad you asked that, Riley. You see, when your *sister* showed up at the base, I knew I had to get the hell outta there. And, gee, with nowhere else to go, I came home." He pauses for dramatic effect.

"I left my brother sitting in a hospital room by himself because I had to get the hell outta there!"

He's oblivious to the irony oozing from that statement. *He expects us to feel guilty that he had to leave Dan behind, yet he was the mastermind behind kidnapping my sister.*

I raise my hands in surrender, hoping he doesn't decide to get trigger-happy. I struggle to temper my tone. Hurling accusations isn't going to help us here.

"Look, you can understand how I felt. I didn't want to be separated from my sister. Just like you don't like being away from Dan."

His eyes widen and his mouth twists into a snarl. Immediately I regret opening my mouth. He grasps the gun tighter, pointing it at me like an accusatory finger.

"This is all *your* fault! All you had to do was go home and leave us alone!" he booms. Spittle chases his forceful words, as though he's barely hanging on to any last strands of control.

Why did I bother trying to reason with him? I should have known it was pointless.

Riley drops the sweatshirt she's unconsciously balled up in worry. She dashes across the floor, stopping directly in front of me. She thrusts a shaking hand into my stomach, pushing me back toward the wall.

Her spine straightens slightly as she faces Jim. The gun wavers now that his target is blocked. Sweat beads along my hairline, but I don't dare raise a hand and possibly set anyone off. If any rolls down my forehead to sting my eyes, I'll just be thankful I'm still alive to feel it.

"Riley, get out of the way! I'm talking to Quinn right now!"

She crosses her arms and juts her chin out. This is not the Riley I grew up with, but I'm thrilled that *brave Riley* decided to show up right about now.

"Jim, if you hurt her, I will never forgive you. Never." She shakes her head slowly, punctuating her promise.

Glass shatters down the hallway behind Jim. He turns, twisting to see past the kitchen, into the bedroom. I push Riley out of the way and lunge toward Jim. My reflexes aren't as cat-like as I thought, because he turns, narrowing his eyes in annoyance. Swinging the gun around, he slams the handle into my temple. Agony explodes, rattling my brain and igniting a fire across my forehead. I collapse to the floor, squeezing my eyes shut in a useless attempt to suppress the spinning.

Riley rushes to my side, draping an arm around my shoulder. Confident we're no longer a threat, Jim turns his attention to the intruder.

"Get your ass out here!" Jim shouts. "The whole damn neighborhood heard you come in through that window!"

A shrill ringing pierces my ears, further diluting my senses. I raise a trembling hand to my temple, fingertips landing in warm wetness. Crimson stains my fingers but the pain dulls, shifting into numbness. Riley stretches an arm across me, snatching a lace doily that once resided on a nearby overturned end table. She presses it into my hand, guiding me to staunch the blood.

I focus my energy on that, silently wishing for this nightmare to end. Every time we make an inch of progress, something else comes along, pushing us back a few miles.

When Riley gasps, I force my eyes open. Jeff stumbles through the bedroom doorway, wearing a sheepish grin. The smile fades when he zeroes in on Jim's threatening stance.

With the gun aimed at Jeff's chest, Jim spits out, "I know you! You're one of those damn rats sniffing around here a few weeks ago." A maniacal smile flashes across his face. "What the hell are you doing back here?"

Jeff raises his hands in surrender and gently raises his eyebrows as if he's trying to calm a cornered animal. "Look, no one's here to cause—" Jim cuts him off, turning his attention toward the front door that still dangles on its hinges. Riley's eyes fly in that direction too. I'm guessing they heard footsteps or the damaged door groan.

"I know you're not alone," Jim bellows. "Your little friend better come join the party or we're gonna start a little game of Russian roulette. Starting with this one." He motions toward me, using the gun as a pointer.

Riley trembles beside me. Misery courses through my veins. I'm hanging on the edge of the what-if spiral of despair. *What if we had picked a different week for vacation?* Our parents would still be alive. *What if the government or the news stations had warned people about the earthquake before it happened?* Our parents would have made us over-prepare for it and we'd never be right here right now.

The door swings open. Shoulders hunched in defeat, Aidan steps through the door. His eyes narrow in question when he notices the blood-stained doily pressed to my temple.

A vicious smile carves satisfaction across Jim's face.

"Alright, that's better. Now let's see those hands, rat," Jim commands. Riley, Jeff, and I watch helplessly. Aidan slowly raises his hands, eyes glued to the gun. *There's no one left to rescue us.* Gravity beckons my body to crumple to the floor, giving up.

I let my head drop and squeeze my eyes shut again. The moment of respite curbs the spinning sensation. Two loud pops in quick succession electrify my nerves. A piercing scream rents the air. I'm not sure if it's Riley's or my own, but it's loud enough to penetrate the pounding between my ears. I assume the escalating throbbing has finally burst my eardrums.

Riley tightens her grip on my arm, sending surges of agony coiling around my bicep. Snapping my head up and eyes open, I observe the scene as if I'm removed from it, hovering above and around it but not actively participating.

Chapter 37

Aidan and Jeff wear matching looks of shock, a palpable mixture of disbelief and fear. With a hand still clamped around the gun he had pulled on Ace, Jeff's hand trembles. He looks from the barrel to the bullets' recipient.

Jim lies sprawled out on the floor just inches away from Riley. For a moment he looks as though he's asleep. As if he was crashing here for the night and passed out wherever his body landed.

Lying on his back, he slowly cranes his neck to peer down at the matching maroon spots marring his shirt. Clumsily raising a trembling hand, intent on investigating the wounds, his lips tremble.

Tears streak down Riley's cheeks as her breathing quickens. Aidan and Jeff tentatively step closer. We're surrounding Jim's weakening body. Jeff's hand, the one holding the pistol, trembles. His eyes widen and his breathing quickens. Aidan looks just as stunned and uncomfortable.

DEVASTATION ERUPTS

I'm guessing this moment goes against everything we've been taught our whole lives: when someone is hurt, you help them. But we all remain frozen in place, trying to make sense of the unexpected turn our little world has taken yet again.

Disbelief, rage, and regret flash across Jim's features. He shakes his head as blood coats his twitching hands. His head drops back to the floor. Those beady eyes, draining of life, dart between me and my sister. Although he fixates on us, I know his words are for everyone in the room.

"This isn't how it was supposed to be!" He coughs, a gob of viscous red mucous raining down on the shabby carpet between him and Riley. "You can go to hell!"

Riley inches closer. Although careful to avoid what just landed before her, the move is the exact opposite of what my instincts scream. She brushes away flowing tears and leans over Jim.

"No, Jim, I'm not going with you ever again." She turns toward me and rises to her feet. Turning on her heel, she strides to the isolation of the bedroom.

Jim's mouth opens and closes as if he's a fish out of water, gasping to breathe, but no more words come. His eyes flutter until they close and his body slumps into the thin carpet, arms giving way to gravity's endless pull.

Jeff nods toward the bedroom. "Why don't you go check on Riley? Maybe she can help patch you up? We can take care of things out here." He clamps a hand around Aidan's shoulder and tosses his head in a silent send-off. I manage a weak, "Okay."

Grasping the nearby couch, I pull myself up slowly, searching for balance. Aidan offers me an arm, but I wave him off. I don't want to require help just to stand up.

Lurching down the hallway, I lean against the wall for support. I find Riley sitting on the bed, arms wrapped around her tucked knees, gently rocking. I slump onto the bed, sitting next to her. She keeps her eyes trained on the crumpled blanket.

"It's awful to say, but this is how it had to be," she finishes her thought with a whisper, "I don't think he would have ever let me go. I would have spent the rest of my life looking over my shoulder, wondering if he was watching, just waiting to hurt us."

She turns her head toward me, fresh tears sailing down her cheeks. When she notices the stained doily in my hand, remembering my injury, her eyes fly to the sticky maroon substance clinging to my hair.

"Quinn!" She jumps to her feet, hovering over me. "I…I forgot…Let me see your head." She peels the stained doily from my hand and dabs my temple as she examines the wound. Her mouth forms a small "o" until her eyes catch mine. "It's not that bad," she whispers, but her pinched features contradict the claim. She tugs my hand. "Come on, let's go to the bathroom."

I numbly follow her into the hallway. We both keep our eyes trained on the worn rug to avoid seeing whatever's happening in the living room. Blurring movement shifts in my periphery, but I ignore it. The gnawing ringing in my ears easily tunes out background noises.

Once we're closed within the tight quarters of the bathroom, Riley rushes around me, selecting tools for the task. After a few minutes, she's wiped the wound clean and patched it with an antiseptic cream and bandage. Before we return to the living room, she insists that I swallow a painkiller.

The cool water trickles down my throat, sending a soothing sensation through my body as it carries the medication to my stomach.

We return to the living room to find Aidan and Jeff waiting for us. Neither Riley or I acknowledge the missing body or the red blots that now form an abstract design on the carpet. Although his blue eyes flood with concern, Aidan forces a weak smile. He motions toward my head. "That looks better already."

"It's actually already starting to feel better." I touch the bandage instinctively, unsure if I'm just getting used to the pain or if the ibuprofen is working its magic. The only certainty I feel is a resolve to never return to this trailer again. The family vacation memories have been overridden by the desperation Riley and I fought when we first made it here after our parents died—and we just watched the life drain out of someone right here in this space.

As awful as Jim was, I pray I never have to see anyone else die. A shiver rushes through me.

Running a hand over her face, Riley sinks into the couch, rubbing her temples. Before I can offer comfort, Jeff rushes to her side, drops onto the cushion, and wraps an arm around her.

"Are you okay?" he asks, concern etching his features. Eyes squeezed shut, she nods. Then, like a splintering dam, confessions slip from his lips. "I've...I've never done anything like that before. Maybe we could have talked him out of it. I should have tried to talk to him—"

With a single tear trailing down her scarred cheek, Riley turns to Jeff and wraps both of her arms around him. "No. Jeff, we owe you our lives. I know Jim. He would have hurt every one of you to get to me. You *had* to do it. Please don't blame yourself. It was either him or us and you chose us."

Aidan takes a step forward and clasps Jeff's shoulder. "Yeah, man, you saved us. All of us."

It's my turn to deliver a fresh serving of honesty. "Speaking as the person whose name was on that first bullet, if you hadn't shown up and done what you did, I wouldn't be standing here right now."

Blowing out a deep breath, Jeff gives us a weak smile. "Thanks," he mutters.

Silence descends and the moment passes. I'm eager to move past the thick, ugly haze of shock. We all deserve better, and I have to believe it awaits us.

"Why don't we get out of here?" I say, motioning to the door.

"I think that's a great idea." Aidan steps toward me. With his back to the others, he whispers, "You doing okay?" Letting everything else fade out of focus for this moment, I stare into his eyes and nod. Even with everything I've lost, I'm incredibly thankful for this person standing before me and the care and concern that he freely offers.

As Riley and Jeff rise and follow us through the doorway, Aidan asks, "So, what's the plan now? Chris is home but we still have a ways to go. We really need a vehicle and we're severely lacking in that department." His voice is gentle but serious. And he's right. We don't have time to process what just happened.

"What was it like?" Riley asks quietly. "Taking Chris home. Did it seem…okay?"

The guys exchange a glance before Aidan answers.

"The kid's gonna be alright." His smile deepens as his eyes drift past us, probably returning to the memory of Chris' send-off. "He was living with his mom and her boyfriend. Chris' dad is...was...in the army. When he found out Chris was missing, he got a leave and came back."

"The guy camped out at his ex-wife's house until Chris came home," Jeff adds, smiling. "We told him about what's coming. He said he'll go AWOL if he has to but he's not leaving that kid behind."

"I believe him," Aidan murmurs.

Riley nods in approval.

Relief washes through me. The kid's in good hands, and where he should be.

"So, back to the plan," Jeff claps his hands again but this time we're ready for the short burst of noise. "Anywhere we can borrow a car?"

Like magnets, Riley and I turn our heads toward each other. "Well, I don't know if it'll work, but I've got an idea," she says.

Chapter 38

Riley thinks our best bet is Benny. A year-round resident of the trailer park, he's been a friend of the family for as long as I can remember. Although we consider him more of a family member than a friend. When the area was evacuated for a tornado, one of the neighbors took him to Dover Air Force Base. He should be back by now, and he's got a car. If we tell him about Yellowstone's impending eruption, Riley thinks we can convince him to come home with us, the only catch is that we need to use his car to get there. Oh, and we have to stop along the way to get the satellite phone to Bowen's wife. *Minor details.*

Aidan scratches his head. "It's worth a try. But maybe we shouldn't put all of our apples into one bushel." The others scrunch their faces up, mirroring mine. I'm sure that's not the expression, but we remain silent so he'll continue.

"Quinn, how about you and I see if Rose might have a car we can borrow?" He wants to hike back to the house we took shelter in the night the tornado hit.

"I guess we could try, I mean, she said her daughter was coming to get her, so maybe she has a car she doesn't really need anyway. If she's still there." While I doubt this woman we barely know will just hand over her keys, we don't have many options and time continues to slip through our fingers.

He smiles weakly, brushing his shoulder against mine. "Besides, it would be nice to check on her...and warn her if she is there."

"Alright then," Jeff exclaims. "If Quinn's up for the walk," he nods toward my bandaged head. "Then Riley and I will head over to this Benny's place and you two go see Rose. We *need* a vehicle, so let's just get there as fast as we can and then meet back here. Let's make this happen!"

His pep talk deserves an enthusiastic team cheer or high five but the best we can offer is sullen uncertainty. We part ways and I lead Aidan toward the wooded path at the edge of the trailer park. We dodge downed tree limbs—victims of the tornado that passed through the area the last time we took this trail.

A surge of adrenaline propels my determination, and my body. Although we move at a much slower pace than last time, the dizzying fog clouding my mind dissipates, replaced by anticipation.

We reach the clearing to Rose's yard, but it lacks the overwhelming feline presence of my previous visits. Only a handful of cats laze around the property. Aidan must notice too. He glances at me questioningly. I hitch a shoulder up and point toward the street.

An orange and white box truck sits in the driveway, its opened roll-up door practically beckoning more boxes to be loaded inside it. We scamper toward the front door and cautiously knock.

A moment later the door swings open, revealing the wheelchair-bound woman who allowed two strangers to take shelter in her home just a few weeks ago. For a second, I worry that too much has happened since the tornado, that she won't remember our faces.

When a smile lights up across Rose's cheeks, fueled by recognition, I take a step forward and cross the door's threshold. She clasps a soft, wrinkly hand around mine.

"Well, it's good to see you two," she says. "Glad you're both still in one piece!" Relief ripples through me, clearing the way for my mind to focus on the enormous favor we came here to ask.

Aidan leans in toward Rose and rubs her shoulder. "It's good to see you too, and Jerry." He motions toward the wheelchair she named after her late husband. She pats Aidan's hand, smiling. When her eyes catch mine again, she senses the hesitation building behind them.

"Well what's with you? You look like a corn fritter on shuckin' day. What're you so nervous about?" Her eyes shift between the two of us. "You still got this handsome fella following you around." She juts a shaky finger toward Aidan.

"Well, Rose," Aidan starts, "We came here to tell you something, and to ask you something."

"Well come on inside. Not like you don't know your way around." She rolls the wheelchair backward, swivels it, and proceeds down the hallway. We follow, pausing only to close the door. She leads us to the living room and gestures toward the blue plaid couch. We sink into the cozy cushions. Just as we're about to speak, a petite Asian woman steps into the room, stopping mid-stride when she spots us. She tilts her head, narrowing her eyes, as if she doesn't believe what she's seeing.

"Mom?" she asks tentatively. "Who are these people?"

"Oh, Emily, these are the kids I was telling you about," Rose says. "The ones that kept me company during the storm."

"Oh, the ones that left you here alone with shattered windows and a tarp as the only barrier to the outside?" She raises her eyebrows expectantly. Before we can respond, Rose waves her off.

"I told ya, I had to chase these two outta here so I could take care of the kitties. Most of 'em missed supper because of that damn storm. My babies were hungry." Aidan takes the opportunity to steer the conversation away from Emily's accusation.

"We noticed there aren't as many cats around here," he mentions.

Rose nods in agreement. "Now that they finally cleared the damn roads, my Emily made it." Pride beams from her lopsided smile. "She worked with the local shelter and they took most of 'em. Then one of the neighbors down the road offered to take care of the ones still here."

Her eyes drift past us as if she's recalling the conversation. "Young man, he went to school with Emily. He started coming by the house, petting the cats. Said he loves them."

Aidan rests a hand over hers. "We're really glad you found someone to take care of them." He turns toward me before adding, "We know how important they are to you."

Emily strides to Rose's side, crossing her arms. "That guy was always creepy. I wouldn't trust him with a stuffed animal, let alone the cats. We're finding someone else to take care of them!"

"Not if we're leavin' tomorrow!" Rose snaps. "You're the one who wants to high-tail it outta here in the mornin'."

Aidan gently slices through the tension. "Actually, that's what we were hoping to talk to you about."

Emily turns on her heel. "I'll leave you three alone to talk. I've got more boxes to load anyway." She stomps out of the room, a wave of irritation trailing each step. Rose watches her, a smile stretching across her face. Any hesitation she had about leaving the house seems to be squelched by the love connecting her to her daughter.

Chapter 39

"Don't mind her—she's just tired. Been loading the truck all day." She clasps her hands together. "She doesn't mean to be smart. She's worried about me, and she just wants to get home. We leave tomorrow."

"I'm so glad." A flash of relief swims through me but knowledge of the impending disaster churns in my gut, trying its best to drown and sink any joy.

Aidan leans forward, the weight of what he's about to say transparent in every feature—the sharp determination in his eyes, the strained edge to his jaw, and the clenched teeth peeking out from his tight lips.

"Rose, we got some information about something bad that's about to happen." He glances at me, as if questioning what to say. I nod, silently encouraging him to do whatever it takes to make her understand how important this is.

We take turns explaining the condensed version of what we know. Yellowstone is on the verge of an eruption. People are going to panic. Those that live close to the volcano will lose their homes, or worse. Resources will run dry.

Worry and fear swirl in her pale eyes. She slips her glasses off to wipe away the gathering tears. Aidan gently takes her hand.

"Rose, you and your daughter should leave now. Don't wait until morning. Get supplies, get to her house and barricade yourselves in there as long as you can." He rubs his chin, eyes glazing over in distraction. "First we'll have to worry about the ash. It's going to coat everything. But soon after that, survivors will have to be evacuated and sent to parts of the country less impacted. And supplies aren't going to last forever. Our economy, our environment, our food. They're all going to be strained."

"Dear God," she raises a shaky hand over her gaping mouth. She doesn't question how we know this, but Aidan's demeanor conveys his sincere concern for her well-being. In the short time since we met, he's convinced me that he knows more about this stuff than he could have learned in a college textbook.

"There's one more thing, Rose." He takes a deep breath, preparing for the big ask. "We still need to get ourselves home, to Pennsylvania. And we have no way to get there. We really need wheels." He scrunches his eyes shut as if bracing for impact.

"Well if you're asking for Jerry, you're outta luck!" she says, running her hands lovingly along the wheelchair's arm rests. When Aidan and I just stare at her she chuckles and tosses a hand in the air toward us. "You kids can't take a joke."

She tilts her head to one side. "I've got a car you can take. I owe you two a lot, even if Emily doesn't see that. I want you to be safe. I'll make sure she gets us out of here and we're takin' the rest of the cats with us. I'm not leaving them behind with all this happening. Even though that Jim down the street said he'll take care of them. I'm not leaving them behind."

My eyes narrow when that one word slips past her lips. "Did you say *Jim?*"

"Yeah, he just lives down the road, in the trailer park. He went to school with my Emmy. Just a few days ago he started comin' around, visitin' the cats. I thought he'd take care of them, but I can't leave them here after what you told me."

My startled eyes catch Aidan's. There is no more Jim, but we're not going to be the ones to tell Rose. Especially when she believes he's worthy of entrusting with her pets. Maybe Emily isn't so bad. At least we share the same opinion of Jim.

The pulsing blood sizzles within my veins, electrified by sparks of fury. Jim must have gone home as soon as he left the base. And he must have planned on catching more of Rose's cats to *join* him for meals. If she found him on her property, he would have just explained away why he was there. She doesn't know him well enough to understand what a slimeball he truly is, was. I gulp down my discomfort and glance around the bare walls in search of a clock. They all must be packed.

Footsteps tread down the hallway, growing louder with each step. The front door thuds shut as Emily reappears. Noticing Rose's alarmed expression, she rushes to her mother's side.

"What's wrong, Mom?" She twists nervously, her shoulders hunched with worry. Rose rubs her forehead.

"Em, we've got to leave tonight." Rose's eyes widen. "Go get my keys. Aidan and Quinn are takin' the car."

"What?" The word oozes incredulity. "Mom, you can't—"

"Emily! Get the keys so we can send them on their way. I'll explain everything, but we don't have a lot of time. Trust me, they did us a big favor by coming here." Rose's stern tone commands compliance.

Defeated, Emily rises and strides out of the room. A moment later, she returns and drops the silver cat-shaped keychain in Aidan's palm. We both rise, thanking and hugging Rose simultaneously.

"Git yourselves outta here now! And take care of each other!" Rose shoos us away. Emily stands, her mouth gaping. Our small victory is fueled by adrenaline, and we dash toward the front door, throwing it open and descending upon the light blue Thunderbird.

Chapter 40

"I can't believe it! We got a car!" I cry. "It was almost too easy." After all we've been through, this little win feels like we've hit the lottery.

Aidan smiles, turning the key in the ignition. The engine sputters and our alarmed eyes meet. He twists the key again and we're met with the same crushing disappointment. *Why can't anything go right?*

Slamming his fists against the steering wheel, Aidan drops his head. The violent act startles me. He blows out a deep sigh.

"Alright," he mutters dejectedly. "One more try and then we high-tail it back to your aunt's trailer in case Jeff and Riley had any luck." I nod. He gently grasps my hand, as if it's made of glass, and wraps it around the key. Covering my hand with his, he meets my eyes. "Together?" I nod, unable to hide the smirk tugging at my lips.

In one movement, we turn the key and the engine purrs to life. Tension drains from my head to my toes and we savor this brief moment of success.

Smiling ear-to-ear, Aidan announces, "It's got a full tank of gas!" We buckle up and race back to the trailer park. We pass a few cars, driven by people seemingly out for a leisurely drive. I wonder what the highway would look like if everyone knew what we know.

We roll into the neighborhood, slowing as we near Aunt Grace's trailer. Riley and Jeff pace outside, pausing to evaluate the approaching vehicle. They visibly relax when they realize it's us. Aidan points toward them, "Looks like they failed in their mission. Good thing we didn't." He shoots me a sly grin, which I'm happy to return.

Riley bounces toward the car as Jeff slaps the hood. "You did it!" Running his eyes along the vehicle, he adds, "And she's a beauty!"

We hop out of the car to help load the items Riley's gathered to bring with us—clothes we left behind when we first tried to go home, before Jim and Dan took Riley, and a small assortment of knickknacks that may someday serve as our only reminders of this place.

Jeff scrambles to the driver's seat and yanks the door closed. Aidan wanders to the window, casually leaning on the open pane.

"What makes you think Rose is okay with a total stranger driving her car?" he asks, eyes wide with challenge.

Jeff chuckles, wrapping his hands around the steering wheel. "Well, the way I see it, anyone crazy enough to give you two their car, just *give* away a car, isn't really lucid enough to care if I'm driving it or not." I cringe. Although I believe Rose is completely sane, she did hand over her keys to two near-strangers. We spent a stormy night in her basement together, but she slept for most of that time.

Blowing out a deep breath, Aidan catches my eyes. I raise my shoulders, a silent admission of my nonexistent counterargument.

Riley, Aidan, and I slide into the car. Jeff hoots with excitement and starts the engine. With no time to waste, he rolls onto the highway and drives north. At least we know the general direction to go.

"So what happened with Benny?" I say, but what I really want to know is if Benny is okay. One of the year-round residents at the trailer park, Benny is like a grandfather to us. He's been a family friend for as long as I can remember going to our Aunt Grace's trailer for summer vacation. From what my parents used to tell us, we'd gone since Riley was a baby. I bet they knew him for about twenty years.

Shaking away the memories, my ears tune back to the conversation when Riley's mid-sentence. "So, yeah, he can't leave. They're making him stay at the base."

"What do you mean *it's no big deal?*" I boom. Images float through my mind, visions of Benny strapped to a hospital bed, cringing away from a menacing figure hovering over his immobile body.

The others stare at me in stunned silence, which only encourages me to continue.

"They can't hold him there like he's a prisoner!" My mind switches gears as fast as the words spill from my lips. "And how did you even find out if he isn't home?"

Aidan shifts his eyes from the road, his lips hitched in a smirk. "Did you even hear anything your sister said? She just—"

"Quinn," Riley interrupts. "Benny wasn't home, so Jeff and I went to the neighbor's place. Remember Cindy? She's a nurse and she was checking on Benny." When I dumbly nod, she continues. "Well, Cindy told us that Benny is still at the base because his blood pressure was too high for them to release him. They're trying to control it with medication, but they felt it was too risky for him to leave, especially with all of this crazy weather that's been happening in the area, so he's staying at the base's hospital."

Dammit. I missed some key information when my thoughts wandered. My cheeks flush in embarrassment. "Sorry, guys, I guess I kinda zoned out there for a minute. It all makes sense. I'll try to keep up from now on."

We turn off the main highway, following back roads that curve around sprawling hills and meadows. After about ten minutes, Jeff slows the car, his eyes latching onto something ahead on the right. Squinting, all I see is a farmer's field. Whatever was growing there must have been chopped or harvested because all that remains is smoothed-over soil and rows of low-lying, browning vegetation.

"Look at that!" he barks, pointing to the field. *Great. Now he's got one hand on the steering wheel and no eyes on the road.*

"How about you look at where you're driving?" I retort. He shoots me a mock glare.

"It's just a plowed-over field. What's the big deal?" Aidan throws his hands in the air.

Ignoring us, Jeff pulls to the side of the road when we're

right next to the field. *What in the world is he doing?*

"Wait, I see it too," Riley says, her eyes glued to the window. "All those black spots. What are they?"

"That's exactly what I want to know," Jeff says, an expression of concern sweeping across his face. I hover over Riley's shoulder, scanning the field.

"We aren't gonna figure it out from here!" he says. "I'm going to check it out."

Suddenly I miss "serious" Jeff. He doesn't appear too often, but this changing world needs him. "Carefree" Jeff ought to take a back seat right about now.

"That would be trespassing," Aidan says. "Whatever it is, it's none of our business. Plus, we've got somewhere to be. It's just not a good idea." He looks to me for support. Before I can back his cause, Jeff throws a door open, calling over his shoulder, "Won't be the first bad idea we ever had!" he says just before he jumps out of the car and darts into the field.

"Kinda feels like *Jurassic Park* when they're on the tour and one guy just jumps out of the car. After that, all hell broke loose. Or should I say, all dinosaurs broke loose." Aidan shakes his head. "You know we're gonna have to go out there. He won't just come back on his own."

All three of us stare outside, unmoving. Jeff dashes about twenty yards into the property and stops short. Sweeping his head back and forth, his expression turns serious as if understanding has seeped into his bones. He scans the ground. After just a few strides of searching, he picks up a narrow stick. Turning toward the car, he motions for us to join him.

"And there it is," Aidan exhales. "Let's get this over with. It'll be the fastest way to get back on the road." Rolling my eyes, I can't contain my annoyance. *Why did we let Jeff drive?*

All three of us climb out of the car. Aidan and I trudge toward Jeff. Riley reaches him first, obviously the most interested in his findings.

Jeff crouches, jabbing the closest black lump with the stick. When he flips the lifeless object over, Riley and I gasp, taking an instinctive step back.

The iridescent black feathers on its wings and head are perfectly smooth, not one out of place. They're a sharp contrast to the tiny tufts of black jutting from the once-smooth curvature of its belly. Slight movement catches my eye, but it can't be the crow stirring. Its thick, slightly-hooked beak is opened as if frozen in a silent shriek. It's clearly dead.

Chapter 41

Grasping the stick, Jeff pokes its belly. As if its contents were secured by a flimsy piece of taut plastic wrap, it splits open. A mini-cluster of legs, antennae, and bean-shaped bodies spill out. They tussle briefly, ensnared within each other's limbs as they attempt to separate, fleeing their former prison. *How can they be alive if they were eaten? Wouldn't the bird's digestive juices have smothered or dissolved them? I probably should have paid more attention in Biology class.*

Turning away in disgust, I survey the rest of the clearing. Sure enough, the other nearby black lumps mirror this one's size and shape. There must be at least thirty of them.

Leaning closer, Jeff bobs his head in various directions, conducting a thorough visual inspection of all angles. He inches nearer the dead body.

"Don't touch it!" Aidan snaps. "You could get some virus or something if that's what killed it."

"I wasn't planning on touching it," Jeff huffs. "I just want to see if we can figure out what happened."

"I don't feel so good," Riley says, thrusting a hand over her mouth. Aidan's concerned eyes land on me. "Why don't you two go back to the car? We'll be there in a minute." I nod and wrap an arm around Riley's shoulder, leading us both away from the ground-level grave site.

She shakes her head, "What do you think happened to that one? Do you think they're all like that?"

I hunch a shoulder. "I don't know. I mean, that one looked pretty healthy. You know, other than being dead and having its stomach split open. How could those bugs still be alive and so active if—"

Riley pales, raising a delicate hand. "We don't have to guess. It's okay."

Trudging back to the car, we claim the front seats, indirectly relieving Jeff of his driving duties. Then we sit in silence, looking anywhere but outside.

Aidan and Jeff return to the car and slide into the back seat. "Ready to go?" Aidan asks a little too cheerfully. Riley starts the car and pulls onto the road. I twist in my seat to face the guys.

"So, did you find anything back there? You know, figure out how they died?" The guys share a pinched look before Jeff answers.

"Well," he stretches his arms casually, as if we're just catching up on last weekend's activities. "We checked four more and they all looked the same. Other than their stomachs, nothing was out of place. But some of them," he runs a hand through his hair. "Some of the others had really swollen stomachs."

Aidan nods. "And those were the ones that had hardly any bugs…coming out of them." He shakes his head and takes a gulp, muttering, "I don't get it."

"It's like the bugs did this," Jeff adds, rubbing his chin. "From the inside out."

"Lethal bugs?" I scoff. "I know there are poisonous spiders and frogs, but are there bugs poisonous enough to kill?"

Aidan's head drops and he squints his eyes shut. "Guys. It's like Wes."

Heavy silence consumes the car. *Aidan's right.* Riley doesn't ask any questions, but I had told her about the guys' friend Wes. He was traveling with us to Langley Air Force Base. He didn't make it.

Along the way, he became progressively weaker until he just couldn't go any farther. We discovered he had a tick attached to him. Only instead of the typical red-ringed bullseye rash, his was black. We didn't have access to a hospital or a doctor, so we don't know for certain what prevented him from ever waking up again.

I peer out the window, watching the scenery roll past. Desperate to break the awkward stillness permeating the car, I turn in my seat and scan the baggage nestled between Jeff and Aidan in the back seat.

We continue along the highway, but we need a clear destination and now's as good a time as any to set the GPS. Digging out the satellite phone, I follow the steps Bowen showed us to input an address. Foggy details swim through my mind as the screen blinks, awaiting input.

"Who has the photo of Bowen's wife?" I ask no one in particular. The address was printed on the back of the framed picture the sergeant gave us.

Aidan shuffles through the bags resting at his feet. His deft fingers search slowly at first, but turn slightly desperate when he reaches the last one. Breathing out a sigh, he elbows Jeff. "You could help look, too, you know."

"You probably just missed it," Jeff says. "Move aside, *I'll* check." I glance at Riley as her knuckles grip the steering wheel tighter. Worry lines crest her forehead as she pushes a long brown lock behind her ear. Riley's always been detail-oriented. And Aidan seems like he is too. If she's not the type to skip right over something she's looking for, a tingling sense tells me that Aidan wouldn't either. Unless it isn't there to begin with. Bile rises in my throat, the blinking screen mocking us.

Aidan's questioning eyes slide toward me. I raise my eyebrows and hitch a shoulder in response. With deliberate concentration, Aidan investigates each bag thoroughly, placing the ones he's checked on the floor. Almost as soon as he discards a bag, Jeff grabs it, tearing through its contents.

When their little assembly line completes its task, Aidan and Jeff stare blankly at each other. "It's gone. We must have left it in that asshat's car," Jeff mutters, shaking his head.

"Now what?" Aidan's eyes shift to each of us. "We can't just keep going without a destination." *Another failure.* I look to the sky, seeking wisdom or comfort. Instead, the darkening clouds forecast doom, as if they swirl within an enormous cauldron that's conjuring the ingredients for an onslaught of lightning bolts.

"We have to call Bowen," I utter. "He can give us the address. We don't have time for anything else. We'll just have to admit that we lost the picture."

A succession of beeps explodes from the radio. *I didn't even realize it was on.* Aidan's hand shoots toward the dash and he cranks the volume up. The pattern repeats before a brief static sound diminishes to silence. A robotic voice, eerily calm, holds our rapt attention:

> *This is the emergency public broadcast system. The U.S. Geological Survey has confirmed seismic activity indicating that the Yellowstone Caldera is on the verge of eruption. Evacuation zones span as far west as Oregon to Wisconsin and Illinois in the east. These areas constitute the primary and secondary ash zones based upon the current wind conditions.*
>
> *Areas along the East Coast should prepare for a population influx as evacuees seek shelter. Further information will be provided as it becomes available.*

Chapter 42

My stomach twists and goosebumps surge along my forearms. A chill sweeps through my body. I focus on stilling my fingers enough to dial Bowen. After a few misdials, my fingers finally get the numbers right.

We wait, anticipation weighing down the air. The phone rings at least a dozen times but there's no answer on the other end. I glance at Riley. She blinks rapidly, probably fighting the release of worried tears; her hands twitch as if they are the sole keepers of her nervous energy.

"He's not picking up," I mumble. Letting the phone fall away from my ear, I let the ringing continue though I know it won't make any difference.

"It's okay," Jeff says, placing a hand on Riley's shoulder. "Just keep driving. You said we're heading to Maryland, right?"

Riley and I both nod. She answers him. "Yes! Towson! He said Towson. Can you plug that into the phone, so we'll know we're going in the right direction at least?"

I set the navigation, releasing a gasp when the robotic voice alerts us that it will take two hours. *And that's not even counting how long it will take to get home after we stop there.*

"I don't know, guys, those clouds look pretty nasty," Jeff says, pointing out the window. "And nothing's even happened yet."

"We should check in with our parents," Aidan mutters to Jeff. He retrieves his phone and hands it to his friend. Although we only hear one side of the conversation, it's clear Jeff's parents heard the emergency broadcast. He assures them that he's on his way and tells them not to worry.

I fix my gaze out the window. I can't bear to face my sister. I'm guessing the same blend of jealousy, regret, and sorrow swirls within both of us. We should be with our parents right now. Or at the very least, we should be calling to tell them we're okay and on our way home.

Our first stop is our Aunt Robin's house to retrieve our family dog, Snickers. But we don't even have her phone number. It's saved in the address book of our cell phones. But they now reside somewhere along Route One—maybe lying in a ditch along the shoulder or crumpled within the remains of our smashed car. Either way, I'm praying she'll be home and ready to hand over Snickers, because we won't have much time to explain.

I tune the conversations out when Jeff wraps up his call and Aidan begins his. I don't even realize that Aidan's hung up until Jeff starts firing questions at him.

"So, you must understand more about what's happening."

Jeff leans against the door, twisting so that he faces Aidan. "What do you think's gonna happen around here?"

Aidan blows out a deep sigh, shooting me a worried glance. The crystal hue to his irises darkens, as if signaling the hesitation in his words. "The warning was right. We're not exactly in the projected ash zone but if this eruption is major and the Jet Stream is strong, it can carry ash all the way to Pennsylvania."

"And what if it does?" Jeff asks. I twist in my seat to listen as if my eyes have to see what my ears are hearing. I study their expressions as they talk, searching for clues that this really isn't as bad as the hairs rising on the back of my neck suspect.

"Sounds kinda minor compared to flowing lava," Jeff mutters, shooting me a sly grin. My eyes volley to Aidan, but his lips don't even tug at the corners of his mouth. They seem to tighten, forming a pursed line.

"Ash is basically rock and glass. Even if it doesn't blanket the East Coast, it would cause a lot of damage in the Midwest. It would kill plants and animals, collapse buildings, and destroy electrical equipment. Communication's been spotty with cell phone towers out from the earthquake. This would be a hundred times worse, and it would take a lot longer to repair."

The smile falls from Jeff's face when his jaw drops. Riley chews on her fingernails, one hand at a time, listening intently. My heart crashes within my chest, sending frantic jolts through my extremities. The relaxed, caring college guy I met just a few weeks ago seems to have aged by ten years in the past ten minutes.

"Do you know how much of our food is produced in the Midwest?" He pauses, but not long enough for any of us to answer. "That's where most of our meat comes from. Not to

187

mention crops. This could have a major impact on the food supply."

"And that's not even considering that volcanic eruptions release sulfur dioxide." He turns, running his eyes over each of us as if awaiting a response. When we remain silent, fixated on his knowledge, he continues. "In the atmosphere, that causes acid rain."

Silence descends, cloaked in distress. I nearly skyrocket through the roof when the satellite phone practically screams its mechanical tune. I must have inadvertently turned the volume up when I tried calling Bowen. *Bowen! He must be calling!*

My fingers fumble over the smooth black surface and the phone tumbles to the floor. Aidan and Jeff shout obvious commands from the back seat. "Pick it up!" "Hurry, before he hangs up!"

I scramble to accept the call, squeaking into the receiver, "Hello! Hello!"

"This is Sergeant Bowen," the familiar voice answers. But the usual seriousness has been replaced by an unhinged urgency.

"Look, we don't have much time. The eruption's happening faster than predicted. You aren't going to make it home before it happens. Get to Rossana and take cover with her." His words fly at us in a rush. "Stay inside until the ash settles. As soon as it does, drive straight home and tell Rossana to drive to the base as fast as she can. Do you understand?"

All I can manage is a half-hearted "Yes."

"Good." He barely breathes between words. "Before you leave, tell Rossana to give you our ham radio. Take it and listen to it every day. You'll need it to get any updates on conditions. Be careful and stay safe. I'm counting on you to send my wife down here. You're the last chance I have."

Guilt and failure swirl within my core. We've already failed at getting home before all hell breaks loose. And now we probably won't make it to the sergeant's wife in time.

"Sergeant," Riley's timid voice surprises us all. "We, um, might have misplaced the address to your house." The responding deep sigh hums through the receiver clearly.

"You lost the picture with the address written on the back of it?" he clarifies.

"Yes." I hang my head in shame even though he can't see. I decide not to volunteer that we also lost some of the weapons he provided us. No need to offer up information he really doesn't need right now.

"If there's anything you learn from me, it's that you should always have a fail-safe," he says. I envision him squinting his eyes and pinching the bridge of his nose. He proceeds to talk me through a series of keystrokes. Apparently, he programmed the address into the phone for us. That way if we lost the frame, we had our destination in the phone. And if we lost the phone, we still had the address on the picture. That just would have been a little trickier if we didn't have at least one working cell phone to guide us.

After confirming that the phone is leading us in the right direction, Bowen bids us farewell.

"At this point, don't let anything stop you. Get to my house and take cover. I'll talk to you then."

Chapter 43

Between Aidan's explanation and the sergeant's warning, the conversation dwindles to an uncomfortable lull. I have so many questions, but no one has the answers. Bowen said to make sure we get a ham radio from his wife in case there are future announcements. Remembering the emergency broadcast message we heard earlier, I switch the radio back on.

Pop music rolls from the speakers. No one seems to notice or care. I glance out the window, wondering what the sky has in store for us. Will it come crashing down and snuff us all out of existence? Will it scatter flecks of poison into our water and air, choking us from the inside?

I'm jolted from the cyclone of morbid thoughts when a series of harsh beeps blares from the radio. My hand shoots toward the dial, turning it up.

Static, then the robotic voice announces a message from the Emergency Broadcast System. Silence stretches across the airwaves. Goosebumps crawl up my arms as my heart thunders in my chest. After what feels like an hour, a voice splinters the silence. This time there's no mechanical inflection. The deep voice oozes confidence:

> Citizens of this great country, good evening. This is President Taves addressing you from the Oval Office. Tonight's address is different from any other I've ever given. It is with grave concern that I am speaking to you under the current circumstances.

> Our homes, our communities, our very way of life. They are all in danger right now. We sit on the brink of disaster. And although we can't fight this enemy with weapons or technology, we stand together as citizens of this great country, and we will prevail.

> I received word today that the Yellowstone Caldera in Wyoming is poised to erupt within the next few hours. Now I know this information is alarming, but the most important thing we can do right now is to stay calm.
> Our military forces are prepared, and they are uniting to assist those with the greatest need. The Yellowstone National Park area is under an evacuation order. This includes Wyoming, Montana, and Idaho.

> Please stay tuned after my address concludes for local

emergency plan announcements. In general, military bases, educational facilities, and municipal properties throughout the country will open their doors to assist citizens until further notice. These safety communes will provide food and shelter, as well as basic necessities.

If you are in an immediate jeopardy zone, I encourage you to gather your family and minimal belongings and report to the closest military base, school, or municipal building for instruction. If you are not within the Yellowstone National Park evacuation boundary, stay put until further notice. Specific information will be provided based upon your location.

I wish everyone a safe evening. Good night and God Bless.

"Okay, first of all, he said he found out today. Sergeant Bowen told us days ago, so the military knew." I slump into my seat in frustration. "It's just like the earthquake. They knew about that, too, but they didn't warn people. The only reason they're announcing it now is probably because the news stations started talking about it."

Aidan's face twists in confusion. "What do you mean they knew about the earthquake before it happened?" Before I can answer, he mutters to himself. "Of course, they knew. That kind of seismic activity would have triggered warnings." He scratches his chin. "The real question is why. Why didn't they warn anyone? And how did they keep it under wraps?"

"It doesn't really matter now, does it?" Riley cries. "The clock is ticking. All that matters is that we get to our next stop before the ash falls."

"Yeah," Jeff agrees. "At least they did the right thing now and told people. Even if they did wait until the eleventh hour. I mean, it's better than nothing."

"I guess," I shrug, not convinced. Riley's right, though, there's nothing we can do about it and it doesn't change our situation.

The rest of the ride is quiet as we all process the impending disaster. Bitterness pits in my stomach as I imagine the widespread panic sweeping our country right now. Our small group has had a few days to digest what's happening, but most people heard it now for the first time. What a cruel twist that the roads were just cleared, and power was just restored.

How many will disbelieve the warning? How many didn't hear it?

My mind wanders back to when we were trying to find Riley, driving in the Malibu Jeff had *borrowed* that ended up getting swallowed by a sinkhole. The group was together—me, Aidan, Jeff, Chris, Jasmine and Wes—talking through what was happening with the environment. The earthquake, the tornado, and temperature extremes.

I remember Jasmine saying something about Mother Nature being angry and tired of human destruction. And that maybe nature was setting some sort of mass extinction plan into motion. A chill sweeps up my spine, triggering an involuntary tremor through my limbs.

Resting an elbow on the door, I lean against it, dropping my head into my palm. When my finger brushes the bandage sticking to my temple, I flip the visor down to check if it's bled through. I have no idea what year this car was made, but it's old enough to lack basic necessities, like a visor mirror.

I squeeze my eyes shut, cringing when I realize that a mirror isn't a true necessity. *I think we're all about to find out what we can live without.*

Chapter 44

"You have arrived at your destination," the mechanical voice chimes. Riley shoots me a side glance as she eases up on the gas pedal. Aidan and Jeff pitch forward, gripping our seats as they sway back and forth to survey our destination.

The car drifts across the narrow blacktop driveway, rolling to a stop. Nervous anticipation electrifies the air. We take a quick inventory of the supplies Bowen gave us and throw the doors open.

Bags slung over our shoulders, we follow the winding walkway to the front door. Aidan and Jeff let us lead the way. Locking her brown eyes with mine, Riley hesitates for just a moment before she depresses the rectangular doorbell button. I release a deep exhale in a futile attempt to slow my racing heart.

Awkward silence stretches as we patiently await a response.

"What's her name again?" Riley whispers, panic lacing her words.

"Um…it started with an R." I remember that at least.

"You two are gonna sound real credible if you don't even know her name," Jeff says, crossing his arms and tilting his head. He raises his eyebrows to punctuate his lack of confidence in us.

"Well, doesn't look like it's gonna matter much if no one's home." Aidan plants a leg between us, reaching forward and banging on the door. We all straighten again, just in case someone's in there and heard this time.

The noise draws attention, but not from inside the house. Across the street a low growl morphs into a yapping bark, warning us that we're being watched. And also announcing our presence to anyone who's home.

"Great," Jeff slaps his leg and motions toward the dog. "How come the welcoming committee was so easy to find?"

Riley stares at the barking machine, lightly tapping my arm. "Quinn…that dog. I think that's Bowen's dog!"

I stumble toward the street, craning my neck to see the dog's face. The mass of black fur approaches us with interest. As it draws closer, I recognize the subtle sprinkle of white around the otherwise black muzzle. *Riley's right—that's the dog from the picture!*

I rush toward the yard—shouting calls for me to wait fly past my ears. My steps falter when the dog responds eagerly to my approach. The barking dwindles, quickly replaced by a teeth-baring growl. The sound reverberates, sending waves of fear through my heart and caution to my brain. A hand clasps around my shoulder, startling me. My whole body jolts in surprise and I nearly tumble to the ground when my feet lag behind my brain's reaction. Aidan scolds me. "What were you thinking? Taking off like that, running full force toward an aggressive dog!"

Disappointment coats his words. "You've gotta think, Quinn, you can't just do stuff like that."

I raise my hands in surrender. "You're right," I agree. "That was stupid. I got all excited because I think we found Bowen's dog."

Riley and Jeff join us, their narrowed eyes drilling into me. Before they can express their annoyance, I raise a hand to ward off the impending lecture. "I know, I know. I shouldn't have done that. Sorry."

"So," Jeff starts, nodding toward the house across the street. "You think she's in there?" The dog circles excitedly but stays within the limits of the browning lawn. He scents the air, dark eyes following our every step.

"We don't really have another plan," Riley says flatly. "If she's not here, then what?"

No one answers. No one has an answer.

"Well then," Jeff says, rubbing his hands together. "Let's find out." As he leads the way, we flow into a single file along the driveway. With light steps and a soothing tone, he sweet-talks the dog while slowly easing toward the front door. "Who's a good dog? Are you gonna be a nice puppy?"

Thankfully, the *puppy* tilts its head, captivated by Jeff's charms. Maybe these are words it recognizes. Either way, it's working because the snarling has ceased, and the teeth no longer threaten to chomp into our flesh.

When Jeff pauses and bends at his waist, the dog seems to relax. Its ears ease from their previous upright position and its tail hesitantly sways back and forth in anticipation of a full wag.

The dog approaches and Jeff gingerly extends a hand.

Seemingly confident that the dog has no intention of tearing it off, he strokes the dog's head.

Tired of standing in place, I rest a palm on the closest vehicle, which happens to be parked just a few inches away. My eyes trail the bold design splashed across the pickup truck's side and cap.

Deathtrap Pest Elimination. *Gee, that name says it all.* Beneath the words, a smiling uniformed employee hoists his chosen extermination weapons outward, proud and ready to eradicate any creature that dares cross your path.

An amplified barking yanks me from my thoughts. It's not the vicious kind meant to warn us. This time, it's the jovial announcement of a new friend's arrival. The dog's eyes dance while its tail swishes. Jeff shoots us a nervous glance, his jaw tensing as he cringes.

We animatedly try to shush the dog, waving our arms and begging for silence. Our efforts are fruitless. Before any of us can take another step forward, the house's front door swings open and a stout man bursts onto the porch.

Chapter 45

"Come here, Millie!" he calls. The dog immediately obeys, charging past him and into the house. With her secured, he turns a scrutinizing gaze toward us.

"Can I help you with something?" He crosses his arms and leans on one hip, jutting out the other leg. His tone doesn't convey an offer of assistance.

Running a hand through his hair, Jeff takes a step forward. He dips his shoulders in a non-confrontational way. "Yeah, we were actually looking for someone." He motions for me to come forward. The man huffs impatiently as I stumble past Jeff.

"Um, we're trying to find one of the neighbors," I say nervously, gesturing across the street at the house we just left. "The woman that lives in that house."

Riley appears at my side, close enough to brush my shoulder. "We know her husband, and he has a message for her," she adds.

Surprise flashes through the man's eyes before they turn cold. "No one's there anymore. They left when the warnings started yesterday." He tugs on his shirt collar as the words tumble from his mouth quickly. His face scrunches in annoyance. I can't tell if it's because the neighbors left or if it's because we showed up asking about them.

"But the dog," Riley says, cocking her head. "Isn't that her dog?"

The man's eyes shift, as if he's dangling on the precipice of truth, weighing his best option. "Yep, that's their dog. They knew they couldn't take her where they were going, so they left the dog behind." His lips twitch into a smile, as if he can't contain the cleverness.

Riley and I share a knowing smile. *The whole reason Bowen's wife isn't with him is because she wouldn't leave the dog behind. There's no way she did it now.*

"Sorry for the trouble," Jeff calls, turning back toward the street.

Aidan releases a deep sigh and runs a hand through his hair. "I guess we're done here."

"No, we're not!" I challenge. "She's here and I know it." I plant both feet on the ground firmly and cross my arms. Before the man can respond, Riley starts toward the house, shouting. "Roxanne!" *I don't think that's the right name, but maybe it's close enough to get her attention.*

The man rushes toward Riley, arms extended to stop her progress. "Now I told you—" But before he can finish his thought, Millie charges out the front door, barking wildly as she circles my sister and this stranger.

A lithe figure strides across the porch, approaching the chaotic scene. A dopey smile surges across my face as I recognize the blonde hair and bright green eyes. We lost the picture, but this is definitely Mrs. Sergeant Bowen. She's slightly taller than me but definitely thinner. Darkened half-moons under her eyes betray the worry she carries.

Her eyes track Millie, who swarms Jeff for another round of affection. Planting a fist on each hip, she demands, "What's going on here?" Before the man can begin spewing more lies, Riley responds.

"We're here to see you," she takes a cautious step closer to the woman, conveying the seriousness of what we have to say. "We came from Langley Air Force Base." With those words, the woman's eyes widen and her posture cracks slightly.

"We met your husband, Sergeant Bowen, and he sent us here to give you a message," Riley continues. Stillness surrounds the scene like a peaceful bubble. Even Millie has calmed down, content to sit at Jeff's feet while he rubs between her ears.

The man breaks the silence, "Now we don't know if they're telling the truth, Rossana. We can't trust them." He gestures to us in disgust, as if he just caught us rooting through his trash. She raises a hand to silence him.

"Well, I'm willing to hear what they have to say before I decide anything," she says confidently. Then, shifting her focus to each of us in turn, she smiles slightly and invites us to sit down and talk with her.

Chapter 46

We leave the neighbor behind as Bowen's wife escorts us to her house across the street. Millie follows at her heels, although the dog glances back at Jeff as she trots along. She stays loyal to her human, but she's definitely drawn to at least one of the new humans escorting her home.

Even given the circumstances, a slight bounce boosts each step I take. We *finally* accomplished something on this trip. Well, besides freeing the dogs and getting Chris home. A quiet confidence breezes through my limbs. This whole trip I've been focused on our failures, completely disregarding our successes.

Aidan nudges my shoulder, one cheek hitched in a half-smile. "What're you thinking about?" Fire flushes from my chin to my ears.

"What? Why?" Those deep blue eyes vaporize my conversational skills. The smile overtakes his face.

"You just look…I don't know…content. It's not really a side you show often." He raises his eyebrows, awaiting a response.

"I know. I just realized that we've been through a lot, but we've done a lot of good too. And maybe I need to remember that more often."

"I think you're 100% right," he says, a flicker of playfulness flashing through his eyes. "And I'm willing to accept the challenge of making sure you don't forget!"

He squeezes my hand, just a gentle tug, and releases it just as quickly. As we file inside the house, I practically float over the threshold.

We spill into an inviting living room, each wall bearing a different shade of brown. The fluffy folded blanket on the floor beckons Millie, as she immediately sprawls out on it, watching her human intently. Rossana beelines to the kitchen, quickly returning with a dog-boned shaped treat. Millie rises on her haunches, ears perked in curiosity. Or maybe expectation. I get the feeling this is a regular routine.

Rossana leans down to drop the treat while simultaneously patting Millie's head. She quickly shoots back up and turns to us. "Let's go to the lower level and we can talk."

We all nod and follow her single-file, but I wonder why we don't just stay in the living room.

The steps are just a few feet away, and as we descend them a sweeping room opens up. A fireplace resides on one wall, sitting idly. Rossana comments on how unseasonably cold it's been and selects a small log from the metal basket resting on the hearth. Millie wanders down the few steps to join us. She watches calmly as her human sets the log ablaze, forming mesmerizing flames that reach for the flue.

Two overstuffed couches with matching recliners line the wall adjacent to the fireplace. Rossana plops into the tan recliner closest to the fireplace and motions for us to sit.

I sink into a cushion swathed in a deep chocolate fabric. Aidan quickly claims the seat beside me and we both relax into the sofa. Jeff and Riley take the other couch and Millie coils herself at Rossana's feet.

"Thanks for talking to us," Jeff says. He jabs a thumb toward the doorway. "For a second there, I thought your neighbor was gonna banish us or something."

Rossana waves her hand, dismissing the thought. "Oh, don't mind him. He's paranoid about looters. The neighbors were all getting together to talk about what's happening, but I have a feeling what you have to say will be much more interesting." She leans forward and clasps her hands together. "So, you said you have a message for me?"

Chapter 47

When Riley glances my way, I give her a slight nod. It's my job to explain. I am the one Bowen first approached about this mission.

I don't share Riley's abduction and our pursuit to find her. It's really not relevant to this woman. I explain that when her husband realized we were leaving the base and heading home to Pennsylvania, he enlisted our help since he had lost touch with her. At the mention of them losing touch, her eyes water with sorrow.

"But he's okay," I rush to reassure her. "And we've been talking to him the whole way along our trip here." With those words, her eyes reflect fierce determination.

"What do you mean you've been able to talk to him?" she demands, immediately recognizing the harshness of her tone. "I'm sorry, it's just…we talked on the phone every night for months…since he was sent down there. And then one day, he started...confessing some concerns he had, and the line just went dead. And I didn't hear from him since then. I tried calling, sent letters, but I heard nothing."

She shakes her head solemnly before continuing. "I was getting ready to drive down to that base and demand to see him, but then all these warnings came out and I didn't know what to do." She huffs out a frustrated breath.

My stomach twists as my mind over-processes the information. Bowen confessed to us just before we left that the government knew about the earthquake before it happened and warned no one. Although he didn't say as much, the knowledge seemed to weigh on his soul. *Had he reached a point where he disagreed with his employer's ways? Did someone suspect that Bowen wasn't blindly compliant about withholding looming natural disaster warnings from the public?*

My spiraling thoughts slam to an immediate stop when I realize everyone's staring at me, waiting for me to continue. Heat flushes my cheeks.

"Sorry, I got distracted." Riley shoots me an incredulous look that screams, *"Pay attention!"*

"Quinn, I think we've told her enough for now," Jeff says quietly. "Why don't we give her the satellite phone?"

Rossana immediately straightens, as if anticipation tugs at each nerve. I nod. She's waited long enough to talk to her husband.

Jeff digs into the bag in his lap and pulls out the phone. "Do you know how to use this?" he asks gently. Her green eyes sheen with unshed tears as she shakes her head no. Riley snatches the phone from Jeff's hand and rushes to Rossana's side. She demonstrates the basics, like how to dial the number the sergeant pre-programmed into the phone.

With trembling hands, she takes the phone from Riley and mutters a broken "Thank you…if you'll excuse me…I'll be back." Before anyone can respond, she jumps to her feet, sweeping across the room and up the steps. Millie trails half a step behind.

"Well, that got intense," Jeff says, eyes wide and eyebrows raised.

"Yeah," Riley agrees. "I didn't really think about why they lost touch when we've been able to speak with the sergeant pretty easily."

"I think someone knew." They all turn narrowed, skeptical eyes in my direction. "I mean, I think Bowen was starting to see that the government wasn't doing what it should have, like warning people about dangerous situations."

Their stares remain disbelieving, but I continue.

"So maybe he was, like, flagged as someone who was questioning things and they started watching him more closely? And maybe when he was about to tell his wife about what was happening, they cut off his communication with her." I tilt my head, jutting my chin out, in a satisfied gesture. *Surely they'll all see the genius in my theory.*

Aidan crosses his arms and scrunches up his whole face. "Sounds to me like someone's got a case of the conspiracies."

A high-pitched chuckle escapes Riley before she can yank it back. Jeff shifts his eyes back and forth, mimicking a type of wall clock while he chants, "Cuckoo…cuckoo…cuckoo!"

I cross my arms sullenly. Fine. They don't have to believe me, but the hairs rising along the back of my neck seem to agree.

Chapter 48

After about thirty minutes of idle chitchat, a door creaks open within the house and approaching footsteps grow louder. Rossana and Millie bound down the steps and rejoin us.

Rossana settles into the recliner again. Millie sits directly in front of the chair, leaning her furry body against her human's legs. Pink splotches mar Rossana's face, remnants of tears that must have accompanied the conversation. Her green irises appear brighter, temporarily enhanced by the salty substance that spilled over them.

"I can't thank you all enough," she says with a resolve I didn't think possible given her appearance. Swiping a palm across her cheek, she continues. "It sounds like we all need to lay low for a day or two, but after that Millie and I will be heading to Langley and you all have your own plans." She looks to each of us for confirmation.

"Yes, ma'am," Jeff obliges, shifting forward in his seat.

"Alright, then how about we get you set up with sleeping arrangements: I'll get you all towels so you can wash up, and we all just stay here until the ash settles?" Although she technically asks a question, she doesn't wait for an answer. She rises to her feet and leads us up the steps.

After delivering us to our temporary shelter, Rossana escorts the guys to their quarters for the next few days.

Riley and I dump our bags in the spare bedroom we're assigned. Stark white bedding and olive-green walls give the whole room a modern feel. The décor is all harsh angles and bold fixtures. Impeccably detailed pictures embellish the walls and nightstands.

Riley and I float through the space, admiring each one. A red-throated hummingbird hovers mid-air just beneath a tubular purple flower. Its wings flutter in a tannish-gray blur. A fluffy white owl peers judgingly from a withering branch jutting from a slight pine tree. A deer slopes its mighty neck to a clear flowing stream, the pink tip of a tongue peeking out as it drinks the rushing water.

My eyes marvel at the extraordinary images surrounding us, each moment perfectly captured in a split second. A thud, immediately followed by a metallic squeaking, pulls our attention from the gallery of artwork. Millie yelps, but I can't tell if it's in alarm or excitement.

Glancing at each other, Riley and I meander toward the room's open doorway. We follow a scuffling sound that echoes down the hallway. It leads us back to the living room, where

Aidan and Jeff wrestle with the grayish-green couch. With Rossana directing them, they attempt to free the folded mattress and frame hiding within it.

Something must be stuck, because they awkwardly tug at a metal post that refuses to leave its home beneath the cushions. Millie circles the room, randomly yipping as if she's calling out encouragement.

A giggle escapes me, and Riley quickly catches it, sending us both into a convulsing fit. The room blurs as my eyes flood with laughter-fueled tears. When Riley collapses on the floor, Millie rushes to her aid. I allow my knees to buckle, joining them on the thick area rug.

I can't remember the last time I laughed like that. It's like one small intangible reward for fulfilling part of our mission.

As Riley's chuckles taper off, silence surrounds us. I swipe the dueling tear trails across my cheeks to find three sets of eyes on us. Technically four sets if you count the dog's. Jeff crosses his arms and lowers his chin so that he's literally looking down on us.

"You two done?" he huffs. Planting a fist under his chin, he strikes a thinking pose. "Because maybe instead of laughing at us, you could be helping."

My stomach churns as I notice that, other than Riley, none of the others are even slightly amused. *I hope we haven't offended our host.* Clutching Riley's arm, I yank us both to our feet.

Riley brushes off her knees while eyeing the others uncomfortably. "So, what can we do?" Aidan looks to Jeff and the two carry on another one of their silent conversations. Rossana explains that the metal lever within the skeletal frame is stuck. Then, as if her mind processes possible solutions as she speaks, she thrusts a pointer finger in the air. "We might have a tool in the garage that'll help. I'll be right back."

She sweeps through the nearest doorway, Millie rushing to catch up. I turn toward Jeff and Aidan expectantly. *At least we're trying to help now.*

"So, Jeff," Aidan says. "What did you think Quinn and Riley could do to help in this situation?" Jeff rubs his chin pensively in response before slowly nodding.

"You know, things have been pretty stressful and instead of adding to that stress, I think they should distract us from it."

In one swift move, the guys dive toward opposite ends of the sofa. Goofy grins overtaking their faces, they proudly display throw pillows. Within seconds, they descend upon us, pillows swinging.

Chapter 49

Adrenaline courses through me as I turn on my heel, running toward the safety of our bedroom. Feet pound behind me, a little too close, but I don't turn to see who it is. The echoing footsteps grow louder until the four of us land in a pile-up on the bed.

Giggles overtake my movements, yielding me incapacitated as stray elbows and knees connect with my body. We form a human tangle of limbs and laughter. Barking erupts in the hallway as Millie hunts the unruly humans who have invaded her home. She bursts into the room, her legs pushing faster when she spies us. Her sprint morphs into a jump and she worms her body onto the overcrowded bed. This sends us all into a new round of laughter, which only encourages Millie. She rewards us with wet kisses, lavishing attention on whoever is closest to her in the squirming mass.

When the chaos finally settles, I notice that Millie isn't the only one who's joined us. Rossana stands in the doorway, hugging a pile of folded sheets and blankets, patiently waiting for an end to our antics. When the room falls silent, she gives us a weak half-smile.

"And this is why the boys and the girls have separate sleeping quarters," she winks. "Now, I found a tool that might help us with the couch. How about you guys come see if you can make it work? Quinn and Riley, why don't you help me round up some dinner?" Without waiting for an answer, she turns on her heel and retreats from the room.

Taking just a moment to collect ourselves, we rush to the areas we've been assigned—the guys return to the living room while Riley and I report to the kitchen.

Rossana sets us up to chop tomatoes and cucumbers for a salad. We ignore the clunking and grunting sounds emanating around the uncooperative sofa bed. Just as Riley gathers plates, napkins, and silverware to set the table, a melodious ringtone blasts from the living room. I peek around the corner, tracking the noise. Aidan mutters under his breath, "My dad," before pressing the phone to his ear and rushing down the steps to the lower level.

In the time he's gone, Jeff manages to conquer the sofa bed, even stretching a sheet and blankets over the mattress. Locating an outlet, he takes advantage of the electricity and charges his cell phone. That should serve as a prompt to Aidan to do the same when he's done talking to his dad.

Claiming victory, he offers his assistance in the kitchen. Stirring a bubbling pot of macaroni, Rossana motions toward the backyard with one hand, suggesting that he take Millie outside instead. At the mention of the words "out" and "Millie," the dog's ears twitch excitedly. Jeff smiles and pats his leg, signaling her to come. She rushes past him, swishing her tail back and forth as she waits for him at the door.

When Millie and Jeff have their fill of outside time, they rush through the door in a blur. Rossana calls out the location of the treat stash so that Jeff can present Millie with her earned snack. She carries it into the living room and plops down to enjoy it.

Jeff wanders back to the living room. From the slight shuffling noise, I'm guessing he's relocating cushions and bags, organizing them around the fold-out bed that's monopolizing a chunk of space.

A few minutes later, a set of footsteps join him in the living room and whispering voices carry to the kitchen, although I can't make out any of the words. Rossana strains the pasta while Riley delivers the salad to the table.

As if an imaginary dinner bell has rung, the guys amble through the kitchen toward the connected dining room. They choose seats along the sides of the sturdy oak surface, leaving the head of the table open for our host.

When the pasta, sauce, and bread arrive, the clanking of serving utensils on plates is the only sound for a few minutes.

"Everything looks wonderful," Jeff announces, eyes smiling as wide as his lips.

"And I bet it tastes even better," Aidan adds, although his words are flat, and his eyes lack luster.

With a soft smile, Rossana thanks them. She forks a few noodles before asking, "So, you were traveling across the country recently?" Aidan and Jeff exchange a glance before Jeff answers.

"Well, along the East Coast really. We went from Pennsylvania to Delaware and Virginia and then back up. As soon as everything clears up, we'll head back to Pennsylvania. That's home for all of us," he waves his fork in a slow circle so that its imaginary loop encompasses all four of us.

Gulping down a bite, she casually asks, "So, along your travels, did you notice anything strange?" My narrowed eyes meet Riley's. *What's normal anymore?*

"Strange, how?" I ask, unclear of where this conversation is going. She lays her fork on the table beside the plate and leans forward as if sharing a secret.

"I spend a great deal of time outdoors," she explains. Funny, her pale skin doesn't imply that she regularly soaks up the sun's rays. Brushing aside the observation, I refocus my attention but before she can continue, Riley interrupts.

"That reminds me! The pictures in our room," she smiles, proud of the connection she's made. "It's like you brought the outdoors inside. They're just stunning," she gushes.

"Thank you, I actually shot those," Rossana says humbly. "I'm a photographer. My favorite subject is animals in their natural habitat." Her eyes sweep across us cautiously as if she's weighing how much more to say.

"Well you're very talented," Riley says, raising her glass for a sip of water. "They're amazing."

"Yeah, I've seen some pretty amazing things for my work over the years," Rossana shares, a darkness washing over her distant eyes. "But in more recent months, I've started seeing some strange things too."

Chapter 50

A chill wraps around my soul. Resting the fork on her plate, Riley wraps one hand around the other, asking, "What kind of things?" The lights flicker for just a moment and alarm settles at the base of my spine. We all pause in anticipation of losing electricity, but it must have just been a hiccup.

The delicious food before me suddenly loses its flavor. I subtly push the plate away, toward the center of the table, aligning all of my senses to the conversation.

"Well," Rossana starts, "I started noticing, not too long after the earthquake, that the trees around here seemed to drop their leaves early. Like, really early. And their trunks. Some of them started to darken and wither, as if they were dying."

"I noticed the leaves falling early too," I add. "But that was farther south." She glances at me before continuing.

"And the animals, I've gone to the same spots for years to take photos, but subjects are becoming fewer and farther between," she narrows her eyes, curiosity warring with frustration. "And the few I have seen acted…more aggressive than they normally would."

Jeff plunks his pointer finger down on the table, startling all of us.

"Our friend." His words are shaky. He closes his eyes for a few seconds before continuing with a stronger voice. "Our friend had a tick on him. We didn't even know how long it was there, but by the time we saw it, it was pretty full with his blood." He rubs the scruff grazing his chin.

"But the weird thing about it was that the bullseye mark, you know how people can get that?" After Rossana nods intently, he continues. "It was black. Instead of a pink or red, it was dark as night."

Aidan's eyes focus on no one, as if he's talking to himself. "It's like it was pure poison." Slightly louder, he adds, "He died a few days later. We couldn't get to a hospital or anything. There was nowhere to get help."

My eyes mist over at the memory. Riley stares at her plate. She wasn't there when Wes died. She barely knew him. I barely knew him too, but in the short time that I did, he became a friend and a surrogate family member.

"I'm sorry about your friend," Rossana says softly. Then, looking around the table at each of us, she adds, "A lot of things fell apart in a short period of time. I'm sure you did what you could. It's not your fault things turned out the way they did."

Gulping down emotions threatening to spill, Riley clears her throat and speaks. "I saw something too. When I was…I saw someone get bitten by fire ants, hundreds of them." She's talking about Dan. She still hasn't told me everything that happened when he and Jim kidnapped her. I don't ask, but when she does talk about it, I try to show that I'm willing to listen.

"Anyway," she shakes her head slightly. "I'd never seen anyone with bites like that before, but this was…I can't imagine that's what it's like for everyone." She shudders at the memory. "He had red bumps all over his body, with bulging white bubbles. His eyes got so swollen they were practically shut. He went from barely being able to move to his whole body convulsing."

"I don't know," she admits, "Maybe that's a normal reaction, but I've never seen anything like it." Rossana reaches toward Riley and places a palm on my sister's arm. "Was your friend okay?"

"Oh, well, yeah," Riley adds almost as an afterthought. "We got to the base and the doctors there were able to help him. We were really lucky." She flashes a sorrowful look at Aidan and Jeff.

"Well, that's good," Rossana says solemnly. "And now, I guess we just wait for the ash to fall and settle to see what comes next."

After we all help clean up the kitchen, the four of us take turns showering and then settle in the lower level to relax before bed. Rossana wishes us a goodnight before she retreats to her bedroom, the satellite phone in hand. I'm guessing she's awaiting another check-in with the sergeant.

Jeff plays tug-of-war with Millie, attempting to pry a toy made of thick red rope from her mouth. She loves the challenge but doesn't relent her grip. Riley snuggles in the recliner by the

218

fire, her eyes drifting between them and the billowing flames.

Capitalizing on the hint of privacy the distraction provides, I settle into the couch beside Aidan. When he turns toward me, I whisper, "Is everything okay? You seemed really distracted at dinner."

His surprised eyes turn grateful, as if he genuinely appreciates my concern. He rubs his chin, evaluating how much to share. The blue pools of his eyes turn serious when he says, "My dad kinda changed our plans. I should really tell the others." He runs a hand through his hair, sending tufts in every direction. "I didn't want to mention it at dinner. Rossana has her own problems and she doesn't need to worry about our plans." *Worry about our plans? I don't like where this is going.*

Chapter 51

When Jeff finally tires of letting Millie win their game, he plops onto the open recliner. Aidan glances at me and I throw him a nod of encouragement. Now's as good a time as any to hear his news.

"So, guys," he begins, drawing Riley's and Jeff's attention. "I called Jasmine. I told her about what's happening so that her family can prepare. I just wanted you to know that. After that, I talked to my dad."

Relief shudders through me. *I'm glad he told Jasmine's family. They deserve to know. Although how many other people out there deserve to know too? I'd say just about all of them—except for Ace.*

Jeff shifts in his chair, mild interest washing over his demeanor. "What'd he say?"

"Well," Aidan releases a deep breath. "He was hoping we'd be back by now. But since we're not…he agrees that we should stay put until the ash settles."

Okay, that's not so bad. That's exactly what we were going to do anyway.

"But, instead of just going home, he's taking my mom and sisters somewhere that he thinks is safer." Aidan's eyes drift over each of us. "He talked to your parents, too, Jeff. And they all agreed. We should just meet up with them and kind of hide out for a few weeks, or until things start to clear up."

Riley's worried eyes flash my way. Our next step is finding our aunt. I figured we'd see what she thinks we should do. She's the closest thing we have to a parent right now.

"Where are they going?" Jeff asks. "I mean, I'm fine with it, whatever it is they're planning."

"Couturier Caverns," Aidan replies. "It's not far from home, and my dad thinks we should go underground until the ash clears. He's been gathering supplies and today they're taking everything there. He says we should just meet them there as soon as we can."

Jeff nods thoughtfully. But Aidan's answer just opens up a new round of questions for me.

"How is he planning to get in there? I mean, are you all going to just break in?" I cross my arms, attempting to compress the misplaced annoyance creeping through my veins. They're making plans without us—which, of course they are—but the reality stings. They still have parents to return to. The four of us are not a family, and every trip we've made together has been to fulfill a temporary goal. I have to accept that we're destined to part ways.

Confusion swirls in Aidan's eyes and he speaks slowly. "It's near where we grew up." He swirls a finger between him and Jeff. "I was kind of…I guess you could say…obsessed with the place as a kid. My parents got to know the owner because we spent so much time there. They became friends."

"Oh, then you guys have a great plan," I admit, trying to conceal my jealousy.

Aidan flashes me a dopey grin. "Well, I was kind of hoping it was your plan too. My dad said you two should come with us. I mean, I don't know if you were planning to go home but you'd probably be safer with us."

My heart swells, warming any residual bitterness into oblivion. Fidgeting her hands, Riley shrugs. "We've got to go see if our aunt is okay. She has our dog and she's our closest relative…but…could she come with us if she agrees?" She hitches a shoulder up, tilting her head my way.

"Yes! That's a great idea," I agree. "I'm sure we can convince her! And it's not too far from our house either. I remember going there on a field trip as a kid."

"Good," Aidan says, beaming. "Then it's settled."

Jeff claps his hands together once and adds, "And that dog of yours, you should bring him along too. If I'm gonna be trapped underground for who-knows-how-long, I could use a little canine companionship." He rubs Millie's ears as she gazes at him with sleepy eyes.

We sit in thought-consumed silence for a while, each of us envisioning the days that lie just ahead.

After several minutes, Millie's ears twitch and her tail thumps the floor. She hears the approaching footsteps before the rest of us do. Rossana breezes down the steps, stopping just before me and Aidan.

She thrusts the satellite phone toward us. "Someone would like to speak with you. All of you." When Aidan tentatively takes the phone from her hand, she turns and strides up the steps, leaving us in privacy.

"Hello?" I say, glancing at the others.

"Hello," the deep voice is easily recognizable. I smile, realizing this is the first time he hasn't identified himself when he answered the phone.

"I hear you're all preparing to depart soon, and I wanted to talk to you before you go. Rossana's going to give you a ham radio. Do not lose it. Keep it with you, wherever you go and turn it on a few times a day to see what messages you pick up. Can you do that?"

Our voices overlap in an eagerness to respond.

"Yes."

"Yes, sir!"

"We will."

"Good." He sounds pleased. "Now, remember…try to always have a fail-safe. If you have any backup plan to make sure a mission doesn't fail, do it! Whatever it takes, do everything you can to ensure your success." We nod even though he can't see.

"Also, I have reason to believe that units will be deployed to locate survivors and," he coughs as if his mouth doesn't want to form the words, "round them up."

"What do you mean *round them up*?" Jeff interrupts, his face awash with anger.

Bowen releases a sigh, fueled by enough tension to carry it clearly through the airwaves.

"Let's just say," he says sharply. "That some of my privileges have been suspended and although I no longer have access to that information, it appears as though military forces will be strongly encouraging citizens to report to designated safe zones."

"Safe zones?" Riley questions. "Will people have a choice? I mean some people might—"

"I don't know," Bowen's voice cuts to a sharp-edged whisper. "Look, if you see any Humvees or military vehicles, avoid them. Get to your homes and stay out of sight."

Stunned by his harsh tone, silence swells on our end. Fearful eyes meet each other, searching for reassurance. Riley dazedly reaches a shaky hand to her nose, covering her trembling lower lip.

"Look, I don't know what the right answer is here." Although we can't see him, I imagine the sergeant's confident façade crumbling before us. "I just know that this is about taking control. If the eruption is as bad as expected, it's going to impact the availability of food and natural resources for years to come. And the government is going to establish who gets what resources and when."

"Thank you," Aidan practically croaks, as if he's speaking through a lump lodged in his throat. His eyes seem to reflect a deeper shade of blue when they're burdened with unending anxiety. "We know you didn't have to share all of this with us, and we appreciate it."

"Well, I appreciate you finding my wife." The wall quickly rebuilds itself and Bowen's confidence returns. "Now, before you hand the phone back to her, make sure you take the ham radio with you. If you don't know how to use one, tinker around with it and figure it out. It may become a lifeline for you."

"Sergeant?" Riley cuts into the conversation. Her voice falters, hesitation slowing her next words. Determination hints in her eyes as she stares intently at the phone. "Do we need to be worried about our trackers?" *So that's where her mind is.* "Like, is anyone watching where we're going? Other than you?"

The guys exchange glances. I'm the only one here without the tracking device in me, but it's not like I'm leaving Riley's side ever again, so I might as well be tracked too.

"There's too much happening right now," the sergeant answers. "They're watching groupings of trackers and patterns of movement but not individuals. That may change if things get worse, but don't worry about it right now. Just stay focused on getting home."

We release a collective sigh of relief. "Thank you, sergeant," Riley responds.

"You're welcome. Now I've got to attend to other matters." He takes a breath before adding, "But one more thing: take care of yourselves. You may become the ones rebuilding this nation someday."

Chapter 52

The call leaves my insides raw. I ache for the simpler times when Riley and I would dash through a sprinkler on a sweltering summer day, or when we'd soar down a snow-covered hill on matching orange plastic saucers. Back then our parents shouldered the worry. Now it weighs me down like a concrete vest, constricting my lungs and hampering my every move. The only way to go is forward, but that terrifies me.

Jeff rises to his feet, stretching. "I think my brain's done enough thinking for one day. I'm going to bed."

Riley yawns in response. "That's a good idea." We return the phone to Rossana and bid her goodnight before retreating to our quarters. Almost immediately my aching muscles and weary mind release me from the darkness of the day.

The numbers on the nightstand's clock announce a new day but the shadows lurking in the corners cast the illusion of late-night hours. I slip out of bed slowly and pry my fingers between the blinds, peering out into the world. Morning has definitely arrived, but the sun makes no effort to kiss the horizon.

A shiver slithers down my spine. Blanketed by a thick rolling fog, the sky projects an unforgiving, callous aura. Any other day, I would brush it off as a foggy morning, sure to evaporate as the sun's powerful rays rise. I would chalk up the swarm of brown leaves choking the lawn to a seasonal change. But today my eyes appraise the hovering clouds of ash, wondering what poisons they harbor and what toxins have already been unleashed.

Figuring there's no rush to wake Riley, I tiptoe out of the room. Wandering down the hallway, I peek into the living room. Two non-moving lumps on the sofa bed confirm the guys are still sleeping. The rich, crisp smell of coffee drifts to my nose, luring me to the kitchen.

Rossana stands staring out the glass sliding door, her hands clasped around a deep brown mug with ribbons of steam drifting from its contents. Millie watches from just a few feet away, curled up in a tan bed with patterns of white dog bones dancing along the fabric.

"Good morning," I whisper. Rossana turns toward me with a half-smile that doesn't reach her solemn green eyes.

"Morning," she murmurs, her eyes shifting back outside.

"Well, it's happened." Ambling across the marbled tile floor, I join her. Raising the mug to her lips, she takes a long sip before continuing.

I'd honestly rather avoid windows right now. The view is depressing. My gaze floats to the sky, which bears a constant reminder of the pollutants threatening to suffocate every last molecule of oxygen.

"You see that stream," she asks, beckoning ahead slightly to the left. I follow her nod, peering into the distance. Although my view is distorted by the smoky haze, the far back corner of the yard slopes to a rocky edge. Thinning patches of grass dot the landscape just before it drops to an opening. That must be a stream. She doesn't wait for my answer.

"The neighbor across the street, he works for an exterminating company." Her eyes remain fixed on the yard. "His truck, the tank ruptured somehow. Leaked chemicals into the stream."

She turns to face me. A sheen of sadness glistens in her eyes.

"The water was all murky, frothy along the edges. I don't know, it was like it was just oozing with sludge." She shakes her head sadly. "I knew I wouldn't be taking any pictures there for a long time."

The description reminds me of the stream Aidan, Chris, and I saw at the campground at the beginning of our journey. We figured pollution ruined it, snuffing out the life that once flowed through it. I don't want to relive that memory, so I let it slither right back out of my mind just as easily as it tried to slither in.

The two of us stand in comfortable silence, mourning what has been lost as well as the losses sure to come.

"I know we agreed to stay here until the ash settles, but I'm tired of waiting. And what if things get worse the longer we wait? Maybe the ash isn't as bad now, but maybe the longer it's out there, the worse it will get?"

I can't argue with that, and patience has never been one of my virtues. As if Rossana's words stir her to action, Millie rises and gallops through the kitchen toward the living room.

"So you want to leave today?" If she goes, I assume we will too. Who's going to let four strangers camp out in their house with no supervision?

"Yes, after breakfast. I just need to pack a few more things, get you guys the ham radio, and load the car." The finality in her tone leaves no room for discussion. Plus, she's an adult. She's not going to let some kids talk her into changing her plans.

"I'm not going to alert the sergeant of our plans," she adds. Her eyes trace my features, searching for dissent. She won't find it here, though. I want to get home just as much as she wants to see her husband. "He'd just try to talk me into staying here, waiting out the ash. But I've made the decision for myself. For both of us." She smiles when she notices the return of her loyal companion.

Just as quickly as she left, Millie barrels back into the room, her nails clicking on the tile. She pauses to glance behind her, twisting with excitement when Jeff rounds the corner. Rubbing his eyes, he mumbles, "I thought I smelled coffee. Mind if I grab a cup?"

"Sure thing, help yourself," Rossana says, motioning toward a mug tree on the counter. She slides a griddle from a lower cupboard before gathering a red box of buttermilk mix and a pint of blueberries. Jeff dodges her moves, careful to stay out of the way while he prepares a cup of caffeine.

Jeff and I sit at the table, and Rossana shares her plan while flipping fluffy pancakes onto a serving platter. Jeff's hazel eyes grow more alert with each sip he takes. In silence, he absorbs the information and slowly nods his agreement.

"You're right," he rubs his stubbly chin as he speaks. "Nothing's gonna get better, at least not in the timeframe we have to work with. Let's go now, before everyone fleeing from the West clogs up the highways."

I listen mutely as they agree to load up the cars and depart as soon as everyone finishes breakfast. The promise of home is close enough now to become a reality. Even if it takes us two hours to get there, that's nothing compared to everything we've done and everywhere we've been so far.

Leaving half of a syrup-soaked pancake on her plate, Rossana excuses herself. She calls a quick *"Good morning"* over her shoulder when Aidan and Riley wander past her, into the kitchen. Millie watches her human intently but remains planted at Jeff's feet.

Riley yawns before slipping into a seat. "Why didn't you wake me?" I start to answer but close my mouth when she notices the stack of blueberry goodness, forgetting the question just as quickly as she asked it.

As she and Aidan load their plates with food, Jeff and I clear the dirty utensils and glasses away. We glance at each other and I throw him a tight-lipped nod. *We've got to tell them.* Clasping his hands together in front of his chest, he announces, "Guys, we have a slight change in plans."

Chapter 53

Riley's chewing slows and her face pales as Jeff's words sink in. While he waits for Jeff to finish speaking, Aidan physically protests, pushing his plate away, crossing his arms, and releasing a series of frustrated sighs.

Jeff stresses that our host has changed her plans, and that we really don't have much say in the matter. Struggling to keep his voice to a strangled whisper, Aidan objects, "She has no idea how bad it is to breathe that stuff. It's basically ground up glass and rock. You breathe it, it gets into your lungs. You walk around in it, it gets in your eyes and on your skin. And not to mention that time is the only thing that clears it from the air. It's going to get worse before it gets better."

"Look, I didn't launch into a lecture about volcanic ash health hazards and their long-term effects," Jeff retorts, raising his hands. As much as I appreciate the fire in Aidan's eyes and his concern for our well-being, this isn't really up for discussion.

"Aidan, this isn't ideal, but what can we do? We're guests here. We can't exactly demand that she let us stay here without her." I reach out and rest a palm on his bicep. Fighting the urge to squeeze the muscle, I attempt to stay focused even though he's especially cute when he's all fired up about something.

"Could we somehow protect ourselves? Like cover our faces with shirts or something to block out the particles?" Riley asks timidly. Her face takes on a greenish hue and I'm guessing she's done eating, her appetite squelched by the situation.

Aidan scratches his head, disappointment lingering on his squared jawline. "If we really have to go, then I guess that's the best we can do. But anytime we're outside, we have to keep our nose and mouth covered. Safety glasses would be good too."

"Guys, I just remembered," Riley interjects. "We need gas. I thought we had a few days to figure it out, and I sort of forgot about it, but we were almost on empty when we rolled in here yesterday."

"I'll talk to Rossana," Jeff volunteers. "Let's hope the sergeant's the kind of guy who keeps an extra gas can or two lying around for the lawnmower."

With nothing left to say, and no further interest in eating, we clean the kitchen, scraping scraps into the trash and stacking plates and silverware in the sink. Fighting the discomfort of peeking inside someone else's cupboards, we search for containers to store the remaining uneaten pancakes. I'm not sure there's any point to sealing them up in a refrigerator in a house that's about to be abandoned for who knows how long, but we can't just leave them sitting out.

When we finish, Riley and I retreat to the spare bedroom

to gather our belongings and make the bed. Once the room is back in order and we're as ready as can be, we wander out to the living room to join the guys. Although they're nowhere in sight, the pull-out mattress has transformed back into a couch and the guys' bags sit stoically on the cushions. Voices guide us to the kitchen, where Rossana, Aidan, and Jeff crowd around the dining room table.

The black device demanding their attention looks like a cross between medical equipment and a CB radio. A series of black digital numbers illuminate on a credit-card-sized green display. About a dozen buttons and switches surround the display, with a large dial directly to the right of it. A coiled black cord snakes around the device, connecting the boxy bulk of it to a handheld receiver.

Their conversation pauses for a moment as they acknowledge our presence. As the guys bend down to tinker with the radio's buttons, Rossana excuses herself.

"Let me see what else I can find for you in the garage. I'll be right back." She sweeps down the steps to the lower level with Millie following close behind.

Riley and I plop down in dining room chairs while the guys play with their new toy. When the radio emits a haze of static, the guys straighten with pride. Riley and I narrow our eyes at the thing. *Surely it does more than that.*

Before we can ask what else it does, Rossana returns with a small blue and white package. A smile plays across Aidan's face as he reaches for the box of disposable dust masks. I can't help but smile seeing the joy a white coffee-filter-like face covering brings him.

He opens the package and begins doling out its contents. He looks around to each of us and advises, "From here on out, wear this anytime you're outside." When he reaches Rossana, he realizes that although it's a five pack, there are only four masks remaining. Aidan's serious eyes shift uncomfortably.

"Don't worry about me. I saw an old one on the workbench in our garage. That'll work for me. You take these." Aidan expresses a solemn thank you before she offers us one last gift.

"And we do have a gas can in the shed. Whatever's in it is all yours. I'll show you where it is." Planting a fist on each hip, Jeff announces, "It's go time, guys!" before he follows her out the door.

Masks in place, we load both cars and say our final goodbyes to Millie and Rossana. Aidan even convinces her to wear a mask too, so we look like a band of bank robbers readying for a heist. We're the only ones outside, the neighborhood's like a ghost town. I'm sure people are there, though, in their homes, curiously peering out at us behind the relative safety of brick and vinyl, fingers cautiously separating curtains and blinds.

Although the overcast clouds paint a somber mood, excitement swirls within me. *We're finally going home.*

Chapter 54

Riley and I command the front seat. She drives since she has a better memory of the general route we need to take. Without the satellite phone, we've lost access to a GPS and Aidan wants to conserve his phone battery, using it only to talk to his dad.

The guys attempt to master the ham radio in the back seat, deep in discussion until a ring tone plays through the small space. Aidan scrambles to answer his cell phone. We politely pretend that we aren't straining to hear the conversation on the other end of the phone. Aidan's responses consist of a string of "yeah," "okay," and "alright." He voices a few "buts" that drop without further protest.

The moment the conversation ends, all eyes drift to him in anticipation. He runs a hand through his messy brown hair. I'm starting to prefer it that way. He'd look strange with every hair neatly in place. Besides, his perfectly chiseled features more than make up for the chaotic mane. He releases a deep breath.

"Well, the plan is a go. My family is already at the caverns, setting up camp for all of us." His eyes pierce mine when he says *us*. "So, here's what we're thinking."

Before going to sleep last night, the guys strategized a plan. They were going to run it by us today, but when our departure date was pushed up there really wasn't time to discuss the details.

Aidan and Jeff need the car, and they're hoping that our aunt will loan us hers—or better yet, come along with us. They propose dropping us off at our aunt's house, which is only about a mile away from our home. We can collect our dog and convince our aunt to take us home to quickly gather any belongings we deem useful for the foreseeable future, including layers of clothes. Aidan adds that, if we have any to contribute, we should gather canned food—nothing perishable. Otherwise, Aidan's and Jeff's parents are planning for the extra mouths to feed.

While we're preparing to join them, Aidan will drive Jeff home so he can also gather some useful things, and then they'll head to the caverns. All we need to do is meet them there.

It sounds easy, but if there's anything I've learned over the past two months, it's that I can't trust anything to work out the way it's supposed to.

The rest of the drive is quiet, the eerie calm of the monochromatic landscape washing over us. We pass few other cars. Thick clouds of fog-like ash roll through the atmosphere, like an unending stream. Highway signs flash big orange letters at us, the font practically screaming: PUBLIC HEALTH EMERGENCY. SHELTER IN PLACE UNTIL FURTHER NOTICE.

Aidan reiterates general directions to Couturier Caverns. Riley seems to know how to get there. Vague images of a fifth-grade class fieldtrip flit through my mind. Other than my friend Wendy twisting her ankle when she jumped from one giant rock to another, the trip wasn't exactly notable. Plus, I haven't been there since. Aidan snaps his fingers beside my ear, yanking me from the memory.

"Quinn! When we reach the cave, I'll wait for you two and your aunt. You'll need to call my cell phone so I can guide you to the right entrance and meet you there." I nod. Even though Riley and I both lost our cell phones in a car crash, our aunt has one. I'm sure she'll let me use it.

Insisting that we write down his cell phone number, Aidan suggests that I search the compartment between my seat and Riley's for anything we can use to record it. We're still in Rose's car, but judging by the dusty dashboard, I'm not sure how much use it got in recent years. Hopefully, she saw the value in stashing a pen and paper somewhere.

I rummage through sunglasses, a mini ice scraper, a narrow box of tissues, and a wad of long-expired coupons. With no luck there, I fumble through the glove box. *Success!* A matching notebook and pen, adorned with purple lilacs and yellow butterflies, hides beneath the owner's manual.

I glance out the window, but the landscape is consumed by fog. There's not much to see beyond the highway's asphalt and shoulder. Even surrounded by the isolating and gloomy remnants of Yellowstone's wrath, hope grows within me. Maybe we can still beat this, or at least outlast it.

When I wave the notepad set in the air in victory, Aidan

swipes it from my hand, smirking. He leans over it, eagerly jotting down his number.

"We're getting close," Riley mutters nervously.

"We won't drive away until we know your aunt is home, okay?" Jeff assures us. "You give us a signal, and if she's there, you call Aidan as soon as you get on the road for the caverns."

"Got it!" I answer for both of us. Aidan passes me the notepad and pen. I shove them into my backpack and turn my attention to the familiar surroundings. Though they're blanketed by haze, in my mind, I can clearly see every grocery store, mini market, and fast food place.

"Don't forget to bring warm clothes," Aidan advises. "It's cold down there. Change into pants and long sleeves and make sure you pack sweatshirts and stuff like that too."

"We can do that," I promise.

With one last nervous smile, Riley turns onto our aunt's street. Rolling past each familiar house, she shifts the car into park when we reach the driveway. A thick layer of powdery ash smothers the smooth asphalt. What was once a rich black surface now bears the battered remains of what looks like thousands of crushed sticks of sidewalk chalk.

The last time we were here, our whole family sat in this very spot, in our parents' car. We made quick work of dropping off Snickers, figuring we would return in one week to pick him up. Part of me is amazed that Riley and I made it this far. It's an accomplishment that we're still standing after everything that's happened.

Aidan reminds us to affix our dust masks before we throw our bags over our shoulders and slip out of the car. Donning their masks, the guys move fast, exiting the backseat and commanding the driver's and passenger's seats.

They watch intently as we dash toward the two-story brick house belonging to our mother's sister. Other than the fresh layer of ash coating the usually windswept yard covered with crunchy dead leaves and thin, gnarled branches, the house looks just as I remember it.

Before we can ring the doorbell, barking erupts inside the house. The single tear trailing down Riley's cheek confirms what I sense. Snickers is here. And if he's here, so is our aunt.

Chapter 55

When the door flies open, our startled aunt stares in shock. Her jaw gapes open as her eyes widen. Her mouth moves but no words spill out. Tears gloss over her dark irises, threatening to overflow.

Her expression grows more confused as her gaze traces the people and objects before her—from our masks to the running car at the end of the driveway. Before she can say anything, a blur of brown and white fur pushes past her and clamors at our knees.

I turn toward the guys and wave them off. They've got their own stops to make. Riley motions to our aunt, pointing inside the house. Muffled by the mask, she says, "We've got to go inside." With a sharp nod, our aunt beckons us in and closes the door as soon as Snickers' tail clears it.

We peel off our masks and drop our bags. Hugging us with an unexpected but likely relief-fueled strength, Aunt Robin volleys between indignation and gratitude. "I can't believe you're really here! Where have you been? I kept trying to call all of you, for weeks. Even when the phone lines were restored. I just got nothing." Her brown eyes crest with tears. "I watched the news and imagined the worst."

Her resemblance to our mother is both comforting and disarming. The dark, shoulder-length hair and deep brown eyes serve as a reminder of the ones I'll never see again. Right now, it's easier to push the memories aside.

With false hope, our aunt questions, "Your parents?"

Closing her eyes, Riley slowly shakes her head side to side.

"Where are your parents? What happened?" Her voice wavers, the emotion palpable. She glances toward the door, as if magically summoning our mom and dad to appear.

Riley and I tag-team, reliving only the briefest details possible to convey how our parents perished. What was supposed to begin a family vacation at the beach turned into a living nightmare in a matter of seconds.

We've had a head start on grieving, although we're nowhere near done. Our aunt teeters between relief that Riley and I survived and mourning that her sister and brother-in-law did not. Before our eyes, she crumbles into wracking sobs.

We give her time to grieve, silently offering comfort through closeness. After several minutes, she swipes the tears away and pulls us even closer. Her eyes narrow as they sweep across my sister's face. "Riley, honey, what happened to your cheek?"

Riley's hand shoots up to cover the scar. I've gotten so used to it, I nearly forgot it's there. I wonder if she did too. She traces a finger along the healing skin gingerly and motions toward the sofa. "Can we sit? It's a long story," she says simply.

Completely oblivious to the conversation, Snickers yips at my shins. I drop to my knees, sitting on my haunches so he can maul me with stinky dog-breath kisses.

We explain everything that happened over the past weeks, breezing over the details. *We'll have plenty of time for detailed discussions when we're hiding out underground for weeks.* Aunt Robin fills us in on what's been happening here—the weather, local news, and advisories.

When we tell her the plan to hide out underground for a few weeks, her forehead crinkles and her eyes narrow. "They said on the news we're supposed to shelter in place. That was before the power went out, but that's what they said to do." She looks back and forth between us.

"But the people we met, they know a lot about what's happening, they know what we should do to stay safe until the ash clears at least somewhat," I try to explain. Riley nods, encouraging me to continue.

"And it's not just the volcano. Everyone out west has to go somewhere. The ones east of Yellowstone will come this way, looking for shelter and food. It's only a matter of time until infrastructure crumbles and resources dwindle." I guess I paid more attention than I realized when Aidan droned on and on about the impending disaster. Despite my words, a small smile tugs at my lips. He's only been gone for a few minutes, but I miss him already. His long, boring speeches and his messy hair that stands on end most of the time.

"Girls, I know you were out there in…this," she waves a hand toward the door. "But I've got to do what feels right. And if the local authorities are saying to stay home, then that's what I'm doing." Disbelief courses through my veins, fraying my nerve endings. Riley's hands twitch, aching to twist and turn away her worry.

Snickers settles at my feet and leans against my legs, sensing the room's anxiety-charged energy.

"But Aunt Robin, things are going to get worse, and the ash is really really bad to breathe. That's why we were wearing dust masks and you should wear one too if you go outside. Everything outside is or will be covered in it, it damages crops and…" Riley's words rush from her lips like a tidal wave of warning, but they do no good.

"I love you girls like daughters," Aunt Robin says, swiping a tear from her cheek, "and I…I just can't bear the thought of losing anyone else. Your parents…they'd want me to keep you safe." Her voice cracks on the last word. She tousles Riley's hair affectionately, but the nonchalant gesture doesn't disguise the distress buzzing within her. She retrieves her hand and buries her face in her palms. Tears glisten, trailing a path from her covered eyes to her trembling chin.

Riley looks to me, her shoulders sagging as her spirit withers. I never want to see my sister broken again. Her sadness fuels my motivation.

"But Aunt Robin, we *will* be safe." It takes every ounce of energy my cells can muster, but I hold my voice steady. "The people we're going with, they've been preparing for this. They say that the only way the ash will clear is with time. That's why they're going underground. They want to wait it out and stay somewhere safe until the atmosphere has some time to clear."

My words seem to calm Riley's nerves slightly. She rests a palm on our aunt's arm and adds, "I agree. Mom and Dad would want us to stay together and they'd want us to have food and shelter. Our friend Aidan's family is offering us that. And I think Mom and Dad would want you to come with us." *Check, mate. We've made our case.*

Silence descends over the charged air. After several minutes of Riley and I staring at her expectantly, Aunt Robin tugs her lips into a half-hearted smile. Swiping the tears from her cheeks, she defeatedly concedes, "If you were my kids, I'd make you stay right here."

She takes a deep breath, as if the words she's about to say physically pain her. "But I know you're almost adults now and you won't listen even if I forbid you from walking out that door. You're both strong-willed, like your mother." Her eyes glisten once again, and she releases a humorless laugh.

"Girls, this is all temporary. Maybe just a week or so. And whatever comes, I've got to face it on my terms. I'm staying right here in my home and I'll take my chances. I won't deny you that same right. If you feel that your best bet is going to this cave, then so be it. I won't stop you. I'll worry about you and I'll miss you, but I won't stop you from doing what you believe is right."

We all lean in for a slobbering group hug. Riley and I don't even need to discuss our plan. We know this is goodbye, for now. Our best bet is staying with the "family" we formed this summer. They seem to know what's happening and how to best survive it.

Chapter 56

We leave our aunt's home with one win and one loss—our plan to meet the guys is still intact, but our aunt isn't coming with us. Packing into her car, she drives the three of us, and Snickers, to our house. As she follows the path she's driven hundreds of times, she alternates between glancing at Riley, in the passenger seat, to meeting my eyes in the rearview mirror.

"Since I'm staying here, that means you'll have a place to go if this cave of yours doesn't work out. Just promise me that if you have any doubts, you get yourselves right back here." A stern motherly tone emerges in her words. We both nod sharply. *She means business.*

"Now I can't give you my car or my cell phone," she continues. "But I'm going to drive you to the cave after you get what you need from your house. That way I'll know exactly where you are. And that way, if *I* change *my* mind, maybe I can catch up to you!"

A hint of a smile plays across her face. Chewing her bottom lip, she mutters under her breath, "I just wish I had a way to get in touch with you."

The car falls silent. I glance out the window and study what awaits on the other side of the glass. The ash seems to be creeping closer to the Earth, or maybe I'm just imagining it. It feels like no matter which direction we face the clouds follow.

My stomach turns cartwheels at the thought of stepping through that door once again. The last time I walked through it, I was a selfish teenager complaining about having to wake up early for a family vacation.

Now half my family is gone and I'm pretty psyched at the luxury of having a working indoor bathroom to use. For a few minutes anyway. Riley glances in the backseat at me, trepidation lurking in her gaze. I know she's facing the same hesitance at returning to our once happy home. I say a silent prayer that we can stay focused and grab just a few personal items and survival essentials before a wave of memories drowns us.

When we reach the house, all three of us spring to the front door. Snickers rushes past us, twirling in eager circles on the front step. Our aunt produces a spare key and promptly unlocks and throws the door open. *Thank goodness she thought to bring it.* Riley and I lost more than our parents in that car crash.

Stale, dusty air reaches my nose, threatening a sneezing fit. My eyes sweep across the foyer and past it, to the living room. The gray walls are shallow husks of what was once a vibrant space. Frozen moments in time line the hallway—formal school portraits, Riley's first theater performance, and a still-frame of me crossing the finish line at a track meet. Now each smile looks hollow. Riley brushes my shoulder, startling me.

"Come on, let's gather our things and go." She's right. There's nothing here for us anymore. We part ways, launching to our respective bedrooms. I tear into my closet, digging out as many old backpacks and cinch sacks my fingers can grasp. Shoving clean sweatshirts, pants, and underclothes in the bags, I toss each one to the door when it's stuffed to capacity.

Lingering at my desk, I grasp the silver guardian angel charm, turning it in my hand. It fits perfectly within my palm. One continuous, smooth metal wire curves into wings, a halo, and a body. It's been there as long as I can remember. I think our parents got one for me and one for Riley. I didn't know what to do with it, so I set it on my desk, figuring I could use the most help when I was slogging through homework. No matter how much I prayed, the answers never magically appeared, though. I slip it into my pocket before dashing down the hallway to our parents' bedroom.

A shiver races down my spine and goosebumps send every hair on my arms standing. Wasting no time, I swipe a silver-framed photo from the dresser. It was taken the day we adopted Snickers. My dad set the timer and we all crowded around the cowering dog. His fearful eyes latched onto Riley as she tried to comfort him while plastering a ridiculous smile on her face. Facing the camera, she didn't notice that her hand was actually blocking Snickers' eyes when the picture snapped. It looks like she was trying to surprise him or shield him from the camera. I allow myself one brief sentimental smile before cramming it into the only bag with a smidge of space left in it.

Stepping into the middle of the room, I slowly turn,

memorizing each crack in the plaster and every snag in the carpet. It helps to focus on the menial details when the unflattering glimmers of my teenage self threaten to reappear. My eyes pool with hot tears as I hear echoes of myself, from just weeks ago, unable to respond to my parents' questions or observations without injecting frustration:

"Why can't we go somewhere else for vacation just once? It's always the same boring place."

"Yes, the shoes fit but you got the wrong color. I can't wear those!"

"Can't I go out with my friends again tonight? It's so lame at home."

Of course, now that I have sincere apologies to offer, there's no one to hear them. I'll carry a thousand sorrys in my heart until it no longer beats.

Shaking away the pain, I swipe the salty tears from my cheeks and take one last look. *Wherever you are, if you're maybe watching over us right now, please know that I can see now how awful I was. So many times. If I could take it all back, I would. If I could just talk to you one more time, for even a few minutes, I'd trade anything.*

There's no point. My pleas will go unanswered and time is slipping away. I've got to grasp the positive and let go of the bad for now.

My arms loaded with memories I can't leave behind I barrel down the stairs to the front door. Aunt Robin stands sentinel, Snickers now leashed and assaulting a pile of treats. Just the sight of my aunt, or rather her physical similarity to our mother, washes a renewed wave of guilt over me. If I didn't look closely, or saw her first thing on a groggy morning, I'd probably mistake her for the parent I'll never see again. Just that thought pierces my heart. I have to look away from her.

Black trash bags line the entranceway. An appreciative smile crosses my lips when I notice Snickers' belongings peeking out from the cinched sacks. A cushion from his favorite bed. The corner from an unopened bag of his kibble. My aunt hitches a shoulder, tilting her head toward it.

"He can't exactly pack for himself, right?" I allow the bags weighing me down to drop and wrap my arms around her. "Thank you," I whisper into her hair.

Riley's footsteps echo down the hallway, slowing as she nears us. "Everything okay?" she asks, eyebrows raised in concern. Aunt Robin and I nod while Snickers skirts around our legs, tail wagging now that he's consumed the last crumbs of his snack.

Repositioning our masks, we brace for the ash and begin the relay of depositing as many bags into the trunk as possible in the least number of trips. Once we're loaded up, Aunt Robin nudges the vehicle onto the road, and we proceed through the tiny dark flecks coasting on the breeze.

She knows where the cavern is, so now we just need to know exactly where to find the guys once we arrive. She passes me her cell phone and I dig out the paper Aidan gave me with his number written on it.

Chapter 57

I unfold the paper to find more than just a series of numbers scrawled on it:

> *In case you second-guess joining us, I thought I better include a "fail-safe" to convince you...*
>
> *Why is being with a geologist your best option?*
> *Because I'll never take you for granite.*
>
> *Call me as soon as you're on the way!*

All eyes land on me when a giggle escapes my lips. I shake my head. If I had any doubts about what to do, they would have dissolved the moment I read that note. My nerves flutter, reminding me that, even in the midst of disaster, I'm still a teenage girl nervous about calling a cute college guy. I hesitate for just a moment before plugging in the digits.

The conversation is short. Voices in the background vie for Aidan's attention. The initial relief in his tone is quickly replaced by urgency. "Follow the signs to Gate B. If you park in that lot, follow the small paved path to the entrance. There's a big NO TRESPASSING sign covering the gate. Ignore it. I'll be there to meet you and help you carry your stuff."

"Jeff might want to come too," I say. "We kind of have a lot of bags." Between the food, mine, Riley's, and now Snickers' stuff, it'll take multiple trips, and I don't want to add to Aidan's stress more than we have to.

"Jeff's...not here yet," he mutters. "He'll show up soon, though. Okay, I gotta go. I'll see you in a bit."

I relay the details to our aunt. Riley serves as navigator, peering out the window to see as far ahead as possible. Turning Aidan's words over in my mind, I wonder where Jeff is. *His parents knew about the plan, so what's he doing other than grabbing a few personal items?*

I fold and pocket the note, hoping that it stays intact so I can read it whenever I need a smile. Scrolling to the recent calls made in my aunt's phone, I save Aidan's number. I doubt his phone will work underground, but if there's any way to keep a lifeline open, I'm taking it. Maybe it's a *fail-safe*, as Bowen called it.

Reaching over the center console, I stuff the cell phone into my aunt's purse. "One of the people we'll be with is Aidan. I saved his number in your address book."

Her grateful eyes meet mine in the rearview mirror. "Thank you, Quinn."

As we approach Gate B, our tiny space weighs heavy with emotion. I know we're doing the right thing, but it feels wrong to leave our aunt behind. Riley must feel the same. Already knowing the answer, she asks, "Are you sure you won't come with us?"

With a sad nod, she confirms her decision. She parks the car and turns toward us. "It won't be too long before I see you again. I love you girls and I'll miss you, but as soon as it's safe to come up, you find me. Your parents would want you to be safe. And I know they're watching over you."

Riley crashes into her for one more hug. I reach over the backseat and squeeze Aunt Robin's arm.

A sharp knock on the window startles us all. Aidan's bright blue eyes penetrate the safety glasses he now sports. An unspoken burden seems to have aged him in the short time we've been apart. His eyes crinkle, proof of the smile hidden beneath the mask.

Aunt Robin waves at him and moves to lower the window, but Riley quickly stops her. "Don't! You're not wearing a mask. He'll lecture you if you put the window down without wearing one," she explains.

Aunt Robin turns to me for confirmation.

"She's right. He's a total nut about this stuff," I nod.

"Well, I guess you really are in good hands then," our aunt concedes. "Now don't keep him waiting. Go, but call me as soon as you come back aboveground. I'll be waiting to hear from you." With a heartfelt promise and dejected smiles, we unload the car. With her last reach for belongings, Riley scoops up Snickers. Without even discussing it, neither of us trusts him to follow us when there's all kinds of new scents to distract him here.

As Aidan tosses the last bag onto our pile of possessions, I slam the trunk closed. Positioning ourselves by the driver's side window, we wave a final farewell. *I hope this isn't the last time we see our aunt.* She watches, the car immobile, probably waiting to make sure we make it inside alright.

We load up as much as we can carry, but a mound of bags still remains on the ground. As I turn toward the car, a burst of color in the distance catches my attention. The red and blue lights flash, reflecting off the hovering contaminated clouds. It's a police car. And it's headed our way.

Chapter 58

Aunt Robin must see it too because her car's engine churns to life. The tires spin, spitting gravel as they struggle to gain purchase. They quickly catch a grip and the car tears away from us, heading directly toward the police car.

Riley and Aidan stop mid-step, bumping into each other, simultaneously turning toward the sound. Snickers growls as if expressing his annoyance with the collision. Aidan's eyes widen and his voice erupts from beneath the mask.

"Grab the other bags! We need to get underground! NOW!" We converge on the pile, overloading our arms and backs. Riley can't hold much but she does her best to swing some bags over her shoulder while still holding the dog.

Aidan dashes down a winding path that leads to the cavern's private entrance. We struggle to follow closely, gawking at the parking lot through the small army of skeletal trees that block our view.

My shoulders scream from the strain. Aidan leads us down

three flights of concrete steps enclosed by a rusted railing. The last step spills onto a concrete platform, cracked and crumbling around the edges. A rundown wooden structure serves as the shaky doorway to the depths below.

Aidan yanks the industrial-looking metal handle and kicks the narrow wooden triangle propping it open into some nearby wilting grass. The enclosure looks as though a strong wind could blow it over, but the door framed within it stands strong. It reminds me of the heavy-duty kind you'd see at a doctor's office or a school office. The sight of the dank interior sends a rippling wave of doubt through me, but there's no going back now.

Once we're all inside, Aidan pushes past me roughly, grasping the interior handle and slowly coaxing it back into its frame. "It locks automatically," he pants, pushing the mask under his chin to gulp in air.

We lower each of the bags to the ground, relieving our overloaded shoulders and backs. I fight the urge to drop it all in place around me, but I remember that some of our belongings are breakable.

Riley plops Snickers to the ground, who practically pushes off of her in his eagerness to escape her grasp. His tail wags frantically at being set free to explore his new surroundings. He stays close, but happily sniffs the stones and ground.

Eyeing the rusted bolts along the doorjamb, I ask, "Aren't you going to use *all* the locks?" My words rush out in a tone harsher than I mean. I force a few deep breaths, both to recover some of the oxygen my body craves from our mini sprint and to slow my frazzled nerves. *If the police know we're here, will they make us leave? Or what about those shelters Sergeant Bowen told us about?*

Would they make us go there?

He shakes his head frantically. "No. It's too loud. They squeal when you slide them shut. It's not worth the risk of announcing that we've taken up residence here." Narrowing my eyes, I tilt my head in question. Right about now, I want as many bolted locks as I can get.

Ignoring my clear disagreement, he says, "Wait here and stay quiet." His voice is low and commanding, leaving no room for negotiating. "I've gotta tell my dad that someone saw us. We didn't want anyone to know we're here."

Sensing the charged air, Snickers unleashes a low growl, his posture stiffening. Watching us, he awaits our reaction—perked ears anticipate soothing words promising everything is okay or a command to attack. Aidan takes one step, then turns back toward us. "I'm taking the dog. All we need is for him to start barking right here."

Not even waiting for a reply, he swipes Snickers into his arms and bolts down the stone steps. The growling echoes in their wake, quickly chased by shushing sounds. I'm sure Aidan's trying to calm the dog, but dashing down the steps at warp speed isn't exactly setting the mood for anyone to relax.

Nothing about this place feels familiar, but at least I know why we're here. Poor Snickers just got part of his family back and now he's whisked away by a stranger, their destination a dank hole in the ground. I know he's safe with Aidan, but I wish I could explain to him what's happening.

I distract myself by focusing on the immediate surroundings. The steps Aidan disappeared down jut from the ground, smoothly carved from the rock. It's strange to think that I visited this place as a kid and have so little memory of it. *Maybe I wasn't in this part of the cave? It doesn't exactly look like it's part of a tour.*

The faded walls bear the peeling remnants of a moldy avocado-green layer of paint. Exposed lightbulbs dangle from the ceiling, casting the narrow space in a sickly yellow gleam. Must and mildew compete to fragrance the air. A chill washes over my skin, which I attempt to shake off along with the heebie-jeebies. *How are we going to stay* here *for weeks? And what lives down here already? Because I can't imagine anything that likes this environment would welcome us with open arms. Or claws. Or multiple legs.*

Warring thoughts clash within my mind. Maybe Riley and I should go with the police right now and go back to Aunt Robin's house. Without us, she'll be completely alone for whatever comes next. And we're going to be trapped underground like moles.

But then there's the ash. Aidan said the only thing that will clear the air is time and we just have to wait it out. I nearly forget that I'm not alone when Riley tugs on my sleeve. Following Aidan's orders to a T, Riley remains silent but motions toward the door. She mouths, "Someone's out there" and we huddle together, staring at the lone barrier between us and what must be the police.

Leaning as close as we can without actually touching it, we both strain to hear the voices muffled by the door. A thundering knock rockets us both into the air like frightened cats. Somehow, we both manage to restrain from vocalizing our surprise.

Reserving every last molecule of air in our lungs, we don't dare breathe or blink. Pounding explodes again, this time followed by a confident announcement. "State police. We need to talk to you."

DEVASTATION ERUPTS

We freeze, a pair of trembling teenagers attempting to mimic statues. The muffled conversation returns and after one more round of knocking and what feels like an hour's pause, all sound fades completely. Maybe something else drew their attention away, or maybe they chalked it up to a wild goose chase.

Chapter 59

A gentle echo resonates behind us. Aidan's form emerges from the shadowy depths. He slinks his way up the steps, stopping abruptly at the top and staring intently at the door as if willing his eyes to acquire X-ray vision. He motions toward it and raises his eyebrows as if asking, "Are they gone?" Riley nods and whispers, "We think they left. They knocked on the door and demanded to come in, but we didn't make a sound."

Blowing out a relieved breath, Aidan says quietly, "Phew. Well, you two should come down and meet everyone. I think we're okay for now. Besides, the police should have better things to do than sit around watching a door that may or may not have people hiding behind it."

Taking one last glance at the door, I ask, "Should we bolt the other locks now?" He shakes his head. "No, better if we stay quiet. It'll be fine, let's go."

As Riley and I cautiously follow Aidan down flight after

flight of narrow stone steps, horror movie scenes flash through my mind. Why did I have to watch that one about a group of friends trapped underground about a thousand times? They were spelunking and lost their way in a cave system. While trying to find a way out, they discovered they weren't alone in the seemingly peaceful darkness. The movie didn't end well for them.

Shadows drift closer the further we go. A single string of lightbulbs drapes along one side of the cavern. Almost every third light is either dimming or burned out completely. Between that and their sporadic placement, the growing dimness radiates an ominous tone.

Aidan attempts to throw a reassuring glance over his shoulder, but he nearly topples down the slickened steps before righting himself. His shoulders hunch in defeat and probably a splash of embarrassment. Gravity seems to tug harder the further we descend. By the time we reach the bottom, my cramping legs crave flat land, or better yet—a big, soft bed to curl up on.

I fully expect the ground floor of this place to be some pit of doom, so the unexpected view just a few feet from the landing injects a slight spring in my step. The stairway leads to a tunnel completely carved from the rock. Its perfect curvature—from the inviting opening to the smoothed ceiling, is stunning, even in the dim light. Mouth gaping, I can't mask my amazement. It reminds me of the covered bridges just a few miles from here, above ground.

Having already tugged his mask off, Aidan brandishes a full smile, clearly pleased that I can appreciate the surrounding geology. My cheeks flush but I doubt anyone can see. He raises a hand in the air, palm up and asks, "Shall we?"

I can't help it, a giggle slips through my lips and I nod, placing my hand in his. I glance at Riley, who rolls her eyes while a dopey grin overtakes her face. A chill in the air sweeps through me. I'm glad Aidan told us to dress warm.

We trot through the opening. The tunnel's wide enough that Aidan and I can walk side-by-side while Riley trails behind us. Just a few yards long, it leads to a large opening that branches off in three directions. From this vantage point, I can't tell where the tunnels lead or even how deep they run. We've stumbled upon the hub of activity, though.

Half a dozen people move about the cavern, mirroring a human-scale ant farm. They carry boxes and crates from a pile in the center through various openings that branch off from the main room. At the center of the room sits a black fire pit. Its stubby legs raise it about two feet off the ground and a domed mesh screen contains about a half cord worth of small logs I'm suddenly itching to burn.

When he notices us, a tall muscular man strides over, wiping the palms of his hands across his thighs. The dark denim, coupled with the dim lighting, camouflages any dust or dirt his hands deposited.

His messy dark hair and bright blue eyes bear a striking resemblance to our escort. "Hello," he says, eyeing me and Riley. "I'm Scott, Aidan's dad. He said you'd be joining us. Now which one of you is Quinn and which one is Riley?" A playful smile tugs at the corners of his mouth.

After we introduce ourselves and endure his firm handshake, his eyes drift past us. "Isn't there one more coming?" He scratches his head, glancing at Aidan.

"Um…no sir, our aunt isn't coming after all," Riley stutters, toeing the ground with her sneaker. He gives a brief nod and straightens his red and black flannel shirt.

"Oh, well, if she changes her mind, she's still welcome," he says. "We'll do official introductions in a bit. I want to get everything settled first and then we can take a break. Lots more to do to get this place ready."

As we peer around the opening, Aidan's dad continues. "This here is one of the touristy parts of the cavern. Guides bring groups here to explain the history of the cave and point out formations." He motions around the space. Light bounces off the formations circling us. They're all so harsh and ominous— like they're waiting for us to turn our backs so they can thrust those spindly spears at us. "We'll get deeper into the non-touristy parts too, but for right now, this is our main hub."

Before returning to the hive of activity, he points out the others as they breeze past us, scurrying to organize supplies. My thoughts drift as he rattles off names and relationships. Basically, it's just Aidan's sisters and mother, along with Jeff's parents. A comfortable, cooperative air between them radiates through the chamber. They smile and murmur hellos when our eyes briefly meet.

It's like watching a perfectly-harmonized assembly line. They accomplish a greater task while enjoying brief moments of banter. Each plays a role with confident certainty. The bitter tang of jealousy rises in my throat. These people probably finish each other's sentences, and I can't even remember all of their names.

I steal a peek at Riley. She smiles as Aidan's dad speaks,

nodding as if she's hanging on every word. She probably is. If I was polite like her, I'd be listening too. Suddenly I wonder if we really belong here. They work in tandem, each move complementing another's efforts. *Can we meld into the connections sustained by years of familiarity?*

By the time I tune back in to the conversation, Aidan's dad excuses himself and disappears down one of the tunnels. Before I can question what comes next, Aidan faces us both. "Let's cart all your stuff down here to what my dad's calling *the main supply room*." He punctuates the last few words with air quotes. "Then we'll go back up to the door. I've got to call Jeff again to see where he is, and the phone won't work down here." He starts to turn away from us when Riley taps his shoulder.

"Wait, where's Snickers?" she asks. *How did I already forget about our dog?*

Aidan shrugs, "He's having a great time exploring. Last I saw he took off down a tunnel, tail wagging the whole way."

"Alright, as long as he's okay," she says. Aidan leads us back up the steps. I wonder how many times we'll travel up and down these rocks over the next few weeks. At least it puts distance between us and the deteriorating world above. My mind volleys back to accepting that this is the best place for us. *Maybe I could even start running again. If the tunnels reach far enough into the rock to give me some distance.*

It takes us three trips to carry all but two of the bags to the supply room. It would have taken less, but Riley and I refuse to overload ourselves again. Too tired to care, we unceremoniously dump everything in a pile in the middle of the open space. And at least the bags on the bottom layer provide a nice cushion for the rest.

There will be plenty of time later to unpack. For now, our only mission is to horde everything in this one space so it can be sorted and organized.

With tired muscles, we force our feet to fight gravity and make the climb again. Snickers appears and excitedly follows on our heels, seemingly satisfied with his explorations for the time being. Impatient with our sluggish pace, he darts around us and launches up the steps toward the entranceway. Stopping when he reaches the top, he sits to watch our slow progress.

When we crest the last step, Aidan slips the dust mask back over his mouth and nose and pulls safety glasses from his pocket.

"I'm gonna go try to call Jeff. You two stay here and open the door when I knock."

Chapter 60

"But how will we know it's you and not someone else?" Riley asks. I nod, but it doesn't adequately convey my dissent. Crossing my arms, I add, "Yeah, we should come with you. I don't want to just stand here and wait, not knowing when you're coming back."

Sensing a potentially hostile interaction, or perhaps bored with the humans on this level, Snickers rises and promptly asserts his short legs to carry him back down the steps he just conquered.

Conflict flickers through Aidan's eyes and he tilts his head as if weighing our words. "Okay, one of you stays and one of you comes with me. I'll need help anyway. But we need someone to hold the door open."

Building on our rebellious momentum, Riley narrows her eyes and asks, "What *is* going on with Jeff? Why isn't he here and what's he doing?"

DEVASTATION ERUPTS

Tugging the dust mask off, Aidan sighs before explaining that Jeff's parents made a deal with a local sporting goods store. They offered the store owner an exuberant amount of money in exchange for a cache of supplies—guns, ammo, freeze-dried food, lanterns, portable flood lights. Basically, as many survival tools as he could fit into his dad's truck. His parents sent him alone so that every inch of space within the truck could be filled. The store owner agreed to help load the truck, so all Jeff had to do was transport the supplies here.

Once Aidan got us inside and settled, he was supposed to call Jeff and arrange a meeting time so everyone could help to quickly unload the truck and park it away from the entrance. Our little visit from the police altered that plan slightly. Now that we've had the quick tour and our visitors are gone—*we hope*—it's time to get the last of the supplies here and unloaded and then seal up the door.

Riley questions just how tight that door seal will be, in case our aunt changes her mind and decides to join us. Aidan shares that they're trying to create a barrier between us and the poisoned air outside, as well as any potential intruders. When Riley audibly gasps at that last part, he claims that it isn't likely to be a problem. Still, the fear it produces immediately relaxes our stance on leaving the relative safety of the cave.

We promise to wait inside while Aidan phones Jeff. Reaffixing the mask and safety goggles, he slips out the door, quickly closing it behind him. Relishing the privacy, I turn toward my sister, confessing my worries.

"Do you think we did the right thing?" I whisper. "I mean, they're all like one big happy family and then there's just...us...

tagging along."

"I know what you mean," she sighs. "I really wish Mom and Dad were here to tell us what to do." Her eyes water, trepidation drifting through the deep brown irises. "They seem nice enough, but if we decide that things just don't feel right, we can go back to Aunt Robin's and stay with her. We're not prisoners, so if we want to leave, then I say we do it."

"The only thing I don't want to do is go back home," I add. "It's too depressing. I wouldn't mind all my stuff, but I don't want to stay there."

"Same." She nods sadly.

The door pitches open slightly. Aidan's face fills the crack, his plastic safety glasses clinking against the metal. "Hey! I got a hold of Jeff. He should be here in about thirty minutes. Sit tight for now. I'm gonna take a walk around the perimeter and look for any sign of police, or anyone else who might have seen us come here." He retracts from the door opening and pulls it closed without another word. He probably wants to avoid another discussion where Riley and I disagree with him.

Lowering ourselves to the floor, we sit and wait. After a few minutes, Riley wanders back toward the steps, peering into the depths below. "Sniiiiiickers," she calls. The sound resonates throughout the cavern. She clasps a palm over her mouth, likely envisioning the worker bees below stiffening, craning their heads trying to locate the source, which I'm sure they know is one of us.

Her embarrassment quickly fades when the summoning works. Snickers returns her cry with a series of jubilant yelps. The patter of toenails clicking on stone carries through the chamber.

A moment later a cyclone of fur blasts from the depths, swirling around Riley's legs. *At least the dog's happy down here.* When she returns to our makeshift seating, Snickers happily trots between us and settles with a yawn.

"Well you've had an exciting day, haven't you, boy?" Riley ruffles his ears. His eyes brim with love as he looks from her to me and back.

For just a moment, the dingy space fades away and our little family consumes my every sense. *At least we're together.*

Soon enough the heavy door creaks open and Aidan's voice carries toward us.

"Jeff's here. Let's help him unload."

Chapter 61

Affixing a dust mask, I rush out the door to help the guys. Riley juts a foot through the doorway, propping it open. I quickly catch up to Aidan and we stop short when our eyes land on the spectacle before us.

A Jeff-shaped figure leans against a blue pick-up truck, his arms crossed. The frame and height look right but a black wasp-like mask obscures most of his face. This guy isn't wasting time with a dust mask like the rest of us.

"Aidan, I *am* your brother," a breathy voice booms through the mask. We take a step closer and Jeff's smiling eyes come into focus. Aidan slaps him on the back and eyes the overflowing truck bed. He throws a hand in the air toward it.

"Nice work, man! Riley's inside and she's gonna hold the door for us. Let's get this inside. Not all of us have full-blown doomsday gear like you!"

"You got it! And don't worry, I got enough masks for all of us!" Jeff nods his head slowly, which only accentuates his resemblance to a giant insect. He throws me a wheezy "hey" before unlatching the tailgate and loading my arms with a large cardboard box. Thankfully it's not heavy, but its bulk will make traversing all those steps a little tricky.

When I reach the door, Riley promptly holds it open. I wobble inside, squeezing past the frame. The excitement of something new to sniff overcomes Snickers and he rushes to my side, circling my legs. I stumble but catch my footing.

"Down! Stay!" I command, pushing past him. My leg muscles burn with exertion, protesting each move. The relatively flat ground of the cavern can't appear fast enough. I've had my share of descending and climbing these steps for today. But I know we're just getting started with this load of supplies.

Passing Aidan on my way back up, he flashes me a crooked smile. Although the mask covers his passageways, I can tell by the lopsided hitch in his cheek. He must be thrilled with all the goodies Jeff got.

"The others are coming up to help us," he calls over his shoulder as we part ways. "They're just finishing something up and then they'll join us." I nod. The more people helping, the less trips for everyone to make.

At least going through all this stuff will keep us busy tonight, and maybe even tomorrow. I can't imagine there's much to do underground besides eat, sleep, and rearrange your meager personal belongings for entertainment.

Just as I reach the top of the steps, my legs pleading for a break, Jeff barges through the entryway. He struggles to balance a brown cardboard box advertising its contents as six hundred fire starter sticks. The circular handle opening of a large plastic bag loops around each of his wrists. By the way each bag swings like a pendulum, drawn toward gravity's pull, I imagine the contents are heavy.

While I admire his commitment to making the least number of trips possible, it's certainly not the best idea to load up so much that you can barely move. Only Jeff would do that. Rolling my eyes and shaking my head, I rush back to the truck. *I want to get this over with.*

Digging past the heavier packages, I discover a large box of freeze-dried food. *Jackpot!* That's nice and light. Aidan passes by on his way to the truck just before I reach the closed doorway. *This will be about the fiftieth time I cross this threshold today.*

Waiting for a few minutes, until the last second of patience I have expires, I kick the door. *Where is Riley?* Her only job is to stand here and hold it open for us. I think it's time we switched roles. Aidan joins me, nodding at the metal blocking our way.

"What's she doing?" he asks, slightly muffled by the mask. I hunch my shoulders up. "No idea." Setting his stack of boxes down, he pounds on the door. "Hey, open up! We've got another load."

The door careens open and Riley pops out, her features etched with frustration. Before we can ask what's wrong, words spill from her almost faster than I can comprehend.

"Snickers…he got all excited when he saw Jeff. What is with that guy and dogs?" She sighs. "Anyway, Snickers was all over him, barking and jumping at him. Maybe it was the mask? I was trying to calm him down when you guys started knocking. I think

271

I got him to stop." A series of yelps echoing behind her claims otherwise.

Dropping his haul, Aidan pushes past Riley, racing inside. My sister and I lock eyes for just a moment before I plunk down the box of food and dash inside with her.

Devastation erupts in our small safe haven. My whole body quakes as a maelstrom of emotions rattle every bone, muscle, and cell.

Chapter 62

Everything happens at once, in that surreal slow-motion effect where you're powerless to do anything but watch, listen, and breathe. Aidan disappears down the steps, screaming words that run together too quickly to decipher meaning.

A cacophony of sound swarms my ears. Snickers' yelps, morphing into frightened squeals. The thudding impact of multiple heavy objects tumbling down solid rock. Two seconds of silence.

Then an explosion that propels a flash of heat and a roaring boom through the cavern. The ground under my feet quakes and rumbles, derailing my balance. Instincts guide my body to the ground and my knees hit dirt. Riley huddles next to me, her eyes already watering either with unshed emotion or the impact our bodies absorb.

The lightbulbs bounce on their wires, some clanking into nearby stalagmites or stalactites, whichever the ones growing down from the ceiling are called. A few shatter while others flicker, desperately clinging to their source of power.

Riley grabs my elbow. "There's a flashlight by the door. I saw it, hanging on the wall." I nod and rise, bounding toward the entrance. I didn't notice it before, but she's right. The orange and black tube hangs from a rusted hook jutting out of the rock. It resembles a gun, but it's pretty clear the only thing discharging from its flat circular end is a mini-spotlight. I pull the trigger, half expecting it to ignore my prompt but a strong beam of light spills through the plastic lens.

I sweep it across the open space. Dust floats lazily through the air, as if its presence doesn't signify the result of massive destruction. I'm thankful for the dust mask. At least it's keeping some of that junk out of my lungs.

A sense of urgency claws at my brain, muddled by the slight ringing in my ears and an overall fatigue from the events of this day. I push up from the ground and edge toward the steps. Riley clings to my side as if we're velcroed together.

"Stay away from there!" she cries. "Don't go near the edge!" Cohesive thoughts slither through my brain, attempting to connect and spark action.

"Riley, we're going down there." I point to the murky abyss. "We have to check on the guys." Her eyes widen in horror, but she knows I'm right. Her forehead crinkles and she squeezes her eyes shut for a moment before nodding her head sharply.

She clutches my hand and I'm grateful that we have each other. Of all the times I've needed someone by my side, this one ranks high on the list. We hesitantly creep near the edge just as rumbling bubbles from the depths. We jump back in unison, to the relative safety of the entranceway.

The thunderous crash of detaching rocks violently smashing together overtakes the chamber. Instinctively I drop to the ground, tucking my head between my knees. Dust wafts skyward, particles hovering within our open space. Maybe they're searching for an escape route.

"Snickers!" Riley cries feebly, choking out that one word with unmistakable anguish. In that moment, anger ignites in the pit of my stomach. We've already endured a lifetime's worth of fear, despair, and loss. If I'm meant to become one with the pits below, then let's get it over with.

Clenching the fear-fueled tremor in my hands into fists, I rise.

"Quinn, what are you doing?" Riley squeaks. Seeing my sister cower reinforces my determination.

"I'm going down there. Aidan and Jeff are down there, and so are their families." I point to the edge. Before she can protest, I lean over and place a gentle palm on her back. "I'm tired of always feeling like I have no control over anything that happens to us. Someone may be hurt right now and I've gotta help if I can. You stay here. I'll be back soon."

Other than the soft echo of pebbles tumbling to the pit below, the chamber is eerily quiet. Until a sharp clicking sound reaches my ears. It grows slightly louder with each second that passes. Confirming my assumption, a brown ball of fur hurdles over the top step, surging through the clouds of dirt and crashing into us. Snickers yelps but I can't tell if it's in joy or pain. Crimson mats the fur on his back leg. If it's not his, it's from one of the guys. Either way, it's a bad sign.

Riley wraps her arms around him, gently cradling him to her chest. I can't tell if she's trying to comfort him or if she's using him to comfort herself. I touch her shoulder. "Take care of him. I'll be back." I don't wait for the inevitable protest bubbling behind her choked tears. I gain my balance and rush down the steps as quickly as I can without losing my footing. Focusing my eyes on each individual step, I concentrate on not plunging over the edge. Every few seconds, I attempt to plot the safest path by stealing glances ahead, although the dancing dust particles limit my ability to see more than a few feet.

When muffled voices reach my ears, I quicken my pace, driven to reach the others. I nearly wail when my eyes land on a prone figure crumpled on the dirt floor. My heart knows what my eyes refuse to confirm. It's Aidan.

Chapter 63

With no concern for what may be unsteady ground beneath my feet, I dart toward him. Sliding into the gravel on my knees, I lean over his body. Tugging his arm, I repeat his name over and over, an indirect command for him to be okay.

His eyelids flutter, allowing me just a glimpse of those cerulean irises. The slits widen into clouded shock as his eyes search our surroundings. I know our situation is less than awesome, but at least he seems to be relatively unscathed. Relief dares to dance through my soul.

Gulping a deep breath, he immediately keels forward, hacking up whatever oxygen his lungs harbored. Not sure what else to do, I pat his back as if he's choking. *At least he knows someone is here with him.* Seemingly clearing out every dust particle invading his air passages, he continues to cough for several minutes.

"Aidan? Anyone over there?" The words are muffled but I can make them out. It sounds like Aidan's dad.

"It's Quinn and Aidan! Where are you?" I rise, letting the voice guide me closer. The sound leads to darkness though, to the very spot that Aidan escorted me through the tunnel earlier. But there's no tunnel there anymore.

"Oh, thank goodness. It's Scott, Aidan's dad. Is everyone accounted for over there?" Even through the newly-formed barrier, I can sense the trepidation in his question. "Yes!" I assure him. Each of us may be afflicted with fresh emotional or physical scars, but he doesn't need to worry about that right now.

"That's good news. But I fear that's where the good news ends. We had a cave-in on this side and I'm guessing you've got a mirror image of it. Tell me what you see," he coaxes. Aidan slowly sits up, rubbing his head. He listens as I describe the space. The steps remain intact, and they still lead to the flat landing above, but one major component of the area has vanished, perhaps swallowed up by the cave itself.

"Well, the steps are here, but where they're supposed to lead to the tunnel, it's just a wall of rock and dirt now."

"That's what I thought," Scott interjects. He pauses for a moment before continuing. "Jeff was loaded with boxes and bags…he tripped and tumbled down the steps. There must have been nitroglycerin in something he was carrying. I can't imagine what else could cause that kind of damage."

Lowering his voice slightly, it's as if he's suddenly talking to himself. "Why the hell would nitroglycerin be in there?" I can almost envision him raking a hand through his dark hair, like I've seen Aidan do so many times. Refocusing on the moment, he continues. "The packages he was carrying must have crashed together and ignited. Pretty much blew the damn tunnel to bits."

Aidan pushes himself up off the ground, but his gait is shaky. I rush to his side and he immediately wraps an arm around my shoulder for support. I'm grateful he's accepting my help so easily. Grayish streaks mar his cheeks and forehead. His hair scatters in tufts more restless than usual. Sprinklings of dust cover his head and body, enhancing his newly-rugged appearance.

While none of that makes him look any less handsome in this moment, one detail concerns me. Although he leans on me for support, his right leg slightly dangles, as if he doesn't want it even grazing the ground. I search his eyes for answers, but the worry etched there convinces me to stay quiet. For the moment anyway.

"Dad, where's Jeff?" Aidan demands, staring at the mass of stone before us, as if he can see his father through it.

"Oh, son, I'm glad to hear your voice," Scott answers. "He's over here. We have him. But he's in pretty bad shape. He was… very close to the blast…and he got knocked around pretty bad."

I imagine he's over there sighing right now, just a few feet away separated by the impossible barrier.

Aidan attempts to extract more details from his dad, but his shaky limbs confirm that he's struggling to stand, and I know we have more pressing issues. For one, Riley and I need to check his leg.

Scott cuts the conversation short, assuring us that no one else was injured, although they're all anxious and emotional. Jeff's parents especially. He explains that the wall between us isn't solid, so we can hear each other through the gaps. We're going to have to find a way to connect our space to theirs, but he doesn't want anyone approaching the rubble just yet. It may still be settling and the last thing we need is another injury or further collapse.

Besides Jeff's condition, our biggest challenge at the moment is the inability to share supplies. Aidan's dad instructs us to finish unloading the truck quickly so that we can move it away from the entrance and hide it behind the property's maintenance garage. He confirms that Aidan knows where that is.

Guilt courses through me, overwhelming my ears as they mute everything else but the rapid pounding of my heart. His dad has no idea that Aidan was hurt in the explosion too. On this side of the rock wall, we keep our mouths shut about that. *No sense tacking on one more thing for his dad to worry about when there's nothing he can do.*

"All three of you over there, go and unload that truck. Get the supplies inside and then come back, let me know when you're done. We've still got a lot to do. We just have to shuffle around our priorities."

Chapter 64

Every teenager, at some point, has despised being told what to do by an adult. But right now, having someone else in charge, telling us what comes next, is comforting. I imagine my dad would react the same way—taking control of the situation and giving everyone assignments to help however they could. *I wish he were here.*

Searching Aidan's eyes for approval, I offer an encouraging smile when he gives me a sharp nod. Turning our bodies away from the tunnel remains, I guide him toward the steps. It's a long way up when you have two good legs. I don't even want to think about how we're going to do this when he must outweigh me by at least fifty pounds and he's trying to skitter along on one leg and my shoulder.

"So why don't you tell me about what happened to your leg?" Might as well glean any information I can. It'll be a distraction from what I'm sure will be a slow progression up.

He breathes out a sigh that morphs into a lung-cleansing cough. "Sorry," he barks out. Clearing his throat, he explains, "I tried to get to him but before I was even halfway down, I saw him lose his balance." He stops moving, which is almost difficult to distinguish given our snail's pace, and locks eyes with me. "Snickers was running up and down the steps, around his feet. I think that tripped him up."

My free hand flies to my mouth and my shoulders drop into a mortified slump. "Oh my gosh! I feel terrible. This is all our faul—"

He reaches up and rests his palm over my hand. "Look, it's no one's fault and placing blame isn't going to help anything. All that matters now is that everyone's okay."

At least he doesn't blame us. *I hope the others don't either when they find out* our dog *caused this.*

Those blue eyes blaze with emotions—worry, disbelief and, most importantly, hope. Reality returns too quickly when his hand starts to tremble. I know it's not nervousness. Reluctantly removing the warmth of his touch, I press his palm to the railing.

Quickly calculating our only option to navigate the upward trek, I nudge a shoulder under his arm to better support his injured side. "Let's get you up there. You're going to take it easy so Riley and I can check you for injuries and then the two of us will unload the truck. You can't do it in this condition."

"I can't stick you two with all that," he protests. When his good foot slips, momentarily jarring our balance, I simply raise my eyebrows as if to say, "See what I'm talking about?!"

"Alright, fine," he mutters. "But bring everything inside and hide the truck first. Then you can conduct a thorough inspection of my injuries." Out of the corner of his eye, he searches for my reaction. I can't help it, in the midst of our latest disaster, he's given me a reason to smile.

The rest of our ascent consists of small talk and small steps. At least the dust has settled, and the cavern has returned to its former stillness. A wave of relief awakens my aching muscles as we near the top. I don't mind being this close to Aidan, but my back doesn't appreciate the added weight of his nearly six-foot frame.

Riley appears at the top of the steps, peering down at us. She must have rushed over when she heard our approaching shuffle-grunt movements.

"Are you guys okay? What happened? Where's everyone else?" She paces, wringing her hands as she fires off questions.

When we crest the top step, she retrieves Aidan's hand from the railing and wraps his arm around her shoulder. His weight shifts, sending immediate relief to my back and legs.

We ease up against the nearest wall and count to three before lowering to the ground in one clumsy drop. For just a moment we allow our breathing to slow and our bodies to rest.

My eyes drift across the floor, pausing to notice that Riley must have busied herself while she was waiting for us. Two stainless steel bowls sit directly across from us, one brimming with water and the other with kibble. It's a good thing our aunt thought to pack some of Snickers' belongings too. I'm not sure we would have thought to do it.

I brush the dots of sweat lining my forehead away. "Riley, we need to go out and unload the truck. Aidan's dad wants us to finish that and get the truck hidden."

Aidan slides his feet forward, as if preparing to stand, but I quickly shut that down with a warning scowl. "Please, stay here. We can't have you get hurt. Again."

Riley crosses her arms and narrows her eyes. "Don't even tell me you were thinking about lugging heavy objects around when you can barely walk on your own!"

He drops his gaze in defeat. Before he can change his mind, Riley and I scramble to the door and reposition the wooden triangle to prop it open. We can wedge one of the larger boxes from the truck just inside to hold it open wider, but that's going to be a two-person job. *I don't even want to think about how heavy some of that stuff looked.*

Dust masks in place, we push outside. I'm two steps behind Riley when she stops in her tracks. Not expecting an impromptu game of red light-green light, I slam into her back, jolting her forward. Gasping to replace the air knocked from my lungs, I start to demand, "Riley! What the—" but the words die on my lips.

A uniformed police officer stands just a few feet before us, casually leaning one arm on the blue truck's tailgate. Except for his eyes, the full facial mask blocks his features. Still, amusement radiates when he cocks his head to the side and tips his head in our direction. I imagine his lips twitching into a loose smirk behind that respirator as he watches us awkwardly straighten from our collision.

Chapter 65

Although my first instinct is to run, I know that's not an option. He'd just chase us and while I was practically a master distance runner on my high school track team, Riley would never make it very far. And honestly, my legs are pretty much jelly at this point. Besides today's overexertion, every muscle in my body quivers in anticipation of speaking with our surprise visitor.

Either losing patience or bored by our lack of response, the officer straightens and staggers toward us. Riley clasps her hands together and politely calls, "Hello, sir."

He stands before us, a tower of muscles packaged in a light gray button–down shirt and dark gray fitted pants. As if the belt of various self-defense hardware wrapped around his waist isn't enough, he's got to be at least a foot-and-a-half taller than us. His deep voice verbalizes the first question. "Ladies, is this your truck?"

Instinctively, Riley and I turn toward each other. The simple answer is no, but there's no way he'll just accept that and leave. Riley's brain works faster than mine.

"It's not ours, sir, but it does belong to our friend." She always falls back on honesty. *Definitely not my first instinct, but let's see how this approach works for us.*

"And where is this *friend?*" he asks. Although he wears a neutral expression, from what little I can see of his face, doubt lingers in his tone.

"He's kind of busy right now," I say, acutely aware that it's not the smartest thing I've ever said. Silence stretches around the three of us. I use the moment to glean whatever information I can. A silver border frames the black nametag bearing six white letters: CROSBY. No title or first name. I shift my attention to his face, or at least what shows through the clear parts of his mask.

The officer can't be *that* much older than us, but his red-rimmed eyes broadcast an exhaustion that would probably even make SpongeBob nasty. The slight forward tilt of his head beckons me to provide a better answer. *I've got nothing.*

With slumping shoulders and a deep exhale of defeat, Riley answers, "He's inside the caverns." She points to the door we just passed through. "There was kind of an accident and we can't get to him, but we were asked to unload his truck."

The officer's eyes widen in surprise and his spine stiffens. "Take me to where you last saw him," he commands, his voice a low rumble. *This revelation has definitely changed his demeanor. Maybe the truth wasn't such a great choice.*

As if we're being led to prison, Riley and I trudge toward the doorway. Aidan's right on the other side, and now we're bringing him one more reason to worry about his family and what was supposed to be a safe haven.

Grasping the handle, I yank it open and Riley leads the way inside.

Unmoved from where we left him, Aidan looks so peaceful with his eyes closed and his head resting against the stone wall. That lasts for about one second. As soon as Snickers eyes the stranger, he blazes into a barking frenzy, sending Aidan into a panicked alertness.

The officer removes his mask and rubs his head where the seal must have been tightest. Indentations in his hair give him a serious case of hat head. Aidan's shocked reaction dissolves when he meets the officer's tired eyes. Recognition dawns and a smile overtakes his face. The officer rushes past us, dropping to his knees by Aidan's side.

"Matt!" Aidan greets the stranger. They lean toward each other, doing that guy greeting that starts with a high five, shifts into a brief handshake and ends with a quick bro hug.

Chapter 66

Riley and I stare, stunned. She breaks free from the stupor first and grabs Snickers, making her best effort to calm him down. She's largely unsuccessful, so I join her in begging the dog to ignore the excitement that accompanies having a new person to sniff.

The guys talk while we distract the dog. No matter how hard I strain to overhear their conversation, I can't make out enough words to piece together a complete sentence.

After a few minutes, the officer rises. Retrieving a flashlight from his belt, he sweeps the beam of light through the darkness below briefly. With just a moment's pause to evaluate the stability of the railing and steps, he charges downward, inevitably seeking the rest of our party.

With Snickers mostly calmed, I rush to Aidan's side. "Who is that? How do you know him? What's he doing?" Those crystal blue eyes narrow as his nose wrinkles and he chuckles.

"It's okay. That's Jeff's brother. He's with the state police." He runs a hand through his hair, scattering a few dust particles clinging to the ends. "He's not supposed to be here. He works two hours away but just finished up a double shift and came to check on his family."

"I guess his parents probably told him they were coming here, huh?" I don't wait for an answer. I have way too many questions. "Does he know anything about the police that tried to visit us earlier?"

"No, but he's going to swing by the local station after he leaves here and see what he can find out." Aidan shrugs. "If anything, he'll help us. He won't go back and report that we're here or anything. In fact, he'll probably try to keep them from coming back here."

I lean forward, paranoia drawing me closer. "Do you think he'll be mad that Jeff is hurt?" I whisper. "I mean, I know you said you don't blame Snickers, but you aren't Jeff's very tall, very strong-looking brother."

With mock indignation, he crosses his arms. "I'm just as tall and muscular as he is, but I'll let your comment slide on account that particulates may be clouding your vision right now."

I'm still tense from the stress of the unexpected visitor, but a hint of a genuine laugh escapes.

"Anyway, just between us, Jeff and Matt aren't exactly *close*." He emphasizes the last word, raising his eyebrows in an attempt to convey his sincerity. "They're kind of like…ammonia and bleach. Sort of like, when they come in contact with each other, it doesn't exactly end well."

Phew, not that I wish for family discourse, but that may help relieve us from all the blame once he discovers that Jeff's hurt. Obviously, by Matt's reaction, he cares about his family. I just hope he doesn't ask too many questions about how it happened.

Riley wanders over with Snickers. He's finally stopped yapping. She crouches and whispers, "Is everything okay…Are you okay?"

Aidan nods. "The pain is fading already. Nothing's broken. I can tell." Then, as if to distract us from our worry, he extends his arms. "I'll take Cujo. You two better start unloading that truck before it draws attention. Leave the heavy stuff. Matt can carry that in."

"Alright," Riley states. "As long as you promise to stay right here and take it easy until we can take a look at that leg."

"Deal," he says with one sharp nod.

About ten trips later, my arms quiver with exhaustion. We've unloaded and tucked about ninety percent of the truck's contents within every open inch of unoccupied space inside the entrance door. The space is packed, but there's no way I'm carrying all this stuff down the zillion flights of stairs tonight.

The clack of hard-soled shoes bounces off the stone walls, alerting us to Matt's return. *Unless by some miracle he managed to free the others.* A moment later, a single head appears, confirming that the situation below has not changed.

Matt lowers himself to Aidan's side when he returns from the depths. Sensing their preference for privacy, Riley scoops up Snickers and bunches his leash in her palm. Bobbing her head toward the door, she mouths "Let's go." I nod in agreement.

There's really no need to eavesdrop. I've got big plans to grill

Aidan after Matt leaves. And I'm sure Riley will back me up on that.

Besides, the dog could probably use a trip outside, especially since we haven't designated an indoor bathroom area for him. I'm guessing that's what we'll have to do. Otherwise, Riley or I would have to leash him and take him out every few hours. That's not going to work if the plan is to seal the door. *Although not much is going according to plan right now.*

Slinking along the building's perimeter, we lead Snickers away from the parking lot. Although there's no other movement, we attempt to blend into the thinly-wooded patches of growth. After several unsuccessful attempts to hurry Snickers along, we trail behind him as he leads us deeper into the property.

Buildings are sparse, but the few nearby structures are similar to the one that serves as our portal to the depths. I can't tell if they are additional entranceways to the caverns or just random outbuildings. When the ground starts crunching beneath my feet, I stop to examine our surroundings.

Although a smattering of leaves dot the trees, most rest on the ground, frozen in a state of decomposition. If this were October, it would be a completely expected sight.

Now that I look more closely, even the grass beneath my feet bears more yellow than green. Maybe it's just dry and needs water. The ash couldn't have impacted it that fast.

"Riley, why are most of the leaves on the ground in the middle of summer?" I ask, knowing she doesn't have any more information than I do. She stops mid-step and hands me Snickers' leash.

"Maybe this is why," she says, pointing straight ahead.

Chapter 67

S he reaches forward, placing a gentle palm on the narrow tree trunk. I'm not sure what type of tree it is, but it's obvious that the smoky black hue ringing its length is unhealthy. At some point it was probably as thick as a fire hydrant but nowhere near as sturdy.

Bark spikes upward at unnatural angles, shards of the protective outer layer reduced to exposed splintered black innards. It looks as though it was peeled away by massive careless claws that grew bored halfway through the task.

"It looks like it's dying," Riley says quietly. Whipping her head back and forth, her tangled brown locks flop in the corrupt air. "They're all dead. Look at them, Quinn." Tangling her hands together, she practically broadcasts her spiraling anxiety.

"What if this is happening everywhere? What if it's spreading?" she asks. "We can't *breathe* if all the trees die. And something's got to clean this air." She thrusts her hands to the sky as we both sweep our eyes across the immediate ecosystem, and everything that's wrong with it.

Snickers excitedly pokes his nose along the ground, staking claim on the perfect spot. Just as he's kicking up tufts of dried grass with his back paws, an engine revs, slicing through the bleak silence.

As if it's a ringing bell, signifying that recess is over, we wander toward it. I tug on Snickers' leash, attempting to coax him from the irresistible scents that keep his snout planted to the ground.

The blue truck rolls past us, close enough to see that Jeff's brother is driving. *Well, that makes one less thing for us to do—hiding the truck somewhere on the property.*

He acknowledges us with a slight nod. When he was talking to Aidan and removed the mask, I could see the family resemblance. He's like an older, more serious version of Jeff. A much more serious version.

We return to find Aidan limping around the small entrance space, shifting and sliding packages into every sliver of open space like a reverse game of Jenga. Besides slightly widening the path from the door to the steps, he's also cleared away a rectangular area against the wall.

"We told you to rest!" Riley scolds him, rushing to his side and relieving him of the bag he was attempting to wedge into a miniscule opening between two boxes. "We can do this."

He starts to protest, but Riley and I flank each side and escort him to the wall. Backing up against it, he slides down until he lands on his butt. "Why don't you two join me down here? I've got to catch you up on what's happening."

Lowering ourselves to the ground next to him, we listen intently. The dusty dirt floor gives my achy muscles a welcome reprieve. Snickers must be worn out, too. He circles a few times before scuttling between my legs and Aidan's, plopping into a napping position and letting gravity overtake his eyelids.

Now that the supplies are all inside and the truck is hidden, this would have been when we barricaded the door shut and took up residence in the caverns below. Aidan's dad even mapped out how we would use each room and form our own little interconnected mini-city. *Not that it does us much good at the moment.*

The group downstairs continues to unpack and settle. They have most of the supplies—items Aidan's and Jeff's parents started bringing over a few days ago. The rest of the stockpile surrounds us.

Jeff's pretty banged up. They're focusing on relieving his pain, but it sounds like the tunnel collapse nearly broke his back. We have no doctor, but his parents are guessing that he's got some slipped discs and pinched nerves. Every movement hurts and he won't even try to stand, so they're keeping him as immobile as possible. Otherwise, they've been able to patch up the scratches and scrapes plaguing his arms and legs. At the moment, he's stable.

Aidan's dad is insistent that everyone stay away from the rock pile separating us for now. If it's still intact tomorrow, and presumably stable, we'll search for a spot to start clearing away rubble—slowly and carefully. *Sounds like it's going to be a blast.*

Chapter 68

Aidan confirms that Matt is gone for the night. He'll return in the morning with tools to help dig through the tunnel. Apparently, he's the only one Aidan's dad trusts to dig through. That's probably a good thing. I'm sure Matt's much stronger than me or Riley. And Aidan's in no condition for strenuous labor, although I don't know if anyone down there knows that.

Riley stretches, fatigue pouring from her elongated yawn. It quickly catches, Aidan and I following suit.

"Why don't we eat something and try to get some rest," Aidan suggests.

"That sounds good," Riley confirms, rising to her feet. "I'll just check Snickers' food and water first." Bowls clink as she rearranges the dog's dining area, topping off the kibble in one bowl and dumping more bottled water into another.

Scanning the space, dread stretches to my limbs when I note the absence of a certain necessity.

"Um, where's the bathroom?" I ask, fully aware that I won't like the answer.

"So, they don't really have restrooms inside a cave," he shrugs. "You know, a little tough to work in all the piping and components."

Eyebrows raised, I nod, imploring him to continue.

"Soooooo," he hedges, gulping. "My dad has some portable devices set up, you know, that everyone can use. That was part of his whole master plan. Being that we'll only be here for a few weeks."

"Go on," Riley prompts, crossing her arms. As if the pressure bursts inside him, Aidan's explanation is a flurry of thoughts.

"There's a body of water that we can access from a few of the caverns below. So we had this whole plan for bathing and there's even fish in the lake down there. If food runs low, we can catch and cook them." He hitches a shoulder up. In theory, it makes sense, but part of me cringes inwardly as he continues.

I hate seafood. Being expected to catch and eat fish is one tidbit that would have been good to know before we agreed to come here.

"Once the air cleared up and we needed to start moving everything out of here, we were going to make trips to the gift shop. That has a proper restroom. My dad's friend who owns the place even gave him a key. But that's…kind of with my dad, so we can't really get to the key right now."

"Can you pick a lock, like Jeff?" I ask, focused on locating an actual bathroom. *How did I not think of this before?* He shakes his head.

"No, that is one skill I have not acquired. But even if I did know how, I couldn't do that. If we picked it open, we'd have no way to lock it back up. We'd be leaving it open for anyone to just walk up and take whatever they wanted or cause damage."

Riley rubs her temples, pinching her eyes shut. "Alright then," she says. "We've got to come up with a plan, because we can't wait until tomorrow to access even the *portable devices.*" Her distaste for the term is palpable. I share it.

Our attempt at brainstorming yields less results than a defunct think tank. Waning energy and smothering silence clog the air. *We've got nothing.*

With her eyes trained on Snickers' slumbering form, Riley huffs out a final frustrated sigh. "We can't venture very far, and it's got to be getting dark outside by now. Like, darker than it was from the ash. I think we have to take a lesson from the dog here."

"So the plan is to sniff out the perfect spot and drop our drawers outside?" I ask, dreading the inevitable.

Aidan chuckles, but it quickly evaporates when I shoot him a death glare.

"You got a better idea?" Riley counters. I numbly shake my head. I know. *She's right.* And this whole thing is our stupid dog's fault. If he hadn't tripped up Jeff, we'd all probably be sitting around a relaxing fire right now, singing Kumbaya and taking turns using the portable devices.

"What do we do with him?" I ask, motioning toward Aidan.

"I'm not your hostage, and I'm not completely helpless, you know," he vents. "Besides, Matt patched up my ankle."

"What?" Riley practically dives toward the hem of his pants leg to investigate.

"Yeah, he had a first aid kit in the cruiser, so he wrapped

my ankle. He doesn't think it's broken. Just sprained. As long as I keep weight off it as much as possible, I can hobble around."

Rising on her haunches, Riley slaps her thighs. "Alright then, let's do this."

Taking turns, under the cover of night, we follow Snickers' lead and use the nonexistent facilities outside. We tote a disposable water bottle with us to rinse our hands, but the lack of soap leaves me feeling germy.

We pick through the stacks of supplies just long enough to locate a stash of freeze-dried entrees. My excitement for the cheesy lasagna plummets when I scan the preparation directions, which require boiling water. Frustration builds as I scan the other foil pouches. *Why isn't this stuff like astronaut ice cream, where you just tear the pouch and chow down?*

As I'm contemplating tearing open the lasagna pouch and dumping bottled water into it, Riley squeals. She proudly displays the biggest bag of trail mix I've ever seen.

"Good enough," I say, my stomach growling at the sight. My body has two demands right now: food and rest.

I plop down next to Aidan and await my turn for the feed bag. We pass it around, scooping out serving after serving until the pouch is nearly empty. The blend of raisins, peanuts, and chocolate candies eases the churning hunger, leaving me in a dozing state of contentment.

"Guys," Riley starts, her voice timid. "You know the tracking…uh, tracker inside us…well, inside some of us—do you think anyone can pick it up in here?"

A wave of relief washes over me again that I don't have one. The thought of that thing "crawling" around inside Riley makes me itchy, like when the person next to you discovers a spider walking up their arm and flicks it off and you're convinced it's coming for you next.

Aidan scratches his chin in thought. "You know, if this tracker, or whatever it is, sends a signal out, I bet all the rocks in here would block it. Maybe right here, since we're close to an opening, a weak signal might make it through, but I bet once we're down below in the caves, they'd probably never be able to see our dots on that device."

Riley nods her head, a faraway look overtaking her eyes. "I like that idea. No one has the right to keep tabs on me, or any of us for that matter."

I sense that she's stewing about the element of control over unwilling or unsuspecting people, which probably reminds her of her time with Jim and Dan. I push those thoughts from my mind. There's enough clouding my mind right now without adding to it, and thankfully that part of our lives is over.

After a deep yawn escapes my lungs, Aidan taps my knee. "Looks like you could use some sleep." He flashes me a sympathetic smile.

"I'm betting we all could," I counter. My batteries are on serious backup power at this point and they're fading fast. Riley and Aidan must feel the same way, especially Aidan. I'm worried about his injury—that I'm sure he's downplaying. "Let's get your leg elevated and that ankle iced," I say, hopping up for a box or bag to prop below it. "I saw a few instant cold packs in there somewhere when I was digging for dinner options."

It's dark, but the flashlight we have propped in the corner illuminates his shocked expression. "Hey, my years on the track taught me more than how to collect trophies."

He nods in approval and gives no resistance as I slide a pack of supplies under his calf. "Thanks," he says, wincing a bit as I press the cold pack to his ankle while tying it in place with Snickers' leash.

Looking back and forth between us, he says, "Well, this isn't exactly ideal sleeping arrangements, but I thought we'd search the supplies Jeff brought for sleeping bags or blankets and then just crash right here." He spreads his arms out in front of him, motioning across the rectangular clearing that I'd estimate to be as wide and long as a refrigerator.

No one argues. It's better than outside and we have nowhere else to go. It's either right here or at the bottom of the steps. There's nothing in between.

Riley and I approach the stacked provisions once more. This time we give up even sooner than we did in the search for food. When I hold up two bright blue tarps that were stuffed inside a crate of lanterns and flashlights, the others brandish unenthusiastic thumbs up.

"That'll work," Aidan says, pushing himself into a standing position. We spread one tarp over the ground. The other will be tonight's blanket. Riley twitches slightly, an idea popping into her mind. She scurries to one of the cartons she sifted through earlier during our food search.

"I knew I remembered seeing these," she declares. "It's not much, but we can try to use them as pillows." She thrusts three rolls of paper towels toward us, balancing one between the other two. That reminds me, we've got to figure out the sleeping arrangements.

"Great idea!" Aidan says, a weary smile tugging his cheeks.

"So," I say, waving a hand over the tarp. "How do we want to do this?"

Aidan runs a hand through his hair and a slight tic shifts his jaw.

"Quinn, you sleep in the middle," Riley says. "You're the youngest, so you're stuck with the least comfortable spot." She shrugs, tilting her head, as if there's simply no other solution.

Whatever. I'm so exhausted, I could probably sleep on a bed of nails right now.

We tuck ourselves between the flimsy tarps. I flatten my paper towel roll as best I can, but I already know I'll be feeling a strain in my neck for days.

With my back to Aidan, I face Riley. When her brown eyes meet mine, she wiggles her eyebrows and mouths, "You're welcome."

Holding her amused gaze, I call a general "Goodnight" and switch the flashlight off, plunging us into absolute darkness.

Chapter 69

A soft whimpering tugs at the edges of my consciousness. My eyelids flutter open. Raising a hand to my face, I swipe away the crusted gunk that collected overnight in the corners of both eyes.

Every inch of my body throbs in agony. My mind must have blocked the pain while I slept, but as my senses return, every nerve makes its presence known.

The whimpering grows louder, or maybe the fog in my ears is starting to dissipate. Something cold and wet nudges my face, followed by a puff of warm air. *Dog breath.* Snickers must need to go out.

Dragging a sore arm across my chest, I paw at the darkness until my fingertips meet fur. "Hey, boy. You wanna go out?" I whisper. Snickers drags his tongue across my cheek, which normally wouldn't bother me. But given our lack of *facilities,* I'd really rather not have the scent of dog slobber wafting to my nose all day.

"Sure, girl! What'd you have in mind?" a gruff voice asks.

I jab my elbow to the right until it connects with his ribs.

"Oomph!" Aidan grunts.

"Oops, sorry!" I giggle.

"Sure, hit a guy when he's down," he mutters. "I guess that's what I get for trying to come between a girl and her dog."

"Oh my gosh, I forgot you're hurt! I am so sorry," my voice cracks with guilt. I roll on my side toward him. "Are you okay?"

He coughs, a pathetic rattle echoing within our small space. I lean closer but can barely see the outline of his face. "I swear, I wouldn't have done that if I remembered you were hurt."

The light switch snaps on, casting a yellow hue that reveals just how close my face is to Aidan's. We both squint our eyes, adjusting to the dim glow. A tapping sound, fueled by impatience, grows louder and faster, drawing our attention toward the door. *How on Earth did she wake up and get moving before me?*

"Come on, Snickers. Obviously, they're too busy flirting, but I'll take you out," Riley teases, smirking. My cheeks flush with fire and my heart nosedives.

"Thank you," I mouth to her, mortification blazing in my silent reply.

Using the outdoors as our bathroom is trickier this time. The sun glimpses through swirling, murky clouds. A slight breeze churns the haze around us. I can't tell if the air looks slightly clearer or if my eyes are adjusting to its contaminated tinge. Aidan said it would carry microscopic pollutants for weeks.

Either way, morning has dawned and even the limited daylight leaves me feeling exposed. We rush through the motions and return to the confines of our quarters. We devour what's left of the trail mix. While Aidan and I scour through the supplies in search of more food, Riley and Snickers dash downstairs for a quick check-in with Aidan's dad.

Aidan insists his ankle feels better but he staggers with a wavering gait. He wanted to talk to his dad directly, but Riley claimed the task before anyone could protest. I'm grateful she did. The last thing he should do is try to climb back down those steps when he's clearly in pain.

We settle on dried apricots and water for breakfast. While we wait for Riley to return, I refresh Snickers' bowls.

Soon enough, the echo of sneakers padding stone precedes her appearance.

Aidan immediately straightens, anxious for an update on his family and friends.

"Well, it sounds like they're doing okay, all things considered." Her eyes shift between us nervously while she gingerly swishes the toe end of her shoe around the dirt. *She knows what he really wants to ask.*

"Jeff's…not great. He can't feel his legs right now, but they don't have any strong medication to give him, so maybe he's just numb from the pain." She quickly shifts the conversation to a more hopeful topic.

"Matt's supposed to come back today with shovels and trowels, but until then, they're searching for weak spots on the other side." She clasps her hands together. "They want us to stay away from the collapse until Matt returns. They've got more manpower than us, and your dad said it'll be a slow and steady process."

Aidan runs a hand through his hair. "So we're just supposed to sit around and do nothing?"

"Actually, they want us to get that ham radio working," she says. "We're supposed to scan for broadcasts and try to gather what people are seeing and saying."

"Do we even have the radio?" I ask. "Or is it down there with them?"

Riley scurries to the remaining bags we didn't bother to carry downstairs before the collapse. She reaches in each, rooting through the contents, until a smile spreads across her face. "Jackpot!"

Chapter 70

Positioning the radio before Aidan, Riley and I crowd around him. He and Jeff had some time to play with the functions before we arrived here. Recognition flares in his eyes as he manipulates the switches.

He tunes through channels, searching for voices. It's unlike a typical FM radio, in that the sound is either nonexistent or clear. There's no static to blur the message. I wish there were. Our heads tilt to the floor in concentration, as if that helps us hear the broadcast better:

> *...inches, we've got inches of ash on the ground. The phones are down. Electricity's out. We've got food, but it won't last forever. I'll do whatever it takes for my family to survive.*

Does anyone have any idea how many are dead or missing? I'm in South Dakota and I can't reach any of the family I got in Montana. I've got a feeling that we're gonna find out real soon how many got the hell outta there, because they've gotta go somewhere. And we're just over the border.

All hell's broke loose. People are looting, taking whatever they need. I've got to provide for my family, but if I go out there and get shot, where does that leave them?

The more we hear, the less I want to know. While some voices are deeper than others, an air of panic wafts through each of them. Aidan flips the radio off and looks to us. "Maybe we can find an emergency broadcast message. You know, something official. These people we're hearing…we don't know if what they're saying is true."

I don't voice my disagreement, but if these people are lying, they're pretty good at it. They all sound anxious to me.

He turns the radio back on, manipulating the switches until we land on a disembodied female voice that reminds me of a newscaster:

Thanks for joining me today for The Frequence Sequence. I usually talk about timely tips and noteworthy news in the amateur radio world, but today's podcast focuses on a much heavier topic. Yellowstone.

We all know it's erupted. My sources tell me that

Wyoming, Montana, Idaho, and Colorado are smothering under feet of volcanic ash. Like an avalanche of a pretty nasty cocktail of splintered rock and glass.

And right at the source, it sounds like lava is oozing across the landscape—a fiery blob of destruction. We can only hope that anything in its path will escape before it's consumed.

The Midwest is faring a bit better but the ash blanketing its landscape will most certainly kill plants and animals, crush roofs and collapse structures, and short all sorts of electrical equipment.

Riley's hands tremble and my stomach tumbles. Aidan told us a lot of this would happen, but it wasn't real then. It was just a college kid sputtering off textbook scenarios. Hearing it in an official-sounding voice alters our reality once again.

I've got to get out of here, away from the words declaring our nation's collapse.

Chapter 71

Rocketing to my feet, I anxiously snatch my dust mask and Snickers' leash. Stunned, Aidan and Riley snap their heads up.

"I need some air. I've…gotta get out of here for a few minutes." Holding the leash up, I sweeten my tone. "Snickers, you wanna go out, boy?" He obliges, trotting over. I quickly affix the hook to his collar.

"You really shouldn't breathe in that air any more than you have to," Aidan cautions. "I know you've got your masks, but they're not exactly foolproof."

"Snickers needs to go out," I insist, shifting from one foot to the other. Never mind that I planted the idea in his little brain.

Riley rises, swiping dust off her pants. "I'll come too. Unless you'd rather not have company." *She's probably eager to get away from this too.*

"Always room for one more," I say, plastering a smile across my face. I raise my eyebrows at Aidan.

"Alright," he says slowly. "Don't go too far, okay? I'll stay here and keep listening. My dad was right. We've got to know what people are saying out there."

We push out the creaky door, stopping to jam the wooden doorstop into the opening so we can slip back inside upon our return. Trailing behind Snickers, he leads us around the building. The sun's valiant effort to shine is once again thwarted by murky clouds. *I guess this is pretty mild compared to areas that have inches or feet of ash.*

"So, what do you think's going to happen?" Riley asks quietly. "I thought that things would stay relatively calm around here and we'd just need to wait for the ash to clear. But how realistic is that when the other side of the country has to dig itself out with no electricity and phone lines down? What happens when they run out of basic necessities?"

"They're already looting," I say. "And this just happened. I think once they run out of places to loot, they'll move on. To places that still have supplies. To anywhere that's better off than where they are."

"Like East," she mutters. "I really wish Aunt Robin came with us." I nod, worry twisting my insides.

"I wonder where Aidan's cell phone ended up?" I question. "Maybe we could try to call her." Riley nods enthusiastically.

"Yeah, we can still convince her to come with us."

Sirens wail in the distance but otherwise an unnatural calm descends upon the landscape. The air is charged, as if each molecule hovers in anticipation of further injury. The fur along

Snickers' spine raises and he dashes back to the cave entrance. Trusting his instinct, we stumble but keep up and clamber back inside. *Will anything ever be "normal" again? Besides losing our parents, it feels like all sense of structure and society are slipping through our fingers with every passing minute.*

When we return, Aidan's still fixated on the radio. This time a deep voice fills the chamber. The slow, smooth drawl would be best suited for a honey-coated bedtime story; instead, it wields paranoia:

> *Think about it. There are so many ways people set themselves up to be monitored. Cell phones, fitness trackers, GPS systems…if one entity gathered all that information, it could keep an eye on almost all of us. And even for those who don't have any of that stuff, how many live with someone who does? So, bam! Big brother is always watching.*

Aidan switches the radio off and rakes a hand through his hair. His wide eyes intently watch our approach. His skin reflects the dim yellow lights, brandishing an unhealthy pallor. I've never seen anyone display withdrawal symptoms, but that's what comes to mind—a doomsday information junkie who just lost his last connection to conspiracy theorists.

Snickers darts inside, nudging himself into Aidan's legs, knocking the radio aside. My heart jumps in the half-second before Aidan snatches it, saving it from the short tumble from his lap to the ground. He smirks, ruffling Snicker's ears. It wouldn't have been funny if the radio had met the ground violently. That dog has caused enough harm. We don't need him damaging the radio too.

Riley plops down next to Aidan, dropping her hands in her lap. "So, did you hear anything interesting?" A subtle defeat lingers in her tone. She's just being polite. She doesn't really want to know.

"Nothing good." His head sways back and forth in disbelief. "How are we ever going to recover from this? Food, gas, clean air, electricity. It's not like someone can just flip a switch and restore everything."

"Maybe we should just focus on the here and now," Riley says gently. She looks to me for support, but I have no reserve of encouragement, let alone any to share. *He's right. And there's nothing we can do but wait to see what happens.*

The swiveling door handle clicks as someone on the other side attempts to open it. But since it locks automatically from the inside, it doesn't budge. Aidan lifts Snickers, relocating him to the ground before attempting to stand. Riley starts to protest but he cuts her off. "My legs are numb. I've got to get some blood circulating." He pushes away from us, limping toward the door before he cautiously swings it open.

We recognize our visitor right away. Matt's arrival carves a welcome break in the conversation. I'm getting used to people walking around with masks covering half of their face. Closing the door, he tips the bug-like respirator over his head and nods in our direction.

Clasping an arm around Aidan's shoulder, Matt comments, "You're already getting around better. How's that ankle feel?"

Glancing our way before he responds, I sense any answer he

gives will downplay his true condition.

"Pretty good," he murmurs. Pointing toward Matt's back, he asks. "You bring us some presents?"

Matt shrugs off the longest backpack I've ever seen. The yellow and red fabric extends from his shoulders to the middle of his thighs. Its rectangular form reminds me of a tent or canopy case. He lowers it to the ground, the contents clanking with each shift.

Leaning down to unzip the top, he retrieves our digging tools—two black folding shovels and two vicious-looking half-axe, half-murder weapons. I was sort of hoping for some electric tool that did most of the work for you. These look very labor-intensive.

Placing his hands on his thighs, he pushes upright. "We're busting through there today. I'm shipping out tomorrow. I'm needed closer to the impact zone." His hard expression dissuades any questions.

Aidan drops a hand on Matt's shoulder. "Thanks for coming back. And for bringing tools. I really appreciate it." With a solemn nod, Matt grabs the long-handled pick-like tools and breezes past us, starting down the stairs. Riley grabs the shovels and follows him.

I step toward Aidan and quietly suggest, "Maybe you should stay here and rest your ankle. The three of us can handle this."

He raises a palm in protest. "No. That's my family down there. Nothing's going to keep me from getting to them."

I raise my hand. "I understand. Just…know that it's okay if you need a break or anything."

"You'll be the first to know, okay?" he teases. "If you're so worried about me, you should probably escort me down the steps. You know, sort of like a crutch I can lean on."

I smile and nudge a shoulder under his armpit. *So far, this manual labor thing isn't so bad.*

Chapter 72

Our descent down the stairs is much faster than the last time we traversed them. Although it was only a day ago, it feels like so much has happened since then.

When we reach the bottom, Matt's already worked out a plan with Aidan's dad, their raised voices echoing through the chamber. They pinpoint the spot that Aidan's family started digging into on their side. That's where we'll target while they distance themselves in case the rock wall shifts.

Matt confirms that we're breaking through to the other side today. The natural confidence flowing from his words and movement convinces me that he's right. And I'll do anything in my power to fulfill that goal. We *need* to reach Jeff. Although I secretly hope that Aidan's dad exaggerated the injury or that Jeff's made some miraculous improvements overnight, I'm prepared to help him—and anyone else who might have been hurt in the collapse—however I can.

For the next several hours, we slowly and carefully dig away portions of the wall. We take breaks only when needed—either because Snickers demands some outside time or one of us requires a quick trip the non-existent *facilities*.

The process is mostly quiet, other than the clanking of metal meeting stone. Most of the pile is dirt and smaller rock that tumbles away when one of us jams a sturdy tool into a weakened spot. I hope we're doing the right thing and not unknowingly triggering a second collapse. If we end up buried down here, there's no one left to rescue us. Everyone else is trapped even deeper within these depths.

My limbs grow heavier with each round of our choreographed smash-smash-dig-dig routine. Every inch of progress propels dust particles into the air. What begins as a mild cough quickly morphs into Riley's body shuddering as a hacking fit overtakes her. Matt's concerned eyes meet Aidan's.

"Let's take a break and grab some water," Matt suggests. "We could all use some hydration."

We make the climb to the top of the steps—to the cleanest air we can access. I assume my position as Aidan's crutch. It's a comfortable closeness, even amid the dust, dirt, and sweat.

Plopping to the ground, we gulp the slightly chilled water, naturally cooled by the dampness of the dark environment. Spotting the idle radio, Aidan's forehead creases before he snatches it and settles back against the wall.

Switching it on, he deftly scrolls through stations. I'm really not in the mood to hear some nameless voice rattling on about how awful everything is or how it's all about to get worse.

Aidan stills when a succession of beeps screeches from the

unit. Snickers emits a low growl, but Riley quickly shushes him. Anticipation chokes the air, weighing heavy between us.

This is President Taves. As a nation, we are in a full-fledged state of emergency. Some of our homes are destroyed. Some of our friends and family are lost. And for many, hope may feel out of reach right now.

We have one hell of a mountain to climb, but we will climb it. Together. Of that I am certain. I am asking you to remember who we are. The United States of America. When we stand united, we can overcome any challenge. And today I challenge you to reject lapses in judgement and consider the needs of all as we strive to ensure adequate resources for all Americans. Those in both primary and secondary impact zones.

We must maintain order. The next several months will be difficult. There is no doubt. But we will overcome the devastation. I ask you to rise with me to rebuild and restore what has been lost.

I have deployed our military and law enforcement personnel into action. Every American, those facing the direct effects of Yellowstone's eruption or secondary impacts, must follow local authority's direction. This is the only way we can avert chaos and forge ahead on the path to recovery.

If you are hearing this, you are located in a secondary impact zone. Until further notice, you will shelter in place. Once our forces have ensured that impact zone survivors have been assigned to and settled within government-created safety communes, focus will shift to the outlying areas.

Stay safe, follow instructions, and lend a helping hand to your neighbors when possible. I will provide updates of our progress in the coming days.

The repeated succession of beeps signals the end of the broadcast. Aidan switches the radio off and shifts his gaze to Matt. "Is that where you're going tomorrow? Right to the belly of the beast?"

With just a blink of hesitation, Matt nods. I'm not sure if he doesn't elaborate because Riley and I are here or if he's sworn to secrecy. Or maybe he just doesn't want to talk about it.

The reminder of his impending trip escalates the urgency in our task. What's it even like where he's going if people are already looting? Would someone hesitate to shoot if he was the only thing standing between them and food they needed for their family?

I shake the thought away. I can't change what he does. I can barely control what our sixteen-pound dog does, let alone a grown man I barely know who is dedicated to serving in law enforcement.

Swigging the last gulps of water from my bottle, I swipe the back of my hand across the drips on my lips.

"How about we get back to work?" I say, pushing my tired muscles to move. Sleeping on the hard floor last night only compounds my discomfort, but that wall isn't going to remove itself. Aidan and Riley narrow their eyes my way. I know what they're both thinking. *Did* you *really just say that?*

Matt's hazel eyes land on me, too. But they bear respect. He never needs to know how much I hate this task. Or the way my body yearns to flop like a seal on a pier. I can push through if it means he'll get to see his family before he has to leave.

"That is a great idea," Matt agrees, rising to his feet.

Aidan chuckles and pushes a hand through his hair. "Alright, back at it. I just need my crutch." I smile shyly but oblige. This may be my favorite part of the process.

Riley exhales a tired sigh before following. Slightly renewed, we return to the depths.

Chapter 73

By the time we open a viable hole in the tunnel, I'm ready to crumple to the ground and sleep for a week. I don't need a pillow or blankets. Once every cell in my body can ease into a state of rest, I won't care where I am.

Matt tests the opening, jamming the flat head of his digging tool around the edges. Satisfied that the opening is secure, he throws a hand up in a "Stay" gesture. A moment later, he turns and dashes through the opening.

Aidan peers through the hole we made. It's wide enough for two of us to pass through at one time. It's also tall enough for Aidan's nearly six-foot-frame to cross without brushing the jagged, rocky ceiling. Just how long those walls will stand without crumbling, who knows.

What starts as a slow sway of Snickers' tail turns into a full swish thumping the floor. Voices carry to my ears and a broad smile spreads across Aidan's face. Forgetting his faithful human crutch, he pushes through the opening and meets his family on the other side.

Riley and I stay in place, the only ones excluded from this reunion. Snickers takes off, unable to resist the celebration. Hugs and laughter spill through the cavern, drifting past us. A sharp churn in my gut reminds me that we have no part in the overflowing familial joy. We're just two orphaned sisters along for the ride. Again.

When the voices die down, Aidan beckons us. "I think it's safe to come through. Come on over."

With all eyes on us, we mosey through the tunnel and join the group. I can tell by the side-eye glances Riley throws my way that she feels just as misplaced as I do.

Aidan launches into formal introductions. We had officially met his dad already, but we were supposed to meet the others that first night. The last time I saw them, they were all scurrying about the interconnecting rooms, carrying and organizing supplies.

The names and faces blur before me. I nod and shake hands, forcing my cheeks to lift, forming a plastered smile. Bright blue eyes and deep brown hair easily identify Aidan's sisters. They both look younger than me, but not by much. I'd guess they're around thirteen and fifteen. A smattering of freckles dances across the slightly shorter one's nose.

Their mother's hair reminds me of honey. Even in the dull light, it reflects a soft shine. She's the only one in the family without ocean-hued eyes. Her rich brown irises mirror my own.

Matt and Jeff's parents greet us similarly. Their names leave my brain just as quickly as they enter. It's overwhelming being thrust into this cohesive clan.

Riley officially introduces Snickers, but my guess is they've all already heard about him. *Hopefully, they don't blame him, and by extension us, for Jeff's fall.*

Clapping his hands together once, Aidan's dad announces, "I think someone over here would love to see you all." His sad smile doesn't reach his eyes.

Scott leads us to the first opening that branches off to the left of the main room. It's the size of a small bedroom, and other than having a dirt floor and rock walls, it's really not that bad. Worn red milk crates serve as a dresser and end table, flanking the short ends of a blue inflatable air mattress.

Jeff lies atop a crumpled blue sleeping bag, his neck slightly propped up on a thin pillow.

"Hey, it's about time you checked out my bachelor pad." Although the words are definitely something I would expect, they lack his usual playfulness. Although he's in a resting position, his body looks stiff and uncomfortable.

Snickers pushes through our legs and jumps on the mattress to douse Jeff with kisses. "Hey, another visitor," Jeff says, completely lacking enthusiasm.

"What is it about you that drives all the dogs wild?" Aidan jokes half-heartedly. No one laughs.

Matt cuts to the chase. He's got the least amount of time to spend here. Kneeling beside his brother, he asks, "How are you?"

Jeff rubs his chin, smirking.

322

I imagine he's conjuring a response that has to do with how much better off he'd be with some French fries and fountain soda.

Matt stares intently, awaiting a response.

Breathing out a frustrated sigh, Jeff matches his brother's seriousness. "Damn tunnel nearly crushed me. Dad and Scott dragged me out from the rubble. Mom was hysterical. Everything hurt like hell for what felt like weeks. I know it wasn't that long, but it feels like it when you're lying around with nothing to do but focus on the pain.

"They gave me what they had, which wasn't much… ibuprofen…sleeping pills. I can't tell if the pain is starting to fade or if I'm just getting used to it. Whatever part of my body doesn't hurt is just numb. I don't know what's worse. I'm just… broken."

Matt slides toward the other end of the bed and gently grasps Jeff's left foot.

"Can you feel that?" he asks, watching Jeff's reaction closely. Jeff shakes his head *no*. Matt continues, working his reach along the side of Jeff's leg. They pause every few inches, but the routine repeats itself until Matt touches Jeff's side, just above his waist. It's the first time he acknowledges that he can feel Matt's touch.

My stomach drops and bile rises in my throat. His legs are paralyzed. *And it's all our fault.*

Chapter 74

"You guys should have some privacy to talk. Quinn and I will go see what we can do to help around here." Riley places a hand on my shoulder and I gladly oblige, following her out to the main room. My muscles scream at the thought of being pushed even further, but staying here, watching heartbreak unfold, fills me with a strangling guilt. Every nerve in my body demands that I flee. Snickers trails behind us. His biggest concern right now seems to be keeping up with us while attempting to sniff every crack and crevice at or below his eye level.

We find Aidan's dad and Riley asks him how we can pitch in. Clasping his hands together, he asks us to follow him. Leading us through the main room, he makes two right turns, traversing the snaking tunnels before stopping at an opening that reminds me of the one Jeff's in.

"I know it's not exactly the Hilton, but it's yours," he says, sweeping an arm across the space. "This is how we set up all the rooms. And it'll only be for a few weeks."

"Thank you," Riley whispers. Her voice cracks. I know she's overcome with emotion, just as I am. These people don't even know us and yet they took the time to set up a space to make us comfortable.

Just like Jeff's quarters, an inflatable mattress consumes most of the space. It's pushed against the wall with identical green sleeping bags spread over it, topped with two of the smallest pillows I've ever seen. Each is about half the size of a normal pillow. Compared to a paper-towel roll it looks luxurious.

"There are extra blankets in the supplies Jeff brought. Make sure you grab some. We're all going to have to get used to how cold it is down here." Scott's eyes convey an insistence. Although I did notice a temperature drop when we came in from the outside and then again when we descended all the steps, the thick air cooled my overextended body with each trip. I didn't mind the chill, but now that I'm not hauling supplies or serving as Aidan's human crutch, I can definitely see the need for more layers of warmth.

After a quick nod of agreement, I survey the rest of our space. Charcoal gray milk crates line both ends of the makeshift bed. The two closest to the pillow-end contain lanterns and flashlights. Both crates at the foot-end are empty. I'm guessing those are for our personal effects. Most of our bags have been deposited on the floor. We still have a few to bring down all those stairs, but it's nice to see our belongings again.

"Dad." Aidan's voice startles me. I didn't even hear him

approach. Maybe that limp is improving. "Matt's gotta go soon. Can you come talk with him and his parents before he goes?"

"Sure, son." With a brief nod, Aidan's dad retreats.

The three of us stand in uncomfortable silence. In the ten minutes since I last saw Aidan, any hint of lingering happiness from reuniting with his family has dissipated. His shoulders have slumped, and worry etches wrinkles across his forehead.

Riley's eyes flash with concern. "Aidan," she starts gently. "I know everything is not okay, but are you…is there anything we can do?" She stumbles over her words, but her intentions are clear.

He clutches his forehead and squeezes as if ridding his mind of all thought. "There's nothing any of us can do. Jeff needs a doctor, or a hospital, but Matt says it's a mess out there. The military is setting up those safety communes and they're filling up as fast as they're set up."

Dropping his palms to his sides, he squeezes his eyes shut. "Matt was our best connection to the outside world, and to getting any help, and now he's got to go. Their parents are a wreck. There's nothing anyone can do. Everything's just falling apart. Everything my dad planned…it's falling apart."

We're helpless. Even with adults here and making the decisions, there are no clear solutions. Frustration is wearing on everyone. When we arrived, the mood down here was positive and cooperative as the others rushed to sort supplies. Now somberness hangs like dark clouds in the chilled air.

"What about the safety communes?" Riley asks thoughtfully. "Could we go there? If they have medical people there, maybe they would let us in and help us."

"You heard Taves," Aidan mutters with defeat. "He said we're in a secondary zone. We pretty much need to behave and stay self-sufficient until they're able to help us."

"Besides," he adds. "From what Matt describes, these *communes* are like warehouses. Rows of beds and cots with sheets hanging between families as privacy curtains. Community bathrooms and showers. Limited food rations. Other than having no medical people, I think we have it better down here."

"That sounds pretty awful," I agree. At least down here Riley and I have our own room, even if it only has three walls. And I'm not worried about our safety with Aidan's and Jeff's families. But a warehouse full of strangers? With only a sheet to shield us and the last of our belongings from people who will probably grow more desperate for stability each day?

"Anyway, I've got to get back out there. I'd like to catch Matt before he goes," Aidan says.

I already miss the fire that sometimes flares behind those blue eyes. Right now, it's smothered with worry and defeat.

"Do you need some help?" I ask, trying not to broadcast my anticipation. There's so little to look forward to right now but the physical closeness of being his crutch brings me comfort.

"No, I can do it." His words sting. Dropping my gaze to the ground, I swish my stringy hair forward in an attempt to cover my cheeks, which flush crimson with battered pride.

"Oh, hey." He must sense my hurt, but I'd rather his indifference than pity. "Quinn, I love using you as a crutch. It's just...I don't want the others to know about my ankle. Everyone's got enough to worry about. The last thing they need is to see me hobbling around here like I'm half-helpless."

Even in the midst of our setbacks, I suppress a smile. *It's not me. He just doesn't want to worry his family.* "I understand. It's okay." I shake my head casually, as if I've got no cares in the world.

"So, what should we do now," Riley asks, rocking on her heels awkwardly. "We told your dad we could help with whatever he needed. He brought us here to show us our room, but that's as far as we got."

Aidan rakes a hand through his hair, which has lost the wayward tufts I've grown accustomed to. I'm guessing the days of not washing have a lot to do with it.

"Well, I know he's already sent my sisters up to bring down as much as they can carry. I think he wants to get all the stuff down here and then work on sealing the door."

Riley and I nod gravely. We knew this was coming. But we also know that it lessens the chances of our aunt joining us down here. I don't believe she has any intention of leaving her home, but the unknowns frighten me. *What if she's forced to leave? What if someone tries to hurt her?* The unanswered questions will spiral on a repeated loop and consume my thoughts if I let them.

"Let's head back out to the main area. The sooner we can get the rest of the supplies down here, the sooner we can get some rest. I don't know about you two, but I was ready to call it a day about five hours ago."

Too weary to even nod, Riley and I follow Aidan back through the maze of tunnels.

Chapter 75

We find the others crowded together in Jeff's room, alternating between wishing Matt luck and sniffling back their sadness. Aidan's family files out first, heading to the stone steps leading upward. Rather than intrude on Matt's send-off, I nod to Riley in a silent understanding and we trail just a few steps behind Aidan's dad.

Eyes wide with surprise, he waves us off. "You girls relax. You've done enough work today. We'll take care of the rest." Relief floods my muscles, relaxing my entire frame. I didn't realize my neck and shoulders were stiff until those words granted us reprieve.

"Thank you," Riley answers. Together, we return to our room and collapse on the mattress. Lying on my side, I turn away from my sister and allow guilt to silently stream from my eyes. My thoughts turn to Jeff. *As if everything isn't bad enough, he's hurt and if we weren't here, the accident never would have happened.* I hold my body as still as possible, just further fraying my nerves.

After replaying scenarios of how much better off Aidan and Jeff would be if they never met us, exhaustion finally takes hold and my vision floats in and out of focus. Our loyal ball of fur hops onto the bed and curls up between us. Swiping away the silent tears, I bury my face in the tiny pillow. My senses fade and I enter a state of desolate relaxation.

My body must freeze in place because the next sensation I feel is a gentle shaking, pulling me from the dark haze of sleep. Forcing my groggy eyes to flutter open, Aidan's face appears inches from my own.

"Is there anyone alive in there?" he asks as he peers at me, awaiting a reaction. Arching my back, I stretch my arms over my head, compelling my muscles to wake. Everything aches. Warm wetness confirms that my mouth was even too weak to hold back its contents. I swipe away a line of drool dribbling from the corner of my mouth and across my cheek to meet the pillow.

Aidan eyes the darkened wet spot on the pillowcase. "Well, that is definitely yours from now on. You kind of claimed it." He covers his mouth, pretending to hide a chuckle.

"Very funny," I croak. Geez, even my throat craves more rest.

"Sorry." His smile conveys anything but regret. "Anyway, my dad sent me to get you two. And I'm not even gonna try to wake her." He points at Riley. He's known her long enough to shy away from the nearly impossible task of waking her.

"What's up? Did something happen?" Worry expedites my

initial hesitance to move.

"No, no. It's getting to be dinner time and he wants us all to be on the same schedule. Plus, you two need the tour. There's a place for everything and everything has a place. My dad loves to say that." He rolls his eyes. "Just come out to the main room when you're ready."

"Aidan? Is there somewhere we can *freshen up*?" I cringe, already disliking whatever answer he'll give.

"Hold that thought. It's part of the tour."

After several minutes of coaxing Riley awake, I explain that our presence is requested in the main room. The hint of a salty, beefy scent drifts to my nose. I hope it's not some kind of aroma oasis and my mind is tricking me into believing that delicious hot food awaits us.

Riley catches a whiff too. Her eyes perk open wide and she waggles her eyebrows. "Smell that?" I nod. Neither of us can restrain hunger-induced smiles. Hastily, we run fingers through the rats' nests that were once stick-straight brown manes. I track fingertips around my lips, checking for any dried drool spots. Straightening our shirts and pants from any residual slumber bunching, we're as presentable as it gets.

Allowing the aroma to serve as our guide, we stride toward the main room.

Chapter 76

The group's been busy in the time we slept. New stacks of supplies, what must have been the remaining cartons at the top of the stairs, now line the room. Three small metal folding tables are clustered in the center of the space. Folding chairs stand at attention, tucked just beneath the surface of each table. Enough for all of us.

Each of the ten place settings comprises a plastic plate, flannel cloth napkin, and a utensil set that may be a folded pocketknife that grew a fork on one side and a spoon on the other.

Aidan's dad is the first to greet us. "Thanks for joining us. We'll talk more at dinner, but would you two like to visit the washroom before we get started?"

I nod furiously, unable to contain my excitement. "Washroom? Yes!" *Could it be? An actual bathroom down here?*

"Aidan, why don't you show these ladies where they can wash up before dinner?" *Wash up? Like with soap and steamy water?* It feels like the dampness and darkness of our current accommodations have erased any trace of the last shower I had. My only consolation is that Riley and Aidan must be just as dusty and dirty as I am right about now.

Obliging, Aidan moseys over, grabbing a lantern and beckoning for us to follow him. Several tunnels jut out from the main room. He chooses the middle one. The dim light of the lantern bounces off the enclosure as we walk. Sections of the rock wall glisten from drips of water slithering down them. It's unnerving how drops randomly land on me. Where's the source? I could ask Aidan but then he'd probably launch into a twenty-minute explanation. And I've got more pressing questions right now.

Once we're out of earshot, I tap his shoulder. "Why didn't you tell us there's an *actual bathroom* here?"

Slowing his pace, he scratches his head and clenches his teeth as if a sudden discomfort has overtaken him. "Um…well, because my dad likes to…he sometimes likes to make things sound somewhat…better than they actually are."

This time I grab his shoulder, halting any forward movement. "What do you mean exactly?"

Pressed against a wall, figuratively and almost literally, he paints us a mental map of the set-up.

The *washroom* consists of a portable toilet that the dads will take turns emptying. I don't ask where exactly and I hope to never find out. Aidan explains that the full tank can weigh more than thirty pounds, and no one wants that spilling, so only those comfortable lifting at least thirty pounds are allowed to empty it. *I will gladly shirk that duty.* Of course, Aidan interjects that he could easily carry that weight, but he's willing to pretend that he can't in this case.

Allegedly the toilet has some feature to contain the smell. *I guess we'll see.* That brings Aidan to his next point, and the next part of the tour. The *wash* part of *washroom*. Apparently, there's another set of steps at this end of the cavern. They lead to a few small rooms with shallow pools of water as well as one large opening that contains an interior lake. There's even a small dock and a few motorboats that were used to ferry tourists along the canal-like routes between rock formations.

We'll use those only if we have to, but for now we've got to finish setting up this tiny working community.

Next, Aidan introduces us to the bathing room. It's located at the very edge of the cavern, a hike away from the main room. I can see why they chose this one. Thick rock walls enclose all but the narrow opening. We squeeze through to peer into the dark space. Its depth within the cave system offers privacy but with that comes little light.

"You'll need to bring a lantern with you anytime you come here," Aidan explains. "And there's a…*schedule*," he coughs on the word, "so that everyone has privacy and it's clear when this room is in use."

"Geez, your dad really loves details, huh?" Riley asks.

Aidan chuckles. "That's an understatement." He runs a hand through his hair and sighs. "I know it sounds kind of overwhelming, but we do need order, and having a schedule that we all follow just sets this up to work like a well-oiled machine."

I'm guessing that throughout his life he's heard that phrase more times than I can count.

"Okay, so we all share one tiny toilet and the same bathwater. What else you got?" I don't mean to sound unappreciative, but I wouldn't mind some surprise amenity right now. Like maybe there's some stealthy snack bar tucked away down here, and if we just flip a switch, some hot cheesy nachos will pop out of a secret compartment in the wall. Or maybe there's a movie room where they show videos about how the cave formed and other sleep-inducing topics. But we could rig it to show actual movies. Yep, we'll visit the snack bar and load up on junk food and then settle in to watch a movie. As long as it's not about cave-dwelling monsters whose hobbies include dining on humans.

"Wait," Riley interjects. "What about Snickers? Where will he…you know, do his business?"

"My dad has a designated space for that too. I'll show you on our way back to the main supply room." The reality of our current accommodations permeates my muscles like a dense weight. *How long will we have to live like this?*

When I tune back into the conversation, Aidan's explaining something about another room like the one we just left. It will be used to wash dishes.

"And nothing but organic soap," Aidan proclaims. "Chemicals could cause a lot of damage down here, so we have natural cleaners to use when we wash dishes or bathe."

So much for that magic snack bar and movie theater.

Before returning to the main cavern, we take turns using the washroom facilities and rinsing our hands in the bathing room water. *And to think I was once worried about walking around without shoes in an arcade-pizza place.*

Although the tour was a little disappointing, there's still a hot meal coming my way. That becomes more apparent with each step. The heavenly scent grows stronger, sending my stomach into a churning frenzy.

"Ah, just in time," Aidan's dad greets us. He sweeps an arm over the one empty table and motions for us to sit. Aidan's sisters and mom sit at one table, one empty seat for his dad. Jeff's parents sit at the other table. Although Jeff's positioned between then, he's reclined in a lawn chair. *How's he going to eat like that?* His face is downcast, and misery emanates from his spirit like smoke from a doused fire.

Someone must have carried him out here. There's no way he could have walked. Instantly I mourn for the Jeff I met just weeks ago. The one that smiled and laughed all the time. My heart aches for what he's lost, and I pray that it's temporary.

We take our seats and Aidan's dad passes a large bowl of chili to each table. We serve ourselves family-style. While everyone is busy dishing out their dinner, Riley whispers to Aidan, "Why isn't Jeff sitting up?" *I guess she noticed too.* Glancing around as if to gauge if anyone is paying us any attention, Aidan uncomfortably answers under his breath.

"He tried to sit up earlier before Matt left and he got really lightheaded. We had to lower him right back down. I bet it happened again before we got back from your tour."

Inhaling a deep breath, I try to exhale the overwhelming guilt that consumes my mind. If we hadn't come here, Snickers wouldn't be here, and he wouldn't have tripped Jeff on the steps.

I force down a few bites of food, but my hunger has dissipated, replaced by remorse. Since we're all gathered, Aidan's dad decides to use the time to explain how things will work while we're down here. I'm grateful for a distraction.

He explains that all of the cooking equipment is set up now. It includes a camping stove and cook station, among other things I don't know how to use. Although we have freeze dried meals, we'll use up the fresh food first. Then we'll start fishing in the interior lake. In case we end up down here longer than expected, we've got to ration our food carefully.

I hate seafood and the thought of catching, cooking, and eating fish nearly turns my stomach. Pushing the thought from my head—I'll deal with that when it happens. Meanwhile, I savor every delightful bite of chili.

Chapter 77

When dinner ends, we all collect the dirty dishes and utensils. Aidan's mom volunteers herself and her daughters to wash them. His dad approaches us, asking if we can take care of sealing the door. He's got to help relocate Jeff and clear away the folding furniture for the evening. And now that Matt's gone, he doesn't plan on opening it for a few weeks.

Riley and I scrunch our faces, no idea how to fulfill his request. But Aidan nods somberly. "Sure."

We trek back up the stairs empty-handed. Riley and I can claim complete ignorance, but Aidan seems to understand what his dad needs. I'm surprised we aren't bringing any tools with us.

When we reach the top of the steps, the space looks bigger, more open than I remember. Other than a small pile of hardware, some long tubes, and a drill, the lack of boxes, along with the absence of our makeshift camp, colors the space with a dull emptiness.

"So what's the plan?" Riley asks the question that's consuming my mind as well.

Aidan lifts a giant screw. It's longer and thicker than any carrot our garden ever produced. But its sharp point and threaded snaking tendrils create a much more ominous tone than a harmless orange vegetable.

"We're going to take these, a bunch of them, and drive them, like spikes, through the frame and into the door. They'll hold the door in a closed position until we're ready to remove them and open it."

That sounds barbaric. I can tell Aidan's not exactly thrilled about this task, so I don't voice my opinion.

"Then, once it's sealed that way, we take the rolls of plastic sheeting and cover the frame. Kind of a weak attempt to block the air flow. But, it's better than nothing."

"Are you qualified to do all this?" I ask, inspecting the array of tools before us. "Maybe your dad should be here too?" He shakes his head in mock indignation.

"I've helped him with home improvement projects for years. Trust me, I know what I'm doing," he says. As if to prove his point, he sets to work.

Dropping the screw and snatching the drill, Aidan stands tall, eyeing where he'll bore the first hole. Those crystal blue eyes zoom into focus, calculating angles and depth. After a few seconds, he raises the drill but hesitates before depressing the trigger.

"This is it," Aidan sighs, looking at us expectantly. "Your last chance to escape." A hint of insecurity tugs at his toothy smile, as if we might just push past him, leaving him and this place.

"Sorry, Aidan," Riley laughs. "You're stuck with us."

I nod my agreement.

As the first screw punctures the metal door, faces flash through my mind. Sergeant Bowen. Without him, we'd probably still be on that base. Thank goodness he took a chance on us. And gave us a way home.

Jasmine and her parents. Chris. Rose. Benny. I hope they're all okay and that we can see them again. *I have no idea if that's even possible, but I don't want to think about that now.*

Memories of our parents creep from the shadows of my mind, never far from the forefront. I'd like to think they're here with us in some way. Maybe watching over us, sometimes cringing but mostly proud that we've made it this far. And that we're together.

Realization strikes like a lightning bolt. The two people I care most about in this world stand right here, and I'm lucky enough to still have them in my life. Emotion swells in a wave rolling from my chest to my limbs. My eyes glaze over, threating to spill tears.

Any caution or self-consciousness I'd normally hold fades into the shadow of powerful feelings. The moment the first screw is embedded, I wrap one arm around Riley and the other around Aidan, drawing them closer. After a blink of startled hesitation, they both return my embrace. In silence, we allow ourselves to enjoy the simple comfort a hug can bring.

I don't know what will be on the other side of that door when we emerge from here, but I do know one thing. I'll do whatever it takes to keep the people I care about safe and by my side.

AUTHOR NOTE

Dear Reader,

We've made it just over halfway through this series! I hope this installment of Quinn and Riley's story did not disappoint. In a world where our attention is demanded from every angle, thank you for choosing to spend some time buried in my characters' ongoing saga!

If you haven't yet, please consider leaving a review for each of my books that you've read on Amazon and/or Goodreads. Reviews are a huge help to authors, and they help readers find books they are likely to enjoy.

Up next, book 4 in the series will be a novella titled *Allegiance Unravels* and it will explore Sergeant Bowen's back—and side—stories. It will provide a perspective on how decisions about handling natural disasters came to be made and executed. I hope you enjoy this deeper dive into information that Quinn and the gang may never learn.

Until then, let's stay connected. I'm active on social media and distribute an e-newsletter whenever I have news to share. Visit my website to sign up. I also attend several signing events throughout the year, so watch the Events page on my website to check if I'm coming to a location near you!

ACKNOWLEDGEMENTS

Michelle Preast of Indie Book Cover Designs, once again you've created an amazing cover that perfectly represents the story within its pages. Thank you for sharing your amazing skills. I could not be happier with the finished product!

Cate Pearce, MA EMHS, thank you for offering advice and support to the Twitter #WritingCommunity. Your disaster-management knowledge is fascinating! Thank you for helping me shape this book, incorporating what could happen as well as what could be believable in my fictitious world.

Angie and Chris, I cannot thank you enough for patiently answering all of the military-base questions I threw your way. Your willingness to help me in this area of research is much appreciated! And I look forward to asking you many more questions!! ☺

Marilyn Krepps, Kennel Manager at the York County SPCA, thank you for sharing your knowledge of dogfighting operations with me. This was the most difficult topic I've researched for this series and I hope that someday soon this vile activity ceases altogether. Special shout-out to the **York County SPCA:** We met our Jasmine at your shelter and truly appreciate your staff's help in matching us with her and the care they provided when she was found as a stray in the city. She is very loved and pampered, and we thank you for entrusting us with her.

Emily Angeline, Robin Asick & Beth Suit, once again I thank you for the insightful feedback you provide as beta readers!

ACKNOWLEDGEMENTS

Your suggestions challenge the story, thereby improving the plot, descriptions, and character reactions. At this point, I can't imagine writing a book without having your eagle eyes review it before it's released into the world. ☺

Vanessa Anderson at Night Owl Freelance Editing, thanks for always pushing me to flesh out the best concept or phrase—especially with the hardest parts, like the tagline and blurbs! ☺ I love bouncing ideas off of you and your industry expertise continues to amaze me. And your wicked sense of humor is a bonus that deserves its own mention!

Friends & Family Members, I appreciate your encouragement and enthusiasm in celebrating the tiny milestones! Bonus points for those of you who actually read one (or more) of my books and posted reviews!!! Also, I greatly enjoy incorporating your names and fictionalized personality traits into the story—it is definitely fun to write!

Jim Lesher, thank you for sharing your vehicular recommendations with me! You were always so fast to come up with the perfect make and model for my characters—like the Pontiac Fury!!! Perfect name for a vehicle in this series! And I *never* would have come up with that on my own. Also, as I've told you many times, you are **not** the inspiration for the Jim character in this series!!

Carol, thank you for going back and forth with me (so many times!) on book title ideas. Without our texting pow-wows,

ACKNOWLEDGEMENTS

Devastation Erupts never would have been granted such a great name! **Robin and Diane,** I love seeing your familiar faces at book signings and bookstore parties! Thank you for being regular fixtures at these events!

Matt, many thanks for your patience when I asked you question after question for research! I appreciate your willingness to share your knowledge and experience with me and I love that you agreed to have a character named after you!!

Scott, Landon & Aidan, thank you for continuing to support me in this journey. Writing and editing takes an incredible amount of time, and I can't think of anyone other than you that I'd rather have by my side. ♥

ABOUT THE AUTHOR

A. E. Faulkner was born and raised in Pennsylvania. When she's not lost in a book, she loves spending time with her husband and two sons, especially while hiking, biking, or exploring nature. She loves *almost* everything about nature—ticks excluded, and one of her biggest fears is the repercussions we will face when nature can no longer tolerate human destruction. As such, she never tires of reading dystopian-themed tales. Stories about the end of the world absolutely fascinate her.

FOLLOW HER WORK

To learn more visit:
AuthorAEFaulkner.com

She can also be found:

Tweeting @AuthAEFaulkner

on Facebook @authaefaulkner

& on Instagram @authoraefaulkner

To leave a Goodreads review, please visit
Goodreads.com and search for
Devastation Erupts by A. E. Faulkner.

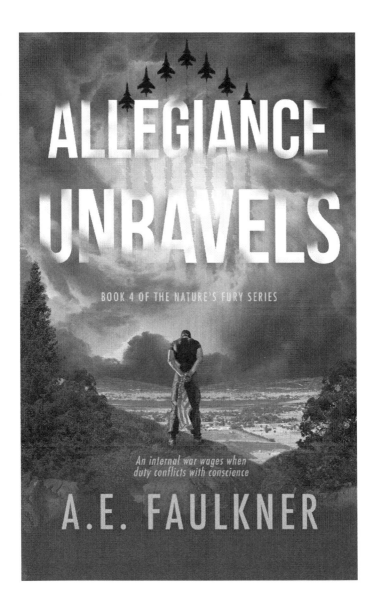

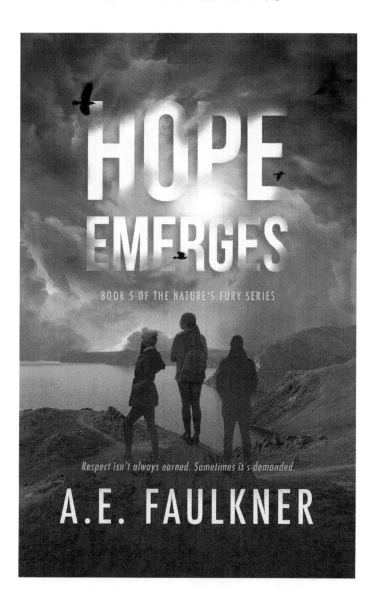

HOPE EMERGES

BOOK 5 OF THE NATURE'S FURY SERIES

Respect isn't always earned. Sometimes it's demanded.

A.E. FAULKNER

Made in the USA
Middletown, DE
10 August 2022

70955783R00215